THE
PERFECT
PATIENT

THE
PERFECT
PATIENT

LUANA LEWIS

bookouture

Published by Bookouture in 2023

An imprint of Storyfire Ltd.
Carmelite House
50 Victoria Embankment
London EC4Y 0DZ

www.bookouture.com

ISBN: 978-1-83790-339-9
eBook ISBN: 978-1-83790-338-2

For Malcolm, Jake and Joseph

PROLOGUE

She sits on the edge of the bed. Dry mouth. Foggy head. Orange light trickles in from the streetlamps outside and sequins shimmer on her dress.

Large numbers on the clock. *12:03 a.m.*

Her arms and shoulders are bare, most of her legs too. Goosebumps all over. The room is a fridge.

Where is her phone?

Blank spaces lie between one thought and the next.

She has to turn the air con down. She wants to find her phone. When she stands up, her limbs are strangely heavy. The carpet is silky-soft under her feet as she crosses the room. Memories take shape now, floating upwards in jagged pieces. A flight of concrete stairs. The bartender's big brown eyes. Voices and music and the taste of something sour. A glass, damp against her palms.

Something more, beyond her reach, hovering around the edges.

There is a half-full bottle of wine on the coffee table. And then she sees her phone, lying right there next to an empty glass. A rush of relief. But when she goes to pick it up, she sees something else, on the floor, in the semi-dark and the orange-filtered light. She can't make sense of it, at first.

A man. Lying on his back. A dark stain spreading out on the carpet beneath him. He is very, very still.

She smells it now, heavy and metallic and violent.

Her heart beats like crazy as she turns to look into the mirror on the wall behind the sofa. She is covered in blood. Smears of blood down her arms and legs; blood turning her fair hair dark.

What has she done?

ONE

Dr Tara Black was still getting used to her new life. She was forty-two years old, she was wearing a new suit, and for the first time in her career, she was her own boss.

At eight o'clock on a sunny summer morning in August, she was in Soho, on the second floor of The Onyx Hotel. The building was tucked away behind Shaftesbury Avenue, modern, with a golden brick façade and vast glass windows interlaced with steel beams. Tara was walking along a vanilla-scented passageway, instead of heading down into the corridors of the hospital where she'd worked as a clinical psychologist for the past fifteen years.

She was both excited and in free fall. Alone.

The manager of The Onyx, Risha Bassi, was as glamorous as her hotel, with black, waist-length hair, dramatic eyeliner, and very high heels. Her shirt was an electric-pink silk. The suit Tara had chosen was tailored and black. Understated. Nothing that would draw too much attention. The two women walked in silence, the textured wallpaper and thick carpet absorbing all sound. Tara found herself reaching for the ribbon of the lanyard around her neck. She missed the familiar feel of it, the way it nestled beneath her hair, against her skin, reminding her that she belonged, that she was needed. Instead, her fingers found the delicate gold chain that had been a gift from Daniel.

They had reached The Red Suite. When Risha first opened the door, the room was in a deep darkness. Then, she inserted her key card into the slot and it burst into brightness. Red leather headboard, red rug, red cushions on a grey sofa.

'As you can imagine, we're not putting any guests in here for the foreseeable future.' Risha walked over to the window and pressed a button. Slowly, the blackout curtains rolled open to reveal floor-to-ceiling windows with a view over the narrow street below. On her way to the entrance of the hotel, Tara had passed a series of trendy boutiques: a perfumery, an artisan jeweller, an art gallery.

Risha's arms remained folded across her pink silk shirt as she stood with her back to the window, watching her. 'So you're working for the defence team?'

'That's right, I'm acting as an expert witness.'

'And you're supposed to work out whether Jade's memory loss is genuine?'

'I can't go into the details, I hope you understand. If there's anything you need to check, you can always contact Jade's solicitor, Valerie Bennett.'

'Right.'

From the anxious undertone in Risha's voice, Tara sensed her presence was an unwelcome reminder of the violence that had taken place in the Red Suite only two weeks earlier, and perhaps of the scandal that must inevitably taint the hotel's reputation. She could not imagine anyone would get a good night's sleep in this sumptuous room, where an ex-police officer had been knifed to death.

'Did you know the man who was killed?'

Risha shook her head. 'He wasn't registered as a guest. I understand Jade met him down in the hotel bar. She'd been working as a waitress in the hotel restaurant, over the summer, and sometimes she would use one of the empty suites after a weekend shift.' Risha did not look particularly pleased about this.

'Was that a problem for you?'

'Jade has certain privileges, given that her father is the owner of this hotel. I worry that it causes resentment among the rest of my staff.' Risha cleared her throat. 'But Jade has a way with her father. And she's pretty well-liked around here too. Or people have to pretend to like her, I suppose.'

'Because of who her father is?'

'Have you met Ray Jameson?'

'Not yet.'

'I'm sure you'll draw your own conclusions.'

Tara had the sense there was more Risha could say about her boss, but instead she smiled to cover whatever it was she'd been feeling.

'Had there been any problems with Jade before this incident?'

'Such as?' Risha's arms tightened across her chest.

'Well, as far as you know, would it have been normal for Jade to meet a man in the bar and bring him up to one of the suites?'

'Not to my knowledge. I mean, the part about bringing strange men up here. Jade would usually be with her friend, Lucy. As far as I was aware, they used the rooms to get changed to go out, or they'd order in room service, or watch TV. That sort of thing.'

The hotel manager was in a tricky position. Perhaps Risha didn't feel able to say anything negative about Jade because Jade's father was her boss. On the other hand, she didn't seem to have anything positive to say about her, either.

Risha looked down at the spot on the carpet between the bed and the coffee table. 'I was in here, after they'd taken the body away.

You wouldn't believe the blood. We had to replace the entire carpet. Not exactly what I had in mind as part of my job description.'

Jade's solicitor had included photographs of the crime scene in the background documents. Tara had them with her, in an envelope in her bag.

Risha checked her watch. 'Was there something else you needed to see?'

'Would it be all right if I stayed in here alone for a few minutes?'

Risha hesitated, then nodded. 'You can leave the key card down at reception when you're done.'

She walked over to the door, her sharp heels sinking into the new carpet, but stopped at the threshold. 'If you decide that Jade really does have amnesia, does that mean she could walk free?'

'I'm sorry. I can't discuss that.'

Risha looked at her thoughtfully. 'I don't know exactly what this assessment of yours involves, but you do know that as part of her bail conditions, Jade is not allowed anywhere near this hotel?'

'I am aware of that, yes.'

When Risha had gone, and the door had closed behind her, Tara took the photographs out and laid them out on the coffee table. She pictured the room as her client, seventeen-year-old Jade Jameson, had described it in her statement: the bed where her memory had come back online; the coffee table where she'd seen her phone lying next to the bottle of wine; the space on the carpet between the coffee table and the sofa where she'd first seen Carl Ress's body. The mirror behind the sofa where she'd seen herself, covered in blood.

Tara knelt down to study the images again. The first showed

Carl Ress, sprawled on his back. At forty-three years old, he was more than double Jade's age. Well-built and in good shape, he was taller and stronger than Jade, but apparently, she'd taken him by surprise. The initial stab wound had been to his back and had punctured his lung.

The second photograph was a close-up of the front torso. There were ten further stab wounds to his chest and abdomen. An orgy of rage. Or bloodlust.

Though it looked like an intensely personal attack, no connection could be found between Jade and the victim. Ress, a retired police officer, had been married. Jade claimed to remember him offering to buy her a drink down in the hotel bar, but said she'd never seen him before that night. No trace of contact had been found on either of their devices or social media accounts.

The investigation was ongoing, but the police seemed convinced they had their killer. Staff at The Onyx Hotel had seen Jade and the victim leaving the basement bar together. Jade was found in the room with Carl Ress's body, and his blood was on her clothes, in her hair and under her fingernails. Her DNA was on the victim's body. By the time the medics arrived, rigor mortis had set in, which meant Jade had waited a couple of hours before calling for help. And her first call had not been to the ambulance or police services, it had been to her father.

The weapon had not yet been found. The police were looking for a small, sharp object. They believed Jade might have disposed of it somewhere in the hotel, or even thrown it out of the window onto the street below.

According to Jade's solicitor, Ress must have been planning to assault Jade before she turned the tables on him. Unfortunately for the defence's version of events, there was no indication of a struggle in the hotel room, no injuries or defensive wounds to Jade's body and no one in the neighbouring rooms had heard any disturbance.

Tara stood between the coffee table and the bed, in the exact same place Jade would have stood when she first noticed the body on the floor. She turned her head and looked into the large rectangular mirror hanging behind the sofa. The bed was reflected behind her.

The temperature in the room dropped. The sheets were twisted and thrown aside. The pillow was soaked through with blood.

Tara closed her eyes. She took a moment to breathe, slowing her heartbeat, pushing back the nausea. When she turned around to look again, everything was back the way it was before. The bed was neatly made up with crisp white sheets. There was no blood-soaked pillow. Of course there wasn't.

TWO

Jade Jameson lived with her parents in a four-storey townhouse in St John's Wood, one of London's poshest suburbs. The house was one of three identical homes, situated at the top of a tree-lined cul-de-sac, in what looked like a new development.

Tara stood in front of the gloss-black front door, between a pair of sculpted bay trees. She had driven over there right after leaving the hotel in Soho, and the feeling of the Red Suite had stayed with her. The savagery. The blood. She hadn't expected to connect to the violence on such a visceral level.

A stocky man with a craggy face opened the door. 'You must be Doctor Black? I'm Ray Jameson. Jade's father.'

His handshake was forceful, squeezing down on Tara's knuckles. 'My wife and I are very grateful you've agreed to help our daughter.'

Tara stepped into a spacious entrance hall and the door shut soundlessly behind her. Chequered marble floors, curving staircase, large gold-framed mirrors. Everything quite lovely on the surface. She had never interviewed an accused murderer at home before.

'My wife sends her apologies, by the way,' Jameson was

saying. 'Sandra runs a fitness studio. She had clients booked all morning so she couldn't be here to meet you.'

Tara followed him through the house, noticing the way his shoulders strained against the seams of his double-breasted jacket. He led her into a large kitchen, all marble worktops and copper hanging lights. Frameless windows looked out onto a compact garden, where tall hedging on all sides ensured it was not overlooked.

'Can I offer you a coffee?' Jameson said.

The thought of a strong coffee was an appealing one, but Tara declined. She didn't want these home visits to ease into familiarity too soon. She was also keen to get started and to meet her client.

'Is Jade ready?'

'She's on her way down. She's a little nervous to meet you.' Jameson gestured to a closed door at the far end of the kitchen. 'I thought we'd set you up in the snug. It's cosy down there and Jade can curl up on the sofa, with the dog. If that's all right with you?'

'That sounds fine.'

'Excellent.' Jameson was flawlessly polite, but Tara could tell he wasn't too happy about having to ask her permission about where to meet with his only daughter in his own home.

'Excellent,' he said, again. This time he smiled, but his eyes were wary.

His daughter wasn't the only one who was nervous. Something inside Jameson was coiled up too. When Tara smiled back, the muscles around her own mouth were stiff.

There was an island workstation in the centre of the kitchen, and a wooden knife block was placed on top of it, in full view. Tara counted six knives of various sizes sticking out of it. She wondered what it must be like, for Ray Jameson and his wife, to live in this house with their daughter who had been accused of stabbing a man eleven times. She wondered if they slept at night.

'You're sure I can't offer you something to drink while we wait?' Jameson said. 'Tea, coffee, orange juice?'

By this stage Tara had noticed the state-of-the-art coffee machine on the counter behind him. Maybe accepting his hospitality would put them both more at ease. 'A coffee would be lovely. Thank you.'

While Jameson was grinding beans and adjusting knobs on the machine, Tara had the chance to study him for a while. He was a powerfully built man, but not particularly tall. His silver hair was impeccably cut; his pinstripe suit tailored. He wore a Rolex on his wrist and there was a sizeable emerald in the pinkie ring on his left hand. Ray Jameson was a man who did not object to being noticed. He wore his wealth openly and with pride. Tara imagined several houses scattered about the world, some for beaches and sunbathing, others for winter snow and skiing. His rugged face though, with a slightly crooked nose that looked as though it may once have been broken, hinted at something different.

Jameson spoke with his back to her. 'So,' he said, 'before you went into private practice, you were head of psychology at the Royal University Hospital?'

'Head of psychology in the Neurology Department, yes.'

'Why did you leave?'

This question was delivered bluntly and she knew it was a test, to see if she would give him an honest answer.

'I'd been in the department for fifteen years. It was a fantastic job, but the higher up the chain I went, the less client work I was doing. I left because I wanted my own practice where I was completely in control of the kind of work I could take on. I also wanted more money.'

He turned to look at her. 'Do you have children, Doctor Black?'

'No.' She was careful to answer in a neutral tone, with no whisper of sadness.

'My daughter is my whole life. Nothing else matters.'

'I'm sorry for what you and your family are going through.'

Jameson was studying her too now, and she wondered what he saw, behind the neutral clothes and the face people tended not to remember.

To her relief, he picked up an electric whisk and turned his attention to foaming the milk. There was still no sign of his daughter.

When Jameson had finally finished preparing the coffee, he came over and stood directly in front of her, holding the cup, but not offering it to her. 'Jade has a gentle soul. I am one hundred per cent confident you will find a way to exonerate her.'

There was pain behind his words, but something else too. Something that made her stomach clench. Tara wasn't quite sure whether what she'd just heard was Jameson's conviction in his daughter's innocence, or a threat. Both, perhaps. And he still had not given her that cup of coffee.

'I'd like to start the interview now,' she said. 'Could you call Jade for me?'

He handed her a perfect cappuccino, complete with a chocolate star. 'My wife is not an easy woman to please, but I do get praise for my cappuccino-making skills.'

This time his smile was genuine, and it took Tara by surprise. Suddenly, he was charming. She almost questioned whether she had imagined his attempt to pressure her. Almost, but not quite.

The coffee was strong, with no hint of bitterness.

'This is delicious.' As she took another sip, Tara had the sense she was crossing over into unsafe territory.

'If you wait down in the snug, I'll go and see if I can find

Jade.' Jameson walked over and opened the door in the corner of the kitchen. Behind it was a narrow staircase.

Intuition. That combination of gut instinct and clinical experience more reliable than rational thought. Tara did not want to go down into that basement.

THREE

Jameson watched as Tara descended the stairs. When she reached the bottom, he shut the door at the top, which seemed entirely unnecessary. Tara had the urge to run back up and check that it wasn't locked. She didn't do it. Instead, she walked around the small living room while she waited.

There was a curved leather sofa, a thick-pile wool rug and an enormous television mounted on the wall. A small window placed high up above the television let in some light, but not much. A standing lamp in the corner had been turned on. On the face of it, the room was cosy, but that wasn't how it felt. When Tara checked her phone, she wasn't getting any reception.

Home visits were a double-edged sword. On the one hand, she got to see the fine-grained details of her clients' lives that she wouldn't have access to in an office consultation. On the other hand, she was on their territory, and there was always a sense of vulnerability. A loss of control.

When the door at the top of the stairs opened, a dog hurtled down into the room, coming to an abrupt stop at the bottom, its ears pricked up, as it stared at Tara, the intruder. When Jade's father had mentioned a dog, Tara had imagined something cute and fluffy. This one was a brute; a large muscular Staffordshire Bull Terrier which reminded Tara of Ray Jameson.

'It's okay, boy, everything's okay.' Tara's client followed behind the dog, moving more tentatively down the stairs.

Jade Jameson was a fresh-faced seventeen-year-old, with long fair hair tucked behind her ears. She was in a white T-shirt and jeans, and barefoot. Delicate-looking, she was a little taller than average, and a little underweight. She paused at the bottom of the stairs, one hand still holding the banister, the other placed on the dog's head. She looked as if she might change her mind and bolt at any moment.

Tara took a step forward. 'Hi, Jade, I'm Doctor Tara Black. It's good to meet you.'

'Hi.' She looked at Tara with wide blue eyes.

Tara was very much aware of the dog standing at Jade's heels, tensed up and on high alert. He hadn't taken his eyes off her. Usually, she loved dogs, but this one set her on edge. She felt her heart rate increasing.

'What's your dog's name?' she asked.

'Ziggy. He's a rescue, so he can be a bit scared around new people. Don't try to pat him, or anything.'

'Right.' Tara took a step back, careful not to make any sudden movements. 'How long have you had him?'

'About seven years. He was already a year old when we got him, so we don't know what happened to him before.' Jade leaned down and scratched the dog behind his ear.

'Shall we sit down?' Tara said.

Jade sat on one end of the curved white leather sofa, tucking her legs underneath her. As there were no other chairs in the room, Tara sat down on the opposite end. The dog jumped up and lay down between them, pushing himself right up close to Jade. The room felt too small for the three of them.

'Before we start,' Tara said, 'I need to make sure you understand that whatever we talk about in our meetings won't be confidential. My report will be shared with your solicitor, and most likely other people after that.'

'I understand. The other psychologist explained everything.'

Anthony Edwards had been the first expert appointed in the case, but he had stepped back due to illness and Tara now had his rather large shoes to fill. Edwards had a much higher profile than she did, he was probably the leading expert witness in criminal cases in London, if not England.

With the delay caused by Edwards' withdrawal, and the time it had taken to choose a replacement, Tara had been left with a tight time frame. She had ten days to complete all the interviews, review the background documents and write up her report. She would be working nights and weekends to fit this in between the rest of her caseload. But the moment Jade's solicitor had told Tara about the case, she had known she had to take it on.

Tara took out a single sheet of paper from her briefcase, a brief consent form, and handed it to Jade.

She skimmed it briefly. 'It's fine.'

Tara handed the girl a pen. Her eyes fixed on the pointed tip as it moved across the page in Jade's left hand. Any sharp object could become a weapon.

Presumably, since she was out on bail and allowed back to live with her parents, Jade wasn't regarded as high risk. Tara could only assume that the solicitor would have warned her if there was any danger involved in meeting Jade alone, in her own home. In fact, it had been Valerie Bennett herself who had asked Tara to go to the Jameson home for the appointments. Apparently, Jade was reluctant to leave the house since being charged. The only place she went was to her local police station, to check in as part of her bail conditions.

Jade handed the form and the pen back. Tara took out her notebook. She preferred to write with pen and paper, rather than sitting behind a laptop screen.

The rest of the first interview was more relaxed. Tara got used to being in the basement, and the tension she had picked up when she first came into the house seemed to dissipate. The dog dozed peacefully next to Jade as Tara asked her about her history. Tara would leave the more challenging questions, about that night in the Red Suite, for their second meeting.

Jade spoke freely about her life before the arrest, but there was nothing in what she said that seemed to give any clue as to why she had committed an act of extreme violence. She had attended a selective public school near to her home, enjoyed her time there and done well academically. She said she had a small circle of good friends. She described her parents as loving and supportive. According to Jade, she had never gone through a rebellious teenage phase. She claimed to have never wanted to try drugs and to drink only in moderation when out with friends.

Jade mentioned a boyfriend, someone her own age whom she'd dated, about six months earlier. She said they had broken up because Jade 'wasn't interested in anything serious' and wanted to focus on her A-levels. Apparently, there had been no unusual or stressful life events in the months leading up to her arrest.

Jade told Tara she wanted to study to be a veterinary surgeon. When she spoke about her plans for her future, Tara saw most clearly the confident young woman she had been before she was confined to the house wearing an electronic tag.

Jade stroked the dog as she spoke. 'My exam results were great, so I'll definitely have the marks I need to get into the

Royal Veterinary College. Plus, I've been working at an animal shelter for years already, so I have a good chance of getting offered a place. Either here, in Camden, or Edinburgh would be good too.'

It was a poignant moment. On some level, Jade seemed to be in denial of the reality of her situation. She was facing a murder charge.

Tara thought about what Valerie had said, about Jade hardly leaving the house since her arrest. Perhaps Jade's fear was not only of the outside world, but also of something deeper: her own recognition of what she'd done, and of the changed future ahead of her. As long as Jade shut herself away in this large house, she could shut reality out too.

They had been talking for almost two hours. Jade was soft-spoken, with a gentle manner. It was difficult to match the young woman sitting opposite her with those gruesome crime-scene photographs.

'Do you have any questions for me before we end for today?' Tara said.

Jade was looking down at the dog, stroking his back. Ziggy's eyes were closed. 'My solicitor says you know a lot about amnesia.'

'I've worked with many people who've had memory loss.'

Jade kept her eyes on the dog. She was still stroking him, as much to calm herself as the animal. 'They say I was in the hotel room with a dead body. For hours. They showed me photos.'

'How did you feel when you saw those pictures?'

'Sick. I could never kill anyone. I couldn't harm a fly. Literally.' Jade looked up. 'Do you believe me?'

Jade was smart. She was trying to get the measure of Tara, deciding whether to trust her. Deciding whether to tell her the truth, perhaps.

'I don't know you very well, yet,' Tara said.

Jade drew her legs up, wrapping her arms around her shins and resting her chin on her knees. The electronic tag around her ankle became visible as the hem of her jeans slid upwards. 'The only person who really believes me is my dad.'

FOUR

Tara was sitting in her car. From where she was parked, she had a direct view of the three houses arranged around the curve of the crescent. The Jameson family lived in the first one, where a Bentley was parked out front, with a driver waiting in the front seat.

Tara noticed there were no cars on the driveways of the two neighbouring houses, no curtains on the windows, no topiaries at the front doors or any other signs of life. If those neighbouring buildings were vacant, then the Jameson family would have absolute privacy. There would be no one to overlook or overhear anything that went on in that family. The thought crossed her mind that Ray Jameson might own all three of those houses.

Thinking back to their conversation in the kitchen, Tara wondered how a man like Jameson might react if the findings in her report were not to his liking.

She called Daniel, wanting to hear his voice.

'Everything okay?' He always picked up when she called, and he always sounded as though he was in a rush.

'Just calling to say hi. How's Zurich?'

'I've barely seen it. I'm either in my hotel room or the client's offices. How's your day?'

'I'm in St John's Wood,' Tara said, 'interviewing for a new medico-legal case. Valerie Bennett's the instructing solicitor.'

'That's great. Who's the client?'

'You know I'm not going to give you a name.'

'Always worth a shot.'

Tara saw the front door of the Jameson house opening. Jade came out alone. Despite the warm day, she'd put on a pale-pink hoodie, with the hood pulled up so it covered all of her hair and most of her face. She walked down the Victorian-tiled front pathway before climbing into the back of the waiting Bentley. She had mentioned to Tara she was due at the police station for her check-in.

'It's a murder charge,' Tara said. 'High-net-worth family.'

There was a pause.

'Dan, are you still there?'

'Sorry, I have to run,' he said, 'but I'm going to try and make it back in time for dinner.'

'Okay, see you later. Love you.'

'Love you too.'

Something made Tara look up at the first-floor window of the Jameson house. A woman was standing at one of the windows, watching as Jade's car drove away. Tall, slender and blonde, the woman resembled Tara's client. Tara was sure that must be Sandra Jameson, Jade's mother. So why would Ray Jameson say she wasn't at home?

FIVE

Later that afternoon, Tara had half an hour's break between patients. She was standing at her office window with a mug of coffee. It had been six months since she'd taken the plunge and left the hospital, and still, every time she looked out at this view, it made her happy. There was a small park across the road, where there was an ancient graveyard with faded headstones, wooden benches and pots full of lavender.

On her first day in that office, standing at the window on the first floor of the mews house in Marylebone, surrounded by the smell of fresh paint and newly laid carpets, Tara had felt sick. And utterly out of place. But this feeling had passed. It was bliss to be able to decide on everything, from her schedule down to the last piece of furniture. She'd chosen pared back mid-century modern pieces from the antique market around the corner from the station: a simple teak desk and two grey-linen armchairs. Built-in bookcases held the books she'd collected over the years. Shutters on the windows created a sense of tranquillity and privacy.

The only thing Tara still missed was Neil's steady presence in the office next door to hers. He had been the neurology consultant on her team, and she'd worked with him ever since she'd started her career. She still consulted with him about some of her complex cases.

Tara was already seeing a good number of patients, though not quite enough of them to cover her costs yet. When she had been asked to work on a report for Valerie Bennett, she felt she'd turned a corner.

A text message pinged through on her phone from Olivia, to let her know her next patient had arrived. He was early, the appointment wasn't due to start for another twenty minutes. When Tara arrived in the waiting room on the ground floor, she was surprised to find that Ray Jameson was waiting for her, sitting on the edge of the sofa, with a cardboard box on his lap.

He stood up when she walked in. 'Good to see you again, Doctor Black.'

'How can I help?'

Jameson patted the lid of the box he was carrying. 'I have some documents here for you.'

'Right. Any paperwork would usually come via the solicitor's office.'

'Ah, I see. I didn't realise that.'

Tara didn't find that particularly convincing. Jameson wasn't naïve, especially where his daughter's legal case was concerned. It was more likely he had some agenda for turning up unannounced.

'These are Jade's medical records,' he said. 'I don't want to risk them getting lost. Now that I'm here, I can take them through to your office for you.'

Tara decided there was no point in making the argument that she could easily carry the small box herself. Everything was information, after all, and what she was learning was that Ray Jameson was a man who needed to be in control. She led the way upstairs, aware of his burly presence on the stairs behind her.

In her office, he placed the box down in the centre of her desk and then took a long look around. 'This is a good building,' he said. 'Good location.'

'Thank you.'

'Are you here on your own?'

'I share the offices with a psychiatrist, Olivia Evans. She has the ground floor.'

'But yours is the only name on the mortgage.'

How on earth would he know that? Had Jameson somehow got hold of a copy of her contract with the bank? Tara didn't even know if that was legally possible.

She was too shocked to respond. She simply stood in silence on the other side of her desk.

Jameson was staring, one hand resting casually on the polished teak surface. 'You put down a sizeable deposit. Very impressive that you managed to accumulate that kind of money on a hospital salary.'

He was looking for a pressure point, a weak spot. Tara was skilled in hiding those, she'd had decades of practice.

She put a bland smile on her face to cover the fact that he was getting to her, setting her off balance. 'If you'll excuse me, I have another appointment.'

Jameson ignored her. He walked over to the windows and tilted the shutters wide open, letting the light in. For a few moments, he appeared to be admiring the view. 'Given the size of your repayments, I imagine you could do with Valerie Bennett sending a few more cases your way. It's really in your best interests to do a good job for my daughter.'

'Of course,' Tara said. 'I always make every effort to do a good job.'

A lot depended on the outcome of her report and Jameson knew it. He didn't like the power she held over his daughter's future, and he was trying to even the playing field.

Jameson reached into the inside pocket of his jacket and

took out a business card. He came over to stand in front of her desk again, offering it to her. Tara had no desire to take it.

'This is my private mobile number. Call me any time. For anything you need. Anything, any time of day or night.'

He seemed to be following up his not-so-subtle threats with a hint at a bribe. Or a prediction that she may find herself in trouble?

His arm remained outstretched. This visit was a power play and Tara knew he would not leave until she accepted what he was offering. Her patient was due any moment. She reached out and took the card, dropping it on top of the box of documents. Her cheeks were burning.

Jameson headed for the staircase leading down to the ground floor, with Tara following behind him. As he reached for the banister, he paused. Suddenly, the burden he carried was visible in the droop of his neck and the slump of his shoulders.

Tara could not help but feel for him. She believed him when he'd told her that Jade was the centre of his world. And that world was crumbling. Jameson was a desperate man, and the extreme pressure he was under might be influencing, or dramatically changing, his behaviour. At the same time though, there was this constant hum of threat whenever she was anywhere near him.

Tara had never been one to shy away from a professional challenge, but Ray Jameson was a different animal. The more she began to understand about her client's father, and the lengths he might go to for his daughter, the more concerned she was about exactly how deep into her affairs he might be prepared to dig.

SIX

NINETEEN YEARS EARLIER

Ray's office was up on the first floor, above the club. At three metres long by two-and-a-half metres wide, it was more of a large cupboard, but the space was all his. He had his privacy and a window overlooking Hunter Street. When he'd first moved in, the glass had been painted black and the frame nailed shut. Ray had managed to prise it open with a crowbar and replaced the glass himself. He'd furnished the room with an old wooden desk and chair he'd found in the basement, first sanding them down and then giving them a coat of oil. His kingdom now consisted of a desk, a chair, a window, a cash box and two sets of ledgers, one true and one for the tax man.

Ray had left school at sixteen to work alongside his father in their newsagent's when the old man's emphysema got bad. When that wasn't enough to pay the mortgage and put food on the table for his parents and younger siblings, he'd got a second job, working nights as a bouncer at Diamonds. Ray had initially been hired for his brawn, but over the years he had gradually taken over many of the day-to-day responsibilities for running the place, including accounts and payroll. He was now managing the club. Given that the accounts needed to be carefully edited before being presented to Her Majesty's Revenue and Customs, and that several of the activities in the club fell into what could be called the 'non-legal' variety, this was a varied and challenging role.

Ray had both ledgers open in front of him, together with the previous night's takings, when there was a timid knock on the door. He called out to whomever it was to come in, closing the lid of the strongbox as he looked up.

It was one of the new dancers. Very blonde, very attractive. She could just about pass for eighteen, but Ray suspected she was a good couple of years younger than that. Inwardly he cursed Charlie who kept an eye on the talent down at the club. Ray suspected he was taking kickbacks to turn a blind eye when pretty girls turned up without ID. And now one of them was standing in front of his desk holding an ugly-looking, spiky plant.

'I came to say thank you,' she said. 'For giving me and my sister a chance.'

'It's a pleasure – remind me of your name again?'

'Sandra.' She was wearing a low-cut vest, cut-off denim shorts and chunky black boots. 'You're Ray, right? The big boss.'

Ray cleared his throat, making a point of keeping his eyes on her face. 'Right. Sandra. I'm sure you'll do an excellent job for us.'

That came out ridiculous and she laughed. She could tell he was nervous.

Those shorts really were very short. Practically non-existent.

'I brought you a present,' she said.

'You didn't need to do that.'

'I know.' She leaned forwards so he could see down the front of her top as she placed the plant on his desk. 'It's a cactus.'

'I guessed as much.'

She smiled at him again, putting both hands in her back pockets and pushing her chest out. Her skimpy top slid upwards and he glimpsed her midriff; taut skin, belly-button ring.

Ray felt a stirring and was ashamed. He had just turned twenty-eight-years-old and he didn't date underage girls. He tried to run a clean shop, as much as that was possible given that he managed a pole-dancing club in Soho. Lots of the girls had tried it on with him, but he had a strict rule never, ever to sleep with any of the dancers. They would go feral if he showed favouritism.

But most of all, there was Noor. Always Noor. He still loved her. He would never get over the guilt.

'It's easy to look after,' Sandra was saying. 'You only need to water it like once a month. And don't water it in winter, or it could die.'

'I think I can manage that.'

Sandra picked up the cactus again and looked around. 'It needs more sun.'

She walked over to the window, which was streaked with London soot. Ray made a mental note to clean it. As Sandra turned around to place the plant on the windowsill, he saw the bruises on her shoulder.

'Who hurt you?' he said.

With her back to him, she reached over and ran her fingers across the marks on her skin. 'My sister's boyfriend is an asshole.'

The old red-hot anger roiled inside of him. All those times he'd seen his mother with black eyes, split lips. Sometimes he didn't know if he was angrier at his father, or at his mother for being so damn helpless.

Sandra walked slowly to the door. That behind of hers. The hair down to her waist. She was perfection and she knew it. She was playing him, and he knew it.

She paused in the doorway. 'I'm not going to be a pole dancer forever,' she said. 'I'm going to be a personal trainer.'

'Is that right?'

'I'm saving up to do a course. I've researched the one I want.'

'Sounds great.'

She turned, as if to leave, one hand hanging on to the edge of the doorframe, swinging herself out, making sure he had an eyeful. Then she changed her mind and turned back. 'Do you ever leave this building?'

'Sometimes.'

'I got the cactus from Camden Market. It's really cool there, have you been?'

Ray shook his head.

'Maybe we could go over there one day, if you feel like it, and get a couple more? For your desk?'

'I don't think so.'

'Plants are good for you,' she said. 'And good for the air.'

He had always managed to resist, until now. 'Maybe.'

'Okay then. Which day?'

At that point, he pretty much knew he was done for. She was smart and she was bruised, and she was looking at him as if he was her prey and he was paralysed in her gaze.

SEVEN

Once she'd finished her last appointment of the afternoon, Tara had a chance to read through the documents that Jameson had unexpectedly dropped off earlier.

Jade's medical records were brief and unremarkable. She visited her GP infrequently and had no history of serious illnesses or injuries. She was not on any medication or birth control. No psychological problems were mentioned. The records matched Jade's own description of her history in her interview with Tara that morning. Basically, there seemed to have been nothing out of the ordinary about her life up until the moment it had imploded in the Red Suite of The Onyx Hotel.

Something was off-kilter in that family, though. And whatever that was, Tara was sure it did not start two weeks ago with the death of Carl Ress.

As she went through the records, Tara realised that they only began when Jade was nine years old. The earlier years were missing. She sent Valerie Bennett a quick email, asking her to chase up the full set of notes.

Later, as Tara was preparing dinner with the groceries she'd picked up on her way home, the Jameson case continued to consume her thoughts. She was left with the same question everyone else involved in the case was grappling with: Why would a teenager, with no history of violence, and no apparent mental health problems, kill a man she'd never met?

Ray Jameson had crossed a line, intruding into her personal life. Not only had he researched her professional background, he'd also been investigating her finances, and he wanted her to know it. That could mean he was afraid of something Tara might uncover; something he did not want to appear in her report. Or, it could mean he was highly controlling and did not leave anything to chance. Either way, his visit to her office had been intended to unnerve her.

Tara marinated the sea bass in olive oil, salt and crushed garlic. Fragments of her conversation with Jade Jameson played on her mind.

They say I was in the hotel room with a dead body. For hours. They showed me photographs.

She cut into a tomato with a paring knife.

I could never kill anyone. I couldn't harm a fly. Literally.

Tara felt a sudden slice of pain.

The only person who really believes me is my dad.

In shock she looked down at the blood gushing from the tip of her thumb. She saw Carl Ress's chest and the dark, spreading stain underneath him on the carpet. That bloodstained pillow. The spatters up the wall. Her mother's body.

Feeling nauseous now, trying to unsee all of this, Tara turned the kitchen tap on full blast, flushing out the wound. She grabbed a kitchen cloth, pressing down hard, trying to stop the flow as she clattered around the cupboards looking for plasters. By the time she'd wound one tightly around her thumb, she heard the sound of the front door opening, and Daniel was calling out hello.

Her hand throbbing, she went to stand in the kitchen doorway to see him. All of his movements were so familiar, so reassuring. He set his travel bag down, hung up his coat and took off his tie. Then he came over to give her a hug.

'It's good to be back.'

'Are you hungry?' She spoke into his shoulder. His white shirt was rumpled and there was a shadow of stubble across his jaw. He'd come straight from Heathrow and his aftershave was overlaid with the harsher scent of a long day's travel.

'Starving. I'll go up and shower first.'

While he was upstairs, Tara gingerly checked the plaster. A little blood had seeped through, but the cut had settled. She was more careful as she finished cutting the butternut. She was using a large Santoku knife now and she didn't want to end up losing a finger over the Jameson case. She tossed the butternut in honey and cinnamon; the oven released a blast of heat as she slid the tray inside.

Daniel came down after his shower and they slipped into an easy routine. He put together a salad, dressing it with olive oil and balsamic vinegar. Soon the kitchen smelled of cinnamon and his aftershave and he was back home, and she started to relax.

As he placed the raw fish in a sizzling pan, Daniel talked about his work trip, which he claimed had been tedious. Office politics were more interesting though. He had been asked to take on an expanded role, which meant a colleague who had been underperforming was being pushed out.

Daniel was asking about her day, her new case. They spoke over the noise of oil, popping and hissing. Tara was thinking about Ray Jameson again as she pushed the back door wide open.

The reason she had been able to put together a sizeable deposit to buy the mews house was partly thanks to Daniel. His work in mergers and acquisitions was impossibly lucrative, and he had wanted to give her the money. He had wanted her to have a clinic of her own.

'Do you know if someone could get hold of my mortgage agreement without my permission?' Tara said. 'I mean, is there a register or something like that?'

'I'm not sure. You could probably find out if a property was mortgaged, but not for how much. I'd be very surprised if you could get hold of someone else's documents. Why do you ask?'

'It's this medico-legal case. The client's father made some odd comments today. He seemed to know that I had a significant mortgage, and that I'd put down a large deposit to buy the clinic.'

'Did he know the exact amount?'

'He didn't go into specifics.'

'Maybe he was fishing? If he'd guessed you bought the mews house, then he could also have assumed that you'd have a big mortgage and that you'd have had to come up with a big deposit.'

'That's true.' For a few moments, she was reassured.

Jameson had been spot on, though. She did need this case and more like it to cover the amount of debt she'd taken on.

They sat down at the kitchen table to eat. The fish was delicious. Soft and fresh.

Jameson would probably also be interested to know that as well as the money Daniel had given her, Tara had used the insurance money from her parents' deaths as the capital she needed to renovate the mews house in Marylebone. For twenty-five years, she had not been able to bring herself to touch that money, but when she'd left her job at the hospital, she had used it to buy her independence. And she wasn't entirely comfortable about it.

Tara was suddenly very thirsty. She got up to fetch another bottle of water from the fridge. 'I have a feeling that this client might look into my background. He's that kind of person. Controlling. Very wealthy. Very protective of his seventeen-year-old daughter. Overprotective.'

'Is he trying to pressure you?'

'He's certainly flexing his muscles. But then, it is a high-net-worth, high-profile family, and the daughter's facing a murder charge, so some kind of pressure probably goes with the territory. I should get used to it, right? I guess that's why they pay me so much money.'

Tara was staring into the open fridge. There was a bottle of rosé in there she'd forgotten about. It had been lying on the bottle rack for months. 'Do you feel like a glass of wine?'

'Not for me, I have an early start. You go ahead though.'

She left the bottle of rosé where it was, it would be a waste to open it for just one glass. Tara had to be up early for work herself. She was going to the Jameson house for the second time.

Later, she lay with her head on Daniel's shoulder. Her hand was on his chest, feeling it rise and fall. He was almost asleep, but her mind was buzzing.

When Valerie Bennett had offered her the Jameson case, Tara hadn't hesitated to accept even though her experience in criminal cases was limited, and maybe she hadn't been quite ready for a case like this one. She wasn't a believer in waiting to be ready though, by doing something, you became ready. Valerie Bennett was one of the top criminal solicitors in London and this was exactly the kind of lucrative and interesting work she was aiming to bring into the private practice.

At the same time, instinct had warned her that the case was too sensational. A young heiress accused of killing a man inside one of her father's hotels was bound to attract attention. A lot of attention. Jade's identity had not yet been released because she was a minor, but that would change. Once restrictions were lifted, there could be tabloid spreads, podcasts, maybe even true crime documentaries and books, churned out for years to come.

The case would be scrutinised from every angle and it was possible Tara would be forced into the frame.

She rubbed her index finger against the plaster on her thumb. The throbbing had settled, but she'd wait until morning to take it off and see the damage. She'd had enough gory visions for one day.

She turned over, onto her back. 'Once this case goes to court and the client turns eighteen, the press will be all over it,' she said.

'Mm.'

'Do you think they could dig up my parents' case?'

'I don't know.' He was silent a while.

'It's unlikely, right?' One small mercy was that it had happened before everything was plastered all over the internet.

Daniel still hadn't answered her.

'What are you thinking?' Tara said.

'I was thinking about the similarities with what happened to you. A teenager with amnesia, who has no memory of a murder.'

'I can't avoid every case where there's overlap between my experience and my client's experience. No psychologist could. And I was never charged with anything.'

'I know. But you asked me what I was thinking.' His hand was solid over hers. 'Put your head on my chest again.'

She laid her head down against his warm skin.

'If this case is going to give you sleepless nights, you can walk away,' he said. 'You're brilliant. There will always be other big cases.'

'Would you step away from one of your big cases?'

'Sure.' Daniel could be annoyingly pragmatic.

'Hmm.'

They didn't say anything more. She didn't tell him about the image she'd seen in the hotel room and how it had come back to her in the kitchen and how she didn't understand how that knife in her hand had slipped. She stroked the plaster on her thumb, pushing the visions away, not wanting to think about what they might mean.

Those gruesome photographs of the murder in the Red Suite must have burrowed into her subconscious. That was all.

She drifted down into sleep.

EIGHT

At nine o'clock the next morning, Tara arrived at the Jameson house for her second interview with Jade. Once again, Ray Jameson came to the front door, wearing a pinstripe suit. This time though, his greeting was less enthusiastic. He didn't make conversation or offer her a coffee.

Tara wondered whether her aloof manner in her office the day before had offended him. Then again, Jameson's changeable moods might have nothing to do with her and everything to do with the acute stress he was under. *My daughter is my whole life. Nothing else matters.*

The smell of toast and bacon and coffee lingered in the kitchen. The room was spotless and there was no sign of any crockery or cutlery on the counters or in the sink. The block of knives stood proud on the polished marble surface.

Jade and Ziggy were outside in the secluded garden. Jade was throwing a tennis ball for the dog and seemed in no hurry to come inside for their appointment.

Tara herself had no desire to go back down into the basement living room. It would be far more pleasant to talk to Jade out in the sunny garden, above ground, but there was too much risk of being overheard. One thing about the snug, at least it was private.

Jameson opened the doors and called to Jade, letting her know Tara had arrived. She came back inside straight away, with the dog close by her side, like a menacing shadow. Jameson gave his daughter's hand a reassuring squeeze and then left, without so much as looking in Tara's direction.

Jade, on the other hand, was perfectly friendly and seemed more relaxed than on the previous day. She was dressed exactly as she had been for their first meeting, in jeans and a white T-shirt, barefoot, with her hair loose down her back. She filled a dog bowl with fresh water and the dog drank eagerly.

Tara knew she was going to ask Jade directly about the night of the killing, and that she needed to do that without Ziggy in the room. Dogs were emotionally reactive, and Ziggy, a rescue dog who had possibly been traumatised himself, might react strongly if Jade became distressed. If the dog perceived her as a threat to Jade, it might attack.

'Jade, can we leave Ziggy up here while we talk today?'

Jade looked down at the dog. 'He won't like it.'

'I know. But I think it would be a good idea.'

Jade lured the dog into his basket with a treat and told him to 'stay' in a firm tone. He obeyed but didn't take his eyes off the two of them as they went towards the door leading to the basement living room.

Tara went down first. This time, Jade shut the door behind them at the top of the staircase. They took up the same positions on the sofa as the day before and Tara opened her notebook. She had reservations about the questions she was about to ask. She would have preferred to move more slowly, to take more time to build trust with Jade, until she felt the relationship was solid enough to talk about the events that had taken place in the Red Suite of The Onyx Hotel. But the time frame for the report made any further delay impossible.

'Jade, I need to ask you about what happened to Carl Ress.'

Jade shifted her position, tucking her hands under her thighs.

'I understand that you were waitressing in the hotel restaurant, and that when your shift ended, you went up to the Red Suite, is that right?'

Jade nodded. In their first interview, she had been adamant that nothing unusual had happened during her shift in the restaurant that night.

'Did you often stay over at the hotel?'

'My friend Lucy works there too,' Jade said, 'and a couple of times over the summer we'd crash in one of the empty suites. The Onyx always keeps one or two rooms open in case a VIP guest turns up last minute, even though they hardly ever do. Lucy works on reception, so she knows which ones are free. We usually just chill, eating pizza, or watching TV, or sometimes if we feel like it, we get changed and go and get a drink or listen to music in Soho.'

That night, Jade had changed into an emerald-green, sequined mini-dress with gold high heels. It was a striking outfit, which made her look older and more seductive. It didn't seem her style. Unless she made a point of looking more innocent, and younger, when she was home with her parents.

'Given the outfit you were wearing,' Tara said, 'it seems like you were planning to meet someone?'

'I don't know.' Jade was looking down at the floor, avoiding eye contact.

Tara put a question mark at that line in her notebook. 'You don't remember if you were going out to meet someone?'

Jade shook her head. Tara knew she was lying.

Jade claimed to have no memory of the few hours she'd spent with the victim. This was possible: she could be suffering from a form of traumatic amnesia. But, given she had no other gaps in her memory, it was not believable that her memory loss extended to her intentions *before* the killing. She would have packed her bag much earlier in the afternoon or evening, and she would remember who she was meeting, and why she had worn that dress. Those decisions would have been made when her memory was working just fine.

But lying did not make you a killer. People lied for all sorts of reasons.

'Jade, I know that isn't true. Do you want to tell me the real reason you chose that dress?'

'Do you have to put everything I tell you in your report?'

'It depends. I can't promise to leave anything out.'

Jade was still sitting on her hands. 'You said all kinds of people could see it? Like the police, and the judge.'

Tara nodded.

'Do my parents get to read it?'

'You'd need to check with your solicitor about that.'

Jade was looking her directly in the eyes now. 'Okay. I have a – kind of a thing for the bartender at The Onyx. His name's Marco. I went up to the Red Suite to shower and get changed before I went down to the bar because I knew he'd be on duty. And my hair always smells of fried food after being in the restaurant kitchen.'

Tara was writing all of this down. She didn't recall the name Marco or mention of a bartender coming up at all in the documents she'd been given. 'How old is Marco?'

'Like, in his twenties.'

'Does he know you're interested?'

Jade shook her head. 'I don't think so. We've never been out or anything like that. My dad wouldn't like it.'

'Why's that?'

Jade shrugged. She changed position again and started twirling a long strand of her hair. 'Just a dad thing. And, Marco works at the hotel, so. That's probably not a good idea.'

It occurred to Tara that Jade could be holding information

back as much because of her fear of her father's reaction as anything else.

'Okay, so after you got changed, did you go down to the bar alone?'

'I was supposed to meet up with Lucy, but she wasn't finished her shift on reception yet.'

'Take me through what happened in the bar, as much as you can remember. Even the small details can help.'

'Well, the place was really packed and I had to wait at the counter a while, until Marco saw me.' Jade closed her eyes. 'I ordered a drink. An Apple Martini. I can see him handing it to me – it's bright green, like my dress – and he's smiling, and I can see his beard, and his big brown eyes and his T-shirt glowing pink in the fluorescent lights... and then everything stops.'

Jade opened her eyes. 'It's all gone. Like when I had my wisdom teeth out. They gave me this injection in the back of my hand, and then I didn't remember anything after that. I didn't remember them taking me into the operating theatre, even though they told me I was awake in there, talking to them.'

Jade had been tested for substances, but nothing had been found in her system. The possibility of a date rape type drug had been ruled out.

'Have you lost time like this before?' Tara asked.

Jade wavered a second too long, her eyes pulling away as she looked up at the ceiling. She shook her head. She was lying, again.

'Had you ever met Carl Ress before that night?'

Jade shook her head. 'Never.'

Given what Tara knew about Jade's personality, and her behavioural history, what Jade was saying didn't add up. First, Jade claimed she didn't even want her father to know she had a crush on the bartender, but then she was bold enough to take a strange man up to one of the suites in her father's hotel. It made no sense.

'Why would you go up to the room with a stranger?'

'I don't know.'

'You must have been thinking about this yourself, right? You must be desperate to know what happened?'

Unless she already did.

'Witnesses saw you talking to Carl Ress in the bar.'

'I don't remember.'

Jade might appear co-operative, but it was clear she was holding something back.

'Jade, I don't believe that you would randomly go up to the Red Suite, alone, with a man who was more than double your age, five minutes after meeting him. You are sensible, intelligent and mature. You told me you don't rebel. So I think you had a good reason for taking Carl Ress into that room.'

Jade was blinking rapidly now. 'The police already asked me about all of this.'

The dog was scratching at the door and Jade was looking up at the top of the staircase, as if she longed to let him in.

'Have you ever done anything like that before, with strangers?'

'No!' Jade drew her knees up to her chest, compressing her body into a ball. Her anxiety was rising, but so was her resistance.

The scratching of paws grew louder and more frantic.

'The police say you attacked him, Jade. They say you stabbed him eleven times.'

Tara had seen a photograph of the dress Jade had been wearing. It was soaked in the victim's blood. She pressed on, knowing she was putting massive pressure on Jade, but aware of the sense of urgency inside herself. 'Eleven times. That's overkill. Bloodlust.'

The dog was barking now, throwing himself against the door. Jade's eyes were flashing, her cheeks were flushed. Tara felt her own face heat up in response.

'Did it feel good, Jade?'

She saw Jade, a knife in her fist, the tip hovering over Carl Ress's heart. She saw the girl plunge the blade hard into his chest, ramming it through skin and cartilage and blood.

Again and again and again.

'Why were you in such a rage? What happened in that room?'

Jade was rocking back and forth. Something in her eyes wasn't right.

Tara saw the blood-soaked carpet of the Red Suite. And then her parents' bedroom. The blood-soaked pillow. Her mother, lying on her back. The walls of the basement were closing in, the ceiling too low. Her breath was stuck in her chest, there was no space in her lungs to take in air.

Jade unravelled her arms and legs and stood up. 'Please can we stop?'

NINE

TWELVE YEARS EARLIER

The phone rang at about two in the morning, when Ray and Sandra were curled up asleep in their bed in the small apartment above the club. Ray disentangled himself, unwrapping his arms from her warm body and turning over to feel along the table beside the bed for the phone. He was expecting it would be the usual, some drama at one of the clubs. He grunted hello.

A woman, sobbing. 'Help me. Please. *Please.* You have to help me.'

'Paula? Is that you?'

She was slurring. 'I'm so scared. Please. Ray? Are you there? Ray? Ray?'

Ray sat up. He and Sandra had got through a bottle of wine with dinner and after that a couple of rounds of Kahlua coffee down at the club. It took him a few seconds to get his thoughts straight. 'Give me twenty minutes. I'm coming.'

'What's going on?' Sandra was on her side, facing away from him.

'Your sister's in a state.'

'Don't go.' Sandra turned over to face him, putting her arms around his waist. 'It won't make any difference.'

He prised her loose. 'I'll deal with it. You go back to sleep.'

'I'm serious. You're not going out on your bike. You've been drinking—'

'Nothing is going to happen to me.' He leaned across and kissed her gently on her lips, but she pulled away. 'Don't worry.'

Sandra was sullenly silent, watching as he got out of bed, pulled on his jeans and leather jacket and laced up his Doc Martens.

'You're encouraging her, you do know that?' The resentment Sandra felt was in her constricted voice. 'Paula knows you'll just come running over and rescue her every time.'

Sometimes, when Paula was out of it, which was most of the time, she tried it on with Ray and Sandra knew that, too.

Ray made his way down the moss-covered steps that lead from the pavement to the front door of Paula's basement flat in Camden. It was pitch black down there and it stank of uncollected refuse, and something worse, like the stench of a public urinal.

He knocked on the door with his right hand, knuckledusters ready and waiting on his left. Paula's boyfriends weren't exactly the friendly type. He'd got a few black eyes on previous rescue missions. Not that it bothered him. If anything, that was the part he enjoyed, gave him a chance to let off a bit of steam.

There was a shuffling behind the door before it opened. Paula was holding a dressing gown around her stick-thin body. Her right eye was already swelling up.

Ray's fingers tightened around metal. 'Is he still here?'

She shook her head.

'You sure about that?'

'I swear.' Paula's pupils were huge black saucers with nothing behind them. She was off her head. Just as well because otherwise she'd be in a shitload of pain. Ray didn't bother asking what she'd taken, she was a chronic liar.

'Right. Want me to take you to A&E?'

She shook her head. He couldn't even look at that smashed up face of hers. Looking at Paula now, Ray didn't think the chances were good she would make it to her next birthday. There was only so much her small body could take.

Sandra was right, her sister was hopeless. They had been trying to help Paula for years already. They'd get her cleaned up, even take her and the kid to their place for a few days, but every single time Paula went back to the drugs. And every time Sandra would make a report to social services about the girl, but nothing ever happened. Nothing changed.

If he had any sense, he'd turn around right now and go back to bed, to Sandra. Only, Ray felt guilty. He had given the green light for Paula to dance at Diamonds. He had known she was underage. And now he could not abandon her. And the girl.

'Where is Jade?' He kept his voice calm.

'I don't know.'

'Jesus fucking Christ, Paula.' He pushed past her. A naked light bulb lit the passageway. A pair of small pink trainers and a pink coat lay in a heap next to the front door. The place was too quiet. It reeked of marijuana and of damp.

Ray wanted to call out to Jade but he didn't in case whoever did that to Paula's face was still there, waiting. Paula was unreliable to say the least. She could have set him up and her latest boyfriend might be looking to jump him and steal his wallet. Paula would do anything for another fix.

He walked down the passage in silence, then pushed open the door to Paula's bedroom. A double mattress on the floor, ashtrays and bongs all over the place. He checked the bathroom. Empty. His real fear was not an ambush from some violent thug, but that one day he'd walk in and see something he could not bear to see. The vision came to him in nightmares, sometimes.

He looked in Jade's room last. Her bed was empty, her pillow on the floor and sheets pushed aside, the mattress indented with her small shape. There was a patch of mould on the ceiling above her bed. As he left the child's bedroom, he saw the bolt on the outside of the door. That had not been there before, he would have noticed. *Paula had put a lock on the outside of Jade's door. She was locking her in.* God knows how long she left the girl alone in there. Anything could happen. A fire, anything. Ray's fist clenched and unclenched.

Back at the front door Paula was on the floor, hunched over, with her arms wrapped around her knees and her dressing gown hanging open. Her wrists and ankles were covered in track marks.

'Look at me,' he said. 'Where is your daughter?'

She looked up. The state of her face. She was so passive, so helpless. Sandra was right, he should not have come. Paula sucked anyone who came too close into her swamp of self-destruction. Sandra was too smart to get involved.

If I let myself get too attached to Jade, she told Ray, *it will be a lifetime of misery. Paula will never change, and that girl is hers. Nothing is going to change that. Paula is Jade's mother.*

But it was too late for Ray.

'*WHERE IS SHE?*'

Paula cowered against the wall, covering her face. Ray felt huge as he loomed over her, the muscles in his arms straining against his leather jacket. He had the urge to hit her and he despised himself for it.

'Check the kitchen.' Paula put her head down again, pulling her knees in tighter into a ball. 'I told her to hide in a cupboard if she heard fighting.'

'Great. That's fucking great parenting.'

Ray went into the kitchen. Old pine cupboards with doors

hanging askew and others completely gone, a sink piled up with dishes and debris, rubbish spilling out of a bin in a corner. Social services knew about the way this kid lived; police knew about the lowlife who beat Paula to a pulp. They were all useless, they all made him sick.

There was a full-length broom cupboard in the corner with a slatted wooden door. He was so afraid of what he would see when he opened it. *Fuck, fuck, fuck.* He tugged at the brass knob and the door scraped open. He was hit by a rush of hot air.

Most of the space inside was taken up by a hot water cylinder in thick cladding, but as his eyes adjusted to the darkness, he saw a small shape. Jade, right at the back, red-faced from the heat and looking out at him with fierce eyes.

'It's me, Uncle Ray.'

Jade blinked a few times. She didn't move. She was petrified. Four-years-old for Christ's sake and she knew she had to hide.

'Do you want to come with me to visit Aunty Sandra?'

Jade loved Sandra.

'Will you come with me, Jadey?'

Ray was getting a very, very bad feeling. Jade didn't make a sound. She didn't move.

'You okay, hun?'

Jade was speaking less and less these days, losing her words instead of finding new ones.

'It's okay to come out,' he said. 'I'm here now. Nothing bad is gonna happen to you when I'm here. I promise.' He held out his hand to her.

Slowly, Jade crept out of the cupboard. Ray did not dare move, not wanting to scare her. She stood in front of him, looking right into his eyes, trying to decide if she could trust him. After a few moments of stillness, she reached out and took hold of his hand.

TEN

After Jade had asked to take a break, she'd gone out into the garden, taking Ziggy with her. Tara waited in the kitchen, watching them. Once she was out of the basement, Jade had quickly settled down and seemed calm again as she threw a tennis ball for the dog.

She'd had an intense reaction to Tara's questions about the night of the killing. This wasn't necessarily a bad sign; it could mean that Jade's memories were not buried too far under the surface. With more pressure, there could be a chance of recovering those lost hours.

If, that was, her amnesia was genuine. Tara still wasn't certain.

Tara's own reaction in the basement snug, the overpowering feelings of fear and claustrophobia, had ambushed her. Thinking back now to those last few moments in the basement, it was difficult to tease out what belonged to Tara and what belonged to her client.

Keeping an eye on Jade in the garden, Tara went closer to the knife block on the counter and pulled one out. A bread knife with a distinctive engraving on the blade: the initials R

and S and J, intertwined. Ray and Sandra Jameson, Tara
assumed. She slipped the knife back into place and pulled out
another. This one was a chef's knife with a wider blade, razor-
sharp edge, and the same engraving.

Tara pulled on the handle of the top drawer in the kitchen
island. It slid open smoothly. Inside, a range of cutlery was
neatly arranged in an organiser. Tara picked out a steak knife
with a serrated blade on a black wooden handle. She checked: it
had the same engraving as the set in the knife block. She put
that one back in place and then counted all of them. Twelve
sharp knives, all engraved with the Jamesons' initials.

The police must have searched this house. They too must
have counted, to check if any knives were missing from the set.

It bothered her, the way these knives were so openly and
casually displayed. Could Jade's parents be so certain their
daughter was not capable of an act of violence? Or was it a form
of stubborn denial?

And it was interesting that Jade's mother had not yet made
an appearance, except for that one moment in the window the
day before.

When Jade came back inside, she said she had a bad
headache and Tara suggested they could leave the rest of the
interview to the next day. She was equally relieved.

It was good to be back in the office, to have a mental break from
the Jameson case. That afternoon, Tara was seeing a new
patient, a woman who had been referred by Neil, her ex-boss at
the hospital.

Melanie Davis, who was twenty-seven, had been experi-
encing severe pain in her arms and legs for which no physical
cause could be found, despite many medical investigations.
Early in the appointment, it became clear why Neil thought she
needed to see a psychologist. Melanie told Tara that when she

had first got her driver's licence, around nine years earlier, she had been driving her younger sister to a party. A little over the speed limit, and on icy roads, she had lost control of her small car and collided with a truck coming in the opposite direction. Her sister had been killed. The agony was still visible in Melanie's face as she told Tara what had happened.

By the time she had shown Melanie out of the building, Tara felt physically shattered herself. Back in her office, after finishing her notes, she opened the window to let in some air. She focused on breathing. Slowly, taking air in right to the bottom of her belly. Usually, the work with her patients grounded her, but this time it felt different. The view did not soothe her.

She questioned why the universe was sending her these cases, one after the other, all of them seeming to revolve around guilt.

Melanie Davis's guilt was eating at her own body, from the inside.

Jade Jameson had blocked out her guilt completely.

And Tara's own guilt. Those images she'd not seen in years. The sense of terror in that basement.

She was overthinking things, reading too much into her cases, questioning her objectivity. She was facing a new kind of pressure, in private practice without the safety net of a team behind her and it was bound to affect her, she was only human. Leaving the hospital had been a major loss, and another massive change in her identity. This feeling of being off balance would pass.

ELEVEN

Tara arrived back at her cottage in the early evening. The fridge was empty, so she settled for slightly stale toast and cheese on the sofa, while catching up on the news on her laptop.

Later, too tired to work but too wound up to sleep, she stood at her kitchen window with a mug of coffee, staring out at the garden, at her beloved cherry tree with its copper-peeling bark. She had known, the moment she had seen that tree, that she would make an offer on the cottage, and also that it was the last place on earth she should be living. She should have found somewhere livelier, somewhere that was not filled with families and children, somewhere nearer the office, anywhere really, except a few streets away from the house where she had spent the first sixteen years of her life.

The dregs of her coffee were cold.

It was still light outside and Tara had the urge to go out for a walk. She turned left out of her low wooden gate and walked along Hampstead Way a while. The Garden Suburb was a secret oasis. Wide leafy streets, woods full of oaks and horn-beam, and homes ranging from chocolate-box cottages like hers to imposing mansions.

She made a left turn onto Meadway Close. For the most part, she resisted this route; when she needed to get out she'd walk in the woods. Sometimes though, the need to go back was too strong. Tara made her final turn, right, into Wildway Close, a short street lined with eight detached houses all in the Arts and Crafts style. At the end of the close, there was an entrance to Hampstead Heath. The police believed that her parents' killer had taken that route after he left the house.

Wildway Close was a beautiful name. The house looked cosy with its brick façade, covered front porch, and timber window frames with leaded squares of glass. The curtains were open and the lights were on inside. Two SUVs were parked side by side on the driveway.

The house had been empty for a while after the murders, but eventually it had sold and a couple of families had lived there over the last decades.

A woman came into the kitchen and stood at the sink. She didn't see Tara standing across the street in the gloom. Tara wondered what might happen if she walked up to the front door and knocked, and what she might see if she walked through those rooms again.

The house had not been a happy home. Tara's father was a man with dark moods. He had never been physically violent, instead alternating between verbal aggression and cold disinterest. Tara and her brother Matthew could never predict which random comment, expression, or tone of voice might set him off. Tara had learned to walk on eggshells. Matthew had become angry, an expert at provoking their father's temper. Their mother had spent long periods in hospital with an eating disorder that brought her to the brink of death.

Daniel had been Matthew's closest friend. He was one of the few people who knew what it was really like inside that family.

When the police found out about Matthew's alcohol problems, and the fraught relationship between Matthew and their father, and then when they found cocaine in the house that night, they assumed Matthew was a killer. Only Tara and Daniel knew that could not be true.

After the murders, her brother had vanished into thin air. Tara had never given up hope that one day he would come back and tell the whole truth. Maybe he would walk straight out of the Heath and onto Wildway Close. Maybe it would be tonight. Every time she came here, that was her secret wish.

The photographs of the crime scene at The Onyx Hotel came into focus, shimmering in the light at the kitchen window. Carl Ress, sprawled on his back, his chest a bloodied mess. Then, another image began to form beyond the glass. Her father with his eyes wide open. Her mother's hair, matted with blood. Tara closed her eyes and took a breath. For a long time, there had been a plate-glass window between her brain and her feelings about the murders. It was better that way.

When she looked again, the young mother was back at the window, peering out into the dusk, as if she sensed she was being watched.

Tara turned and walked back the way she'd come. The plaster on her thumb was irritating her. She stopped at a dustbin, pulled it off and dropped it inside. Underneath, her skin was pale and wrinkled, but the cut was barely visible anymore.

It was late and she knew she shouldn't, but on her way home, she phoned Daniel. His number rang a few times and then the call was rejected.

A few seconds later, a text came through. *Sorry can't speak. All okay?*

She didn't respond. She was angry, though she had no right to be.

If he didn't answer, that meant he was with his wife.

TWELVE

When Tara arrived at the Jameson house the next morning, Ray Jameson opened the front door as usual. He barely greeted her before leading her through to the kitchen in silence.

The whole house was ominously quiet. There was no sign of either Jade or Ziggy the dog, either inside or outside. The door leading down to the basement living room was closed.

'Is Jade down in the snug?'

'She's still in bed. She hasn't got up this morning.' Jameson leaned back against the kitchen counter, bracing his hands on the marble worktop behind him. 'This is very, very unlike her, she's always up early to let the dog out. She's had a bad reaction to your interview.'

'What sort of reaction?'

'Well we don't know, because we haven't been able to get a word out of her since you left. She refused to eat, went up to bed early last night and hasn't come out of her room since.' From his tone, it was clear that Jameson was angry at Tara. He blamed her for whatever was going on with Jade. 'Did something come up in your interview that I should know about?'

'I can't discuss the details of the interview—'

'I need to know what you talked about.'

Tara was uncomfortable being alone with him. 'As I said, I can't discuss the details of the interview. I appreciate you letting me know that Jade might be feeling fragile, I'll bear that in mind.'

It was possible that the questions about the night of the killing had triggered a memory trace that had destabilised Jade, but it was equally possible that Jade was avoiding her. Either way, Tara needed to see Jade herself and check on her well-being as well as her mental state.

'Did my daughter tell you anything different to the information she gave to the police?' Jameson spoke slowly and deliberately.

Tara was stunned at the brazenness of this question. 'I don't know the full details of what your daughter has told the police. Could you please ask her to come down now?'

'Jade is not in any state to talk to you. We gave her something for the anxiety about half an hour ago and she's asleep.'

Jade's parents had known about the interview schedule and were well aware of the tight deadline for the psychological report. Giving her a sedative right before Tara arrived at the house seemed suspiciously like sabotage.

'What did you give her?' Tara said.

'Some kind of tranquilliser.'

'What is the name of the medication?'

'I don't recall.'

Tara did not believe him. 'You gave your daughter a tablet, and she's fallen asleep, and you have no idea what she's taken?'

Jameson hesitated. 'The prescription was for my wife. Xanax, I think it's called.'

Tara reflected that it was strange that she still had not laid eyes on Jade's mother. Sandra Jameson had not made an appearance while Tara was in the house and Tara was beginning to think this must be deliberate. She also wondered how long

Sandra had been on prescription tranquillisers, and why these had been prescribed for her.

'So the tablet you gave her was not prescribed for Jade?'

Jameson shook his head.

Giving someone else's medication to Jade was illegal. And Tara hadn't seen anything about sedatives in her medical records. Alarm bells were going off.

'I need to see Jade, please. I'm happy to go up to her room if she can't come down.'

'You'll have to reschedule.' Jameson's arrogance was something else.

'That's fine. But I still need to see Jade before I leave. I need to see her even if she's asleep. I told Jade's solicitor that I was seeing her today and I'm not leaving the house without doing that.'

Tara caught a look of fury on Jameson's face. She had half a thought he was going to come across the kitchen and strike her. Instead, he reined himself in, calming himself by running his fingers through his hair, the emerald ring flashing.

'I'll check if she's awake,' he said.

Jameson gave in, probably because he could not refuse without it looking extremely suspicious. Tara had a strong feeling she would pay for this victory.

She followed Jameson up the wide and gently curved staircase leading off the entrance hall. His footsteps rang out on the polished wooden stairs as they climbed up to the third floor.

Jade's bedroom was large and airy. There were double aspect windows, one overlooking the street and the other with a view over the garden. The curtains were open, letting in lots of light. Jade was lying on her side, facing away from the door, and the dog was dozing on the foot of her bed.

Tara hovered in the doorway while Ray walked in ahead of her. 'Jade, Doctor Black is here to see you.'

The dog lifted his head but there was no response from Jade.

Jameson went over to stand at her bedside. 'Jadey, are you awake?'

The room was extremely tidy and sparsely furnished, and there was something bland about the space compared to the opulence on the ground floor. Jade's single bed had a beige padded headboard and white sheets. There was a desk and chair under the window. A bookshelf in the corner held files and textbooks, all of them neatly arranged, as well as a childlike collection of soft toys. Everything else must be tucked away in the wall of built-in cupboards, out of sight.

Jade had turned over and was looking at them. There was a glass of orange juice on her bedside table and Jameson went over, picked it up and offered it to her.

Jade manoeuvred herself into a sitting position, half-propped up against the headboard. Her hair, which looked as though it needed a wash, was scraped back into a ponytail, and her face was pale. She seemed like a much younger child as she held the glass of juice with both hands, taking a small sip before giving it back to her father.

'I'd like to talk to Jade alone for a few minutes,' Tara said.

Jameson wasn't happy at all. He didn't budge from Jade's bedside.

'Is that okay, Jade?' Tara said. 'Can we talk for a bit? Just a chat, no hard questions today.'

If Jade had taken a tranquilliser, she might be less guarded about what she said. Maybe Ray didn't want Tara talking to his daughter in that state.

'It's okay, Dad,' Jade said. 'You can go.'

Jameson bent down to give her a kiss on the top of her head and then, reluctantly, he left them alone together. Tara listened for his heavy footsteps receding down the stairs before she went over and closed the door.

She took the chair from underneath the desk and placed it at Jade's bedside. 'Your dad said you haven't been feeling well?'

'I feel so cold all the time. Like in the hotel room.'

Feeling cold was a sign of anxiety. And the trigger for this anxiety may be her lost memories edging closer to the surface after Tara had challenged her the day before.

'Did you remember something more, after we talked?'

Jade's eyes drifted closed. Tara felt another burst of irritation at Jameson, for medicating her right before the interview. There was no way Jade was in any state to talk to her, and she probably wouldn't be for at least a few more hours.

Tara also wondered if medicating Jade might be a pattern in this household.

Jade pulled the duvet up to her neck and slid down again, curling up onto her side with her head on the pillow. 'I wanted to wear her dress, to feel what it was like. The sequins are so pretty.'

She was talking about the dress she was wearing the night Carl Ress was killed.

'Jade, you said you wanted to wear *her* dress. Who does the dress belong to?'

Jade's eyes were still closed. 'It was Paula's dress. Don't tell them. Please. I don't want them to be sad.'

She was half-awake and not making much sense. Tara didn't remember the name Paula coming up in any of the background documents. Maybe she was a friend.

Tears trickled out from under Jade's eyelashes. 'I'm so cold all the time.'

She was shivering and Tara tucked the duvet around her. Strictly speaking, she shouldn't touch the girl, but she looked so young and so vulnerable. She was still a child. Tara reached out and put her hand on Jade's shoulder. She sat quietly beside her for a while.

'Sometimes, I miss her a lot,' Jade said.

'Who do you miss?'

Jade didn't answer. She became still as she sank down into sleep.

When Tara looked up, Ray Jameson was standing in the doorway, watching them.

THIRTEEN

Statement of Lucy Moyo

My name is Lucy Moyo and I am eighteen years old. I am employed part-time at The Onyx Hotel. On Friday, 11 August of this year, I was on duty on the reception desk. My shift started at four in the afternoon and I was due to finish at eleven forty-five.

I had arranged to meet my friend, Jade Jameson, up in the Red Suite of the hotel after my shift. We had permission to use this empty suite from the owner of the hotel. I did not leave the front desk until past midnight because my colleague, Felicity, failed to arrive on time for her shift. My other colleague, Steve, had to leave right on time or he would have missed the last tube home. So I was alone at the front desk and it is strictly not permitted to leave reception unattended. I called Jade on her mobile, to let her know I'd be late, but she didn't answer. I thought maybe she was working late too, or she was in the shower or she had forgotten to take her phone off silent. I was not worried.

At 12.12 a.m., after Felicity arrived and I did a handover, I left the front desk and went up to the second floor in the lift. When I got to the Red Suite, the door was not properly closed which was strange. I knocked and I said Jade's name, but she didn't answer. The lights were off inside. I could smell a man's aftershave. And something else too, but at first I didn't know what the other smell was.

I pushed the door open, slowly, calling, 'Hello, it's Lucy.' There could have been a change to the room bookings, or a last-minute guest had checked in, and I could be walking into some stranger's room by mistake, and about to give someone a heart attack.

I used the torch on my mobile phone to look around the room. That was when I first saw Jade. She was sitting on the sofa. I said, 'Are you okay? Why are you sitting in the dark?'

She said: 'Don't get a fright when you see me. I'm not hurt.' And the next thing she said was, 'Don't come in. Go back down-stairs and call the police.'

I asked her what I should tell the police, but she didn't answer. I felt very worried and I didn't want to leave her alone. I knew something was wrong. I carried on shining the torch on my phone around the room, and that was when I saw the body. A man was lying on the floor, at the foot of the bed.

I'm trained in first aid and I performed all the necessary checks. First I made sure the area around him was clear, in case there was a live electrical cord or sharp glass or something like that. Then I checked his wrist for a pulse, but there wasn't one. He wasn't breathing and he had lost a lot of blood. I did not think it was advisable to give him chest compressions because of the wounds all over his upper body.

I called 999 from my mobile and asked them to send police and an ambulance. Jade was still sitting quietly on the sofa while I was doing all this, it only took a minute or two.

I asked her to come downstairs with me, I said we could wait in the library. She said no. I didn't want to leave her in the room alone, so I sat next to her on the sofa, and I held her hand, and we waited together.

FOURTEEN

As soon as she got back to her car, Tara called Valerie Bennett to let her know about the situation with Jade, and that her client had been sedated without medical advice. Valerie didn't pick up and her mobile went to voicemail. Tara left a message, stressing it was important.

With some free time on her hands, as her time with Jade had been so brief, Tara decided to go back to The Onyx Hotel, to try to track down Jade's friend, Lucy Moyo. Tara had left her a few messages, but Lucy had not returned any of them.

A helpful staff member on the reception desk told her that Lucy was working an extra shift in housekeeping and could be found up on the first floor. Once again, Tara found herself walking along the vanilla-scented passageway. A cleaning trolley stood opposite one of the rooms, and the door was ajar. A brass plaque on the wall read: Blue Suite.

Tara knocked and went inside. The room was identical in layout to the Red Suite, but this one had a blue headboard and blue cushions on the sofa. And this one was in disarray, with towels and empty wine glasses strewn around. A young woman had her back to Tara and was stripping the bed.

'Hi, are you Lucy Moyo?'

'Yes.' She did not turn around.

'My name is Doctor Tara Black, I'm a psychologist working with Jade Jameson. I was hoping you would have a few minutes to talk to me.'

The girl turned around. She was small in stature and rounded in shape. Her shoulder-length dark curls were scraped back behind an Alice band. 'No, not today. I have thirty minutes to get this suite ready and I need to keep to my deadline.'

'Right. Could I talk to you while you work? It's important.'

'I gave my statement to the police. I don't have anything more to add.' Lucy was back to removing the sheets from the large bed and pillows from pillowcases.

Tara took out her notebook and retrieved one of the many pens that were pooling in the bottom of her briefcase. She pushed a bathrobe off the sofa and sat down. It was an unconventional set up for an interview, but on the positive side, Lucy was essentially a captive audience given that she was determined to finish her cleaning.

'You handled the situation so well that night in the Red Suite,' Tara said. 'It must have been a huge shock, finding a dead body.'

'Not really. I'm good at staying calm in an emergency. My mum used to pass out loads of times, so I know the checks.'

'I'm sorry to hear that. Can I ask what happened to your mum?'

'She was an alcoholic. By the time I was four, I knew I was supposed to turn her on her side and to check her airways were clear if she was throwing up.'

When she'd read Lucy's police statement, Tara had noticed how the eighteen-year-old seemed strangely unfazed by coming across a dead body. Now she'd met Lucy in person, the young woman's matter-of-fact response that night in the Red Suite made more sense. Lucy's lack of eye contact and her stiff and awkward speech pattern probably meant she had some broader difficulties in social interaction. She might see the world differently to most people.

'How long have you known Jade?' Tara asked.

On the face of it, Lucy and Jade seemed an unlikely pair to have struck up a friendship. They couldn't be more different, both in appearance and personality. Jade possessed a quiet confidence and an easy conversational style, with the notable exception of when she was pressured to talk about the death of Carl Ress.

'Jade and I met when we were five years old.'

'Were you at school together?'

Lucy shook her head. 'We met at Mrs Martin's house.'

'Mrs Martin?'

'She was our foster carer. We shared a bunk bed. When Jade came, I had to sleep on the top because she was scared of falling out.'

Tara took a few seconds to process what Lucy had just said. She had had no idea Jade had spent time in foster care. There had been no mention of that when she'd asked Jade about her childhood, and no mention of it in the medical records.

'How long were you two in foster care together?' Tara said.

'Three or four years. I came to Mrs Martin's when I was four, and I stayed until I turned eighteen, a couple of months ago. Jade came when she was five. She'd get sent back home, but then she'd come back again, on and off for years.'

'Until she turned nine?'

Lucy nodded.

The information about Jade's time in foster care must be documented in those missing medical records and Tara had to wonder if Ray Jameson had removed those from the bundle himself. Maybe there was information in there about his treatment of his daughter that he didn't want made public.

Tara thought of Jade, sedated and lethargic. Her sense of concern grew. She would try again to contact Jade's lawyer immediately after this meeting. For now, she wanted to try to get more details from Lucy, who was currently her only source of information about this aspect of Jade's life.

Lucy collected all the bed linen from the floor, came over to retrieve the bathrobe from near Tara's feet, and then left the room to deposit it all into her trolley outside in the passage. She reappeared briefly in the doorway with a tray of cleaning equipment, before going into the bathroom where she was out of sight.

Tara went to stand where she could see Lucy wiping down the basin. 'Do you know why Jade was placed in foster care?'

'Her mum was a drug addict. One time, she locked Jade in their flat and went out and didn't come home for days. She could have died.'

The elusive Sandra Jameson. Perhaps this explained why she had been avoiding Tara.

'How about now, is Jade happy at home?'

Lucy paused a second. 'Very happy.'

'Are you sure?'

She nodded.

'How does she get along with her parents?'

'Jade is very lucky with her parents.' There was a sincerity in Lucy's voice. 'I wish I had parents like hers.'

This was a confusing picture. Could the Jameson family have changed so dramatically?

Lucy sprayed glass cleaner across the large mirror in front of her and began wiping it down.

Tara was aware that time was running out, because she had to be back in the office to see a client in an hour. She wanted to move on to the subject of Jade's relationship with Carl Ress.

'You know,' Tara said, 'when I've visited Jade at home, she likes to wear T-shirts and jeans. Comfortable clothes. But I was wondering, when the two of you go out together at night, what kind of clothes does she wear then?'

'T-shirts and jeans. That's her signature style. I think Jade looks like a model, whatever she wears.'

'Right. But the way Jade was dressed the night Carl Ress died was different. It seemed like she wanted to look extra special, don't you think?'

I wanted to wear her dress, to feel what it was like. The sequins are so beautiful.

Lucy shrugged. She began spraying the surface of the marble vanity.

'Why do you think she chose the dress with the sequins?'

No answer. Lucy acted as though she hadn't heard the question.

'Maybe Jade wanted to impress Marco, the bartender,' Tara said. 'She probably told you she has a secret crush on him?'

Lucy paused a moment, then nodded. She was still half-turned away from Tara as she wiped down the taps. 'Everyone around here has a secret crush on Marco. If you ask me, Risha hires her bartenders for their looks. They probably sell more drinks that way. Sometimes I think Risha has a crush on him herself.'

'Right. But Marco is a young guy, in his early twenties, right?' Tara said. 'So, a sequined dress and heels seems a bit of an odd choice if Jade was trying to get his attention. I think that outfit made Jade look a lot older. So I think it would make more sense if she'd worn that dress to impress a much older man. Someone like Carl Ress.'

Lucy set down her cloth. She took out a pair of glasses from the pocket of her tunic and put them on. They were too large for her face and it looked as though she might want to hide behind them. 'I need to finish making up this room and I can't concentrate with all these questions. Mr Jameson basically made the manager give me this job because I'm Jade's best friend, and I can tell you Ms Risha Bassi isn't the easiest woman to work for.'

'Why is that?'

'She watches us like a hawk, trying to make sure everything around here is totally perfect. I guess that didn't exactly work out, did it?' There was a hint of humour in her tone.

Lucy replaced her bottle of cleaning fluid in the tray and then arranged all the bottles so that the spouts faced the same direction.

'Lucy, were you surprised to find out that Jade had come up to the hotel suite with Carl Ress when she'd only just met him down in the bar?'

Lucy frowned. 'Not really.'

Tara was taken aback by her answer. 'Has Jade done that kind of thing before? Come up to a room here with a man she doesn't know very well?'

'No. I mean, no. I don't know.' Lucy wasn't good at being evasive.

Tara had the impression that the girl knew more than she was prepared to admit, but she was conflicted because she was so loyal to Jade. The two of them had a strong bond, going a long way back into childhood. If anybody knew anything about Jade's possible relationship with Carl Ress, Tara would put money on it that person would be Lucy Moyo.

'How about you, Lucy, had you ever met Carl Ress before that night?'

'I work in a hotel. I meet a lot of people. I could have met him and not even known. I've already told this to the police.' Lucy began pouring large amounts of bleach down the plug-holes of the sink, the toilet, and the shower drain.

Given that she had been the first person to find Jade in the room with Ress's body, Tara assumed the police must have looked into her movements that night, and that nothing suspicious about Lucy's involvement had emerged. But Jade's solicitor had stressed that the investigation was ongoing.

Tara was increasingly convinced that both young women had met Ress before, but for whatever reason, were hiding the truth.

The smell of bleach had become overpowering, and Tara had to take a couple of steps back. She had no doubt Lucy wanted their conversation to end. Because Lucy was lying.

FIFTEEN

Back in her office later that afternoon, Tara received a surprise visit from Jade's solicitor. Valerie Bennett sat with her spine straight, her shoulders back and her legs crossed on the opposite side of Tara's desk. Her silver-grey bob was sharply cut around her jaw, her white shirt and black pencil skirt were perfectly pressed, and her tights were impressively sheer.

'Lovely offices,' she said.

'Thank you.'

'I thought it would be good for us to meet in person. You left a message saying there was something important you wanted to talk to me about?'

No instructing solicitor had ever come to Tara's office in person before, and in view of Valerie's reputation as one of the most sought-after criminal solicitors in London, her presence was a clear sign of how important the Jameson case was.

'I wanted to let you know about some concerns I had this morning,' Tara said. 'When I got to the house for our appointment, Jade's parents had given her a tranquilliser. She was sedated to the extent that she couldn't come downstairs or hold a conversation.'

'I understand from Mr Jameson that Jade was in a state of anxiety after you'd interviewed her the day before?'

'Those tranquillisers aren't prescribed for Jade. It's a red flag for me on a couple of levels.'

'I understand. I'll talk to her GP about it, if that reassures you.'

'That would be excellent, thank you.'

There was a pause. Valerie looked down at her hands clasped in her lap. Her short nails were painted a deep shade of burgundy. 'The family was very positive about you coming on board, but I think they are starting to have some concerns about your process.'

Tara had a feeling this visit might be about something else besides the message she'd left earlier and her concern for Jade's welfare. She could still picture the expression on Ray Jameson's face when she had defied him and insisted on going up to Jade's room. He would not let that go without some kind of comeback.

'I'm guessing that Ray Jameson is not happy that I insisted on seeing Jade this morning?'

'I'm afraid it's a little more than that. Mr Jameson is concerned because he saw you touching his daughter inappropriately.'

For a moment, the air was knocked out of Tara's lungs. Jameson really was a piece of work and she was fuming. If anyone was inappropriate around his daughter, it was Ray Jameson.

She collected herself and answered calmly. 'Jade was distressed when I went into her room. I was sitting at her bedside and I leaned over and put a hand on her shoulder for comfort.'

'Mm hmm.' Valerie crossed her legs in the other direction, smoothing down her skirt.

'I can see that was perhaps unwise.'

Valerie nodded. 'You yourself said she was very sedated.'

'I see your point, and I appreciate Mr Jameson's concern. It won't happen again.'

'Thank you. And, of course, a pat on the shoulder for comfort is understandable. A natural response.'

Tara nodded. Relieved. Valerie Bennett was smart and sensible. She was delivering Jameson's message, but she also had the measure of her client. Hopefully, anyway. Because it seemed there was more to come in this conversation.

'So,' Valerie said. 'The family were hoping you would have enough information by this point, having been to the house three times. They would like to know if there's a way Jade could be spared the trauma of further interviews.'

Tara's feeling was that the real reason for this request was that Ray Jameson did not want her finding out anything more about their complex family history. She was beginning to suspect that Jade could be under a form of coercive control where her father was concerned.

'I don't think it's in Jade's best interests to cut short the interview process,' Tara said. 'And it's important that I talk to Jade directly about how she's feeling. Her parents shouldn't be speaking for her.'

Valerie nodded. 'Look, I'll do my best, but you've probably already gathered that Mr Jameson has strong opinions. He might decide to stop the process. To be up front with you, there are other options in terms of experts.'

'I understand.'

Tara sensed that she had Valerie's support. But Valerie herself was no doubt coming under extreme pressure from Jameson who was determined to get his own way. Since Jade was a minor, ultimately Ray Jameson could have the final say.

'If I'm still going to be working on this case,' Tara said, 'I absolutely do need to see Jade again. I've just learned she was in foster care for several years. I need to understand why she was removed from Ray and Sandra Jameson's care.'

Valerie was frowning. 'I think there's been a misunderstanding. Jade was adopted by the Jamesons when she was around nine years old. If she was in foster care, it must have been before then.'

'Right.' Tara was trying to process this, shifting the pieces of the jigsaw around in her mind once again. 'Well, I haven't received any information about the adoption and Jade's early experiences could be crucial to understanding what happened in that hotel room. I assume it's all in the missing medical notes?'

'I'm afraid it's not good news on that front either,' Valerie said. 'I've been trying to chase up those records, but they appear to have been lost. It's unlikely they are going to turn up in time for your report. If at all.'

So crucial information about any early trauma Jade might have experienced was missing. The thought that Ray Jameson might have made those documents disappear did not seem entirely far-fetched at this point.

'Do you know anything about the circumstances of the adoption?'

'Only that it was an adoption within the family. The biological mother was Sandra Jameson's sister.' Valerie checked her watch.

Tara was thinking that she really needed to talk to the elusive Sandra Jameson.

Valerie leaned down and lifted her briefcase onto her lap. It appeared their meeting was drawing to a close.

'I was wondering if any further information about the link between Jade and Carl Ress has been found?'

'No. It was most likely a chance meeting in the bar that led to a situation of a much older man trying to take advantage of an adolescent girl.'

Only Tara did not believe Jade would be so impulsive as to go up to a hotel room with a strange man double her age. She pictured all those knives on display in the Jameson kitchen. Easily accessible.

'One last question,' Tara said. 'Any progress in finding the weapon that was used in the stabbing?'

Valerie shook her head. 'Nothing there either. Forensics took apart the suite and as much of the hotel as they could get access to, but nothing has ever turned up. They are still trawling through a ton of CCTV in the area surrounding the hotel.' Valerie stood up. 'Look, it's DNA soup in that hotel room and my argument has always been that it's entirely possible someone else was in that suite and committed the crime while Jade was in some kind of state of shock. Of course, I'm hoping your report supports that theory.'

Tara knew full well that if her report wasn't to the defence team's liking, they would bury it.

'The police see it differently though?'

'Police can be blinkered. Jade and Carl Ress were seen leaving the bar together, there are no witnesses who saw anyone else going into or out of that hotel room, which is hardly surprising since it's a quiet hotel passageway with no CCTV, and then the victim's blood was all over Jade's body. It's convenient for the police to believe they have the right person because widening the pool of suspects simply means more work for them. My investigators on the other hand are working day and night trying to trace and interview as many people as we can that were on the premises that night.'

Before Valerie left, Tara asked for her help in setting up a series of other interviews. She wanted permission to talk to one of Jade's teachers, to get a different perspective on Jade's personality. She also asked Valerie if she could look into whether Carl Ress's widow might be willing to talk to her. Understanding the victim may be another route in to understanding Jade.

'I'll see what I can do.' The brass buckle of Valerie's brief-case, two interlocking Gs, lit up in a shaft of sunlight. 'I do want to stress though, that your instructions are to give an opinion about Jade's memory loss on the night Carl Ress died. I would be cautious about extending that brief too far. We wouldn't want to intrude any more than we have to into any other matters. For both our sakes.'

SIXTEEN

Due to her unexpected meeting with Jade Jameson's solicitor, Tara was a few minutes late for the early dinner she had scheduled with Olivia. They'd arranged to meet at their favourite Japanese restaurant around the corner from the office. At six, the place was still relatively empty. Olivia was waiting, sitting alone at a table for two along the side wall. She had a menu open in front of her on the table and she was scrolling through her phone.

The two of them had been friends for years before they'd become business partners. Olivia was a psychiatrist, working in a different department at Tara's old hospital, and they'd met by chance when they both joined a lunchtime exercise class at the hospital. It turned out that they had both started thinking about going into private practice at around the same time. When Tara had taken the plunge and invested in the mews house in Marylebone, she had been thrilled when Olivia had jumped at the chance to rent the ground floor office.

Tara hated being late for anything. She apologised profusely as she sat down, explaining she'd been in a meeting with Valerie. She poured herself a glass of water from the bottle

already on the table. It felt like it had been a long and challenging day.

'How's the case going?' Olivia said.

'Not well.' The state of her client when she'd left the
Jameson house was still very much on Tara's mind.

'What happened?'

'My client's parents decided it was a good idea to give her a
Xanax just before our meeting this morning. She was too
knocked out to make any sense.'

'Sabotage?' Olivia said.

'My thoughts exactly. Her mother is avoiding me and her
father is not making it easy for her to talk to me. I think my
client is under a lot of pressure. Maybe it's because of the legal
case, or maybe they're worried about her disclosing something,
I'm not sure yet.'

'That's a tough one.' Olivia knew how pleased Tara had
been when the assignment from Valerie Bennett's firm had
unexpectedly come through. It was the kind of case that could
help build the reputation of the practice.

'Oh, but that's not even the worst of it—'

Their conversation was interrupted as the owner came over
with her notepad to take their order. Tara ordered the usual
assorted sushi, but Olivia said she'd have a miso soup and that
was it. They handed back the menus.

'How's the nausea?' Tara said.

'Relentless. All day. Every day.' Olivia was pregnant with
her first child. It hadn't been planned and had taken Tara by
surprise too. Olivia being on maternity leave wasn't exactly
factored into her business plan.

'What were you saying about the worst of it?'

'I screwed up. When I heard she'd taken a tranquilliser, I
insisted on going up to her room to check on her, and she was in
such a sad state that I reached out and put my hand on her

shoulder, for comfort. The father saw and accused me of "inappropriate touching".'

'Seriously?'

'The lawyer is no fool. She knows he's manipulative. But still.' Tara took another long drink of water. 'I shouldn't have done it. Maybe I am a little over-involved. Over-identified, according to Daniel.'

'Hmm.'

Olivia's hmm conveyed her general disapproval of Daniel. She thought Tara was wasting her time. She was right, of course. But Tara had this fantasy, she'd wait it out, and one day—

'The girl's seventeen?' Olivia was saying.

'Yes.'

'Does she trigger your maternal instinct?'

'She probably does. I never thought of it like that. She seems very lost.' Tara wished she'd ordered a beer. She could do with an ice-cold Asahi and a break from thinking.

They stopped talking as their waitress arrived with their food. Tara hadn't eaten since a quick breakfast before leaving for the Jameson place and she was starving.

Olivia was taking tentative sips of her soup. 'Do you ever think about babies?'

'Yes and no. Mainly no.' But Tara had felt an unfamiliar yearning in her core since she'd heard Olivia's news, and sometimes, alone and late at night, doubts crept in.

'You probably need to decide soon.'

'Thanks.' What Tara loved about Olivia, and what she sometimes found alarming, was that she had razor-sharp vision and no filter between her brain and her mouth.

'Was that insensitive? I'm sorry. My big mouth is even worse than usual. I blame the hormones.'

Tara mixed wasabi into her soy sauce. Daniel already had two children. 'It isn't an option for me.'

Olivia was making a valiant effort to get through her soup. She was looking very pale. 'You know what you said about the client's parents worrying about what she might say because she was so relaxed after she took that tranquilliser? It made me think – there are some really interesting results with psychogenics and memory loss at the moment.'

'You mean like ketamine or psilocybin?'

Olivia nodded, stifling a yawn. 'I used ketamine with one of my patients who wanted to uncover memories of early abuse. Interesting stuff came up. The problem is there's no way to know if it's a real memory or a fantasy because she was essentially tripping. In your case – I'm not sure it would stand up in court.'

Olivia had apologised and left early, feeling exhausted. Tara stayed on at their table for a while, enjoying the buzz of conversation around her as the restaurant filled up. She ordered herself an Asahi. She didn't feel like going home.

She took out her notebook and read through the fragmented interview she'd had with Jade that morning, and then her conversation with Lucy Moyo. Her strong intuition was that for some reason, both girls were lying about knowing Carl Ress.

The final notes that day were from the meeting with Valerie Bennett. Tara liked Valerie's no-nonsense, upfront approach. She very much hoped she would be allowed to finish the assessment with Jade. If she did crack this case, then Valerie might send a lot more work her way. But when she thought back to Jade, woozy in bed after being sedated and the expression on Ray Jameson's face in the kitchen, she knew the road ahead was unlikely to be smooth.

So far, Tara had resisted the urge to research the Jameson family online. She knew from Valerie Bennett that Jade's father was a hotel magnate and property developer, but she had not wanted to know too much more, she hadn't wanted to go into the process with too many preconceptions. Now though, with Ray Jameson's increasingly manipulative behaviour, she decided it was time. She took out her laptop.

A profile piece about Jameson had appeared in the *Financial Times* around five years earlier. Apparently, although he had established his fortune by developing a chain of luxury hotels, before that, he'd had a colourful career. After leaving school at sixteen for a stint as an amateur boxer, he'd worked as a bouncer at a so-called 'Gentleman's Club' in Soho. There, he'd moved up the ranks to become the owner's personal bodyguard, before ending up managing a string of clubs across London. His former boss, who was accused of having criminal connections and being engaged in money laundering, had subsequently landed up in jail.

The rest of the article went on to describe the success of Jameson's hotel franchise and focused more on the healthy state of Jameson's finances than on his personal life. Tara could find nothing else about the family online, though she did find one photograph of Jade and her parents. Then in her early teens, Jade had braces on her teeth and wore a demure floral dress as she stood between Ray and Sandra, smiling for the camera. She looked carefree and happy. Her father's arm was around her shoulders. Sandra Jameson was standing a little way away from the other two, unsmiling. She was sylphlike and lovely and the resemblance to Jade was strong. The caption noted that the photograph had been taken at a cocktail party held for the opening of The Onyx Hotel in Soho.

On impulse, Tara also googled Dr Anthony Edwards, the first psychologist who had been hired to work on Jade's case. His practice was based in Oxford. She sent him a brief email, asking if they could set up a time to talk, though she did not specifically mention the Jameson case.

When Tara checked her email, there was an unwelcome

message waiting for her from Ray Jameson, informing her that Jade was still 'too unwell' to meet with her the next morning. She sent a reply straight back, saying that in that case, she would like to meet with Ray and Sandra instead. To her surprise, he agreed quickly and without argument. At least that was something. But her gut feeling was that Jade was avoiding her, and for whatever reason, it seemed her parents preferred it that way.

SEVENTEEN

Tara met with Ray and Sandra Jameson the next morning. They had once again asked her to come over to their home in St John's Wood, claiming they did not want to leave Jade at home alone.

Jameson was back in charming mode when he came to open the front door and there was no trace of the animosity he'd shown the day before. He once again offered Tara a coffee, which she firmly declined.

She'd had a rough night, with vivid and thinly disguised anxiety dreams. In one, Tara's bed was down in the basement snug of the Jameson house, and she was afraid of a young woman, not Jade but similar enough, who was sleeping in the next bed, holding a knife engraved with the initials R-S-J. Tara had desperately wanted to leave the room, but was too scared to move for fear of waking her.

This time, Jameson took Tara up to the high-ceilinged living room on the first floor. Sandra was waiting for them, standing in front of one of the large sash windows, next to a cactus that was as tall as she was. She was dressed from head-to-toe in white Lycra and sipping from a glass containing a thick green drink.

'Sandra, this is Doctor Black,' Jameson said.

Sandra acknowledged the introduction with a small nod. The resemblance between Jade and Sandra was striking. Both had delicate features, honey-blonde hair, and an ethereal air about them.

'Please take a seat.' Ray motioned towards one of the sofas.

Tara sat, sinking down into the oversized cushions. She placed her briefcase down on the parquet floor close to her chair and took out her notebook, the familiar feel of it reassuring. It took her a few moments to acclimatise to the boldly furnished room. There were butterscotch velvet sofas, large multi-colour abstract canvases covering the walls, and bookshelves filled with vases, photograph frames and glossy hardbacks.

Ray sat down on the sofa opposite and patted the seat next to him. Sandra obligingly came over to sit down. He reached for her hand and she let him take it in a limp sort of way.

As Tara gave her routine explanation, ensuring that the Jamesons were aware that anything they said in the interview could be included in her report, she noticed that Sandra was staring blankly across the room. Tara wondered if she might have taken a sedative herself.

Tara particularly wanted to talk about Jade's experiences while she had been living with her biological parents, and then in foster care, but she began with more general questions, asking the Jamesons if they had noticed any warning signs or changes in behaviour that concerned them in the time leading up to the death of Carl Ress.

They both shook their heads, without taking much time to think.

'Jade is very settled,' Ray said. 'She does well at school, has a good circle of friends.'

Sandra nodded.

When Tara asked about emotional difficulties such as anxiety, depression or social withdrawal, Ray denied Jade had experienced any of these. He was doing all the talking, while Sandra gazed into the distance.

'Has Jade ever been involved in other incidents of aggression or violence before?'

'Absolutely not,' Ray said.

He looked at Sandra, who nodded, after a second's pause. It was becoming clear that Tara needed to talk to Jade's mother alone. With Ray in the room, she would not say anything to contradict him, and Ray Jameson was not diverting from an idealised picture of their daughter. Either because he couldn't face reality, or because he was lying.

Jameson seemed to expect Tara to believe that Jade was a veritable angel who had led a flawless life. But there must have been some sign.

Sandra withdrew her hand from her husband's as she tipped up her glass and drank the last drops of the green liquid. She had not once looked directly at Tara or made eye contact as Tara went through her standard list of questions: Had Jade ever had any difficulty at school with peers or teachers? Had she ever been in trouble with police? Did she ever use drugs or alcohol? Each time Tara asked a question, Sandra glanced at her husband and waited for him to answer, and, as Tara was fully expecting by this stage, Ray Jameson said 'no' to everything. It was Sandra's reactions that Tara was monitoring, but she remained expressionless.

Tara asked about more extreme behaviours, such as stealing, fire-setting or cruelty to animals. If Jade had shown any of these growing up, this could indicate an emerging personality disorder which could go some way to explaining her act of violence.

'Jade adores animals,' Ray said, 'and they respond to her. She has a special way with them.'

'I understand Jade wants to study to be a veterinary surgeon?' Tara said.

For the first time, Sandra offered her thoughts. 'With Jade's school results, she would have had her pick of veterinary colleges. I wanted her to take up a place in Edinburgh, but she insisted she wanted to stay in London, to take up a place at the Camden college. I can't stand it there, it's not a healthy environment for her. But Jade can be very strong-willed.'

Ray patted his wife's hand, as though cautioning her not to say too much. Sandra fell silent again.

'Does Jade have any brothers or sisters?' There had been no mention of siblings in the documents Tara had received so far, but she was well aware by this stage that these documents were far from comprehensive.

'Jade has no full siblings,' Ray said, 'but I have a daughter from a previous relationship. She's a lot older and she's always lived with her mum.'

Sandra leaned forward, putting her glass down on the coffee table. The unusual piece was entirely fashioned out of a thick, blue-tinted glass, the legs sculpted into abstract patterns, like waves. Like everything else in the room, except the old cactus, the table gave the impression of being flashy and expensive. Tara wondered who Ray and Sandra really were, under the affluent veneers.

She had thought at some point one of them might mention the adoption spontaneously, but there was no sign that was going to happen.

The couple sat side by side, holding hands. The pressure they were under showed in their hollowed-out eyes and made itself felt in the atmosphere in the room. Maybe a retreat into denial was their only way of coping. Maybe Jade had picked up on her parents' need for her to be the perfect daughter and had done her best to live up to that demanding and unrealistic role. Until something had gone very, very wrong.

'Such an extreme act of violence doesn't usually come out of the blue,' Tara said.

'We don't accept that our daughter committed any act of violence.' Jameson brushed his hair back off his forehead in a gesture that Tara had come to recognise. It was a tell. Jameson was angry, and trying to calm himself down.

'I need to ask you about Jade's adoption,' Tara said.

Abruptly, Sandra stood up. 'I'm sorry I need to leave. I have clients booked.'

Tara was taken aback. 'It's really important that I talk to you both—'

'It will have to be another time,' Sandra said.

Ray stood up and kissed his wife on the cheek before she left the room. She did not say goodbye as she walked out.

Ray sat down on the sofa again, his palms flat on his thighs. His hands were powerful; thick fingers with old scars across his knuckles.

'I apologise. Her clientele can be very demanding. It's a difficult time.' His voice tailed off. For the first time, he was lost for words and there were a few moments of silence.

'Your wife had a strong reaction when I mentioned the adoption.'

'Sandra's sister, Paula, was Jade's biological mother.'

Jade had spoken about Paula, in her bedroom, while she had been sedated. *It was Paula's dress. Don't tell them. Please. I don't want them to be sad.*

Jade had been wearing her biological mother's dress the night she'd killed Carl Ress.

Ray Jameson rubbed his palms up and down his thighs. 'Sandra feels responsible – for everything. She always has, even though it was all beyond her control. Beyond both of our control.'

'You spoke about Paula in the past tense. Did something happen to her?'

'She died of an overdose, around six years ago now. It didn't come as a surprise to anyone. She'd been a heroin addict since her teens.'

'Could you tell me a little more about Jade's life with Paula?'

'Paula was only seventeen when Jade was born. She didn't even work out she was pregnant before it was too late to do anything about it. For the first couple of years, the two of them were in a mother and baby foster home together, and things weren't too bad. But after Paula moved into her own flat, it all went completely to hell. Drug paraphernalia all over the place, no food, scum in and out of there. They lived in this squat in Camden, that's why Sandra hates the place so much.'

'And how did the adoption come about?'

'One time, Jade had only just turned nine, and Paula disappeared and left her alone in the flat for days. A neighbour called us and we went to pick her up, and that was it. I was out of patience. Sandra never wanted to take Jade away from her sister, and for years I listened to her, but to cut a long story short, I'd had enough. I got a lawyer involved – a good one – and eventually Paula agreed to let us take Jade into long-term foster care. After Jade had been living with us about a year or so, and it was clear Paula wasn't interested in changing her lifestyle, we started adoption proceedings. It was a long process, but it was all finalised by the time Jade turned eleven.'

Tara was beginning to see Jameson in a somewhat different light. He had tried to do the right thing to rescue Jade from a hellish situation. She had to wonder though, how much pressure he might have put on Paula to give up her child.

Tara put her notebook away. She had been hoping Jade might make an appearance. 'Would it be possible to see Jade briefly, before I leave?'

Jameson's response was as she'd expected. He shook his head. 'Jade was upset that you saw her in that state yesterday.

She left strict instructions not to let you up to her room while she's asleep.'

'I understand. I'll be here for the appointment tomorrow then. Hopefully Jade will be feeling much better.'

Jameson took another deep breath, just about stifling his irritation. 'I understand Valerie had a talk with you?'

'She did.'

'Good,' he said. 'Good. As long as we're all on the same page.'

Tara smiled over her own frustration. Jameson would very much like to be able to dictate to her how to do her job. He would like to control her in the same way he controlled his wife and daughter.

EIGHTEEN

SEVEN YEARS EARLIER

Jade was feeling groggy. Ray had given her a sleeping tablet the night before, and then another one before they left for the airport. Walking was hard. He held on to her arm, steadying her, as she walked down the aircraft stairs, squinting into the brightness. The handrail was spongy-soft and warm and she held on tight.

This holiday is exactly what we all need, Ray said. *You'll see.* Big smile. He was acting as though nothing had happened.

Sandra wasn't as good at pretending. She was trying to tuck the fear away, far behind her eyes, but Jade could still see it.

The sun was burning the apples of her cheeks and the bare skin on her neck, between her T-shirt and her ponytail, as she walked across the tarmac. Ray was still holding her arm.

She couldn't remember much. Flashes. Screaming, maybe. Sandra and Ray, fighting. Blood.

The queue inside the airport building moved so slowly; Ray had to half-hold her up now. When it was their turn, the man took ages, checking every page of their passports. Jade's face flushed bright red, her mouth was so dry. Sandra was nervous too, fidgeting. The man was staring, as if he knew. Then he stamped their passports and let them go.

From the outside, maybe they looked like any normal family.

Their suitcases came lurching through on the conveyor belt and Ray loaded them up onto a trolley. Men in uniforms stared as they passed through the sliding doors. No one stopped them.

Outside, everything felt a little better. It was all warm and full of light and air under a blue sky. Jade felt a moment of hope, maybe Ray was telling the truth, and everything could be all right. A holiday could fix everything.

A driver was waiting for them. He and Ray knew each other, and they shook hands and spoke quietly to each other around the back of the van so Sandra and Jade couldn't hear what they said. There were dark black windows and no one could see them once they were inside.

The drive seemed to go on and on as they headed deeper into the unfamiliar landscape, all yellowed earth and mountains. Sandra sat next to Ray, wearing huge sunglasses, not smiling and not looking back at Jade in the row behind them. The bad feeling was back but Jade didn't know if the bad thing had already happened, or if it was going to happen, here. The pills made it hard to think, hard to put things in order, hard to know if she was dreaming or awake.

Sandra slumped against the door. 'Could you put the air-conditioning up, please?'

'Not long now,' Ray said.

The driver glanced at Jade in the rear-view mirror from behind his sunglasses but did not speak. Jade wanted to sleep. She drifted, in and out; she thought she heard herself screaming.

The car jolted, waking her. They had stopped in front of a set of tall gates with barbed wire across the top.

'This doesn't look much like a holiday resort,' Sandra said.

'Wait and see,' Ray said, 'you girls just wait and see.'

A strange thought crossed Jade's mind. *Ray and Sandra have had enough of me.* She thought about the story of Hansel and Gretel and the way their parents tried to leave them behind, lost in the forest. She wiped away her tears before anyone noticed.

NINETEEN

Back at the office, Tara called Valerie Bennett, again, and asked her to set up an interview with Sandra Jameson, on her own, as soon as possible. 'I have a feeling the request might land better coming from you,' Tara said.

'Right.' Given Valerie's resigned tone, Tara had the impression that the solicitor might be having a few challenges of her own dealing with Jade's mother. 'I'll have a word with Mrs Jameson.'

'I appreciate it.'

As Paula's sister, Sandra may have spent more time in that flat in Camden than Ray had, and she would hopefully be able to provide more detailed information about what had really gone on in Jade's earliest years. Tara was hoping Sandra would speak more freely when her husband wasn't watching over her every word. She was also hoping that Sandra might know something that could unlock the case. Because so far, Jade Jameson remained an enigma.

Tara was also beginning to worry about finishing the assessment on time. She'd known the time frame would be tight, but she had not anticipated the limited co-operation from the Jameson family and the cancelled appointments.

She stayed late at her office that day. All of the Jameson background documents and her interview notes were spread out in front of her on her desk. As her thoughts percolated, she typed up bullet points for what would become the final report.

Despite the time pressure, Tara was glad to have this all-consuming case to occupy her mind. She didn't want too much free time because then she might start thinking about how many nights she spent alone. She'd been thinking about that a lot, lately. More than usual. Moving into private practice and losing the sense of belonging she'd had in the team at the hospital had made her more sensitive to the emptiness in her home.

She and Daniel saw each other twice or three times a month at most. He travelled a lot for work, and he'd add on a night to his trips sometimes, then spend it at Tara's place. They tried to sneak a weekend away once a year. It was pathetic, really, the way she accepted crumbs.

But, if she wanted Daniel, she had to be patient and she had always known that. Daniel had made it clear he would never leave Sabine while the children were still at home; they needed him more than Tara did. According to Daniel, his marriage was an unhappy one. He was the one the children were close to, and both of them had a difficult relationship with their mother. According to Daniel, Sabine had struggled with depression after they were born, and in their early years.

Tara had always been free to pursue other relationships. She had tried. The problem was, she had never wanted to be with anyone else but Daniel. There had been others, but she always gravitated back to him.

People married the wrong people all the time, she told herself. Many people stayed in marriages long after the relation-ship had died. Everybody needed and deserved to be loved.

Sabine had a husband, children, and a beautiful home. Tara had the man she loved a few nights a month. Was that so bad?

Some days she could pretend it was working. Since leaving the hospital, though, those days were getting fewer.

It did not improve Tara's mood when an email arrived from Valerie Bennett letting her know that Sandra Jameson was apparently unable to meet with her at any time in the next few days due to her 'busy work schedule'.

There was at least one piece of good news though: Carl Ress's widow, Penny, was willing to talk to Tara, and Valerie had sent through her contact details. Tara emailed her right away, asking to set up a time.

With her laptop still open in front of her, Tara decided to dig a little deeper into Sandra's excuse. It turned out that her teaching timetable was helpfully laid out online. Sandra taught an hour long 'Dynamic Yoga Flow' on the rooftop terrace of The Onyx at seven o'clock each morning in the summer months. Tara decided she might go and see Sandra after this class, without giving her advance warning.

TWENTY

At a few minutes before eight the next morning, Tara was up on the roof terrace of The Onyx Hotel. It was an oasis up there. Tara could hear the chirping of birds above the distant sound of Soho traffic. She was wearing sunglasses and lurking beside a potted olive tree as she observed the last few minutes of Sandra Jameson's yoga class.

Fifteen men and women lay on their backs in Shavasana, Corpse Pose, as Sandra sat cross legged on her mat, reading out a poem about listening to your heart and connection to the self and others.

How bizarre that Sandra could find a state of peace in this hotel of all places. Surely thoughts about what her daughter was accused of doing in the Red Suite must intrude? If they did, no one would ever guess by looking at her.

Sandra bowed her head, the picture of serenity. 'Namaste.'

After some chatter and rolling away of mats, the class dispersed, and Tara was left alone with Sandra on the rooftop. Tara was standing in full view, but Sandra showed no sign of acknowledging her existence.

On the far side of the roof terrace there was an outdoor bar area covered by a thatched roof. Myriad bottles of alcohol were displayed on shelves behind it. Sandra walked behind the bar counter, retrieved her tote bag and began checking her phone.

Tara went a little closer. 'Mrs Jameson?'

'Doctor Black.' Sandra sounded less than impressed. She did not look up from her phone.

'How is Jade feeling?' Tara said.

'A little better. She took the dog out for a walk round the block yesterday evening, that's always a good sign.'

By now Tara was standing right in front of Sandra who still would not look at her. 'If you have a few minutes I'd really like—'

'I told Valerie this week isn't possible.'

'I need to understand more about Jade's life when she was living with Paula. I need to know if there might be a connection to what happened in the Red Suite.'

Sandra froze, but only for a fraction of a second. She pulled a linen shawl out of her tote bag and draped it around her shoulders.

'I know you're pushed for time,' Tara said. 'I'll be brief. Is there somewhere we can speak in private?'

'We can talk here. The bar doesn't open until midday, but my next client will be here in ten minutes.'

The open-air terrace was hardly an ideal setting for a sensitive interview, but they were the only two people around and Tara decided it was better to go ahead given she'd managed to pin Sandra Jameson down, even if was only for a matter of minutes. She might not get another opportunity. For all she knew, guards might be manning the entrance to the roof for Sandra's next class.

Tara sat on one of the high bar stools and took out her notebook.

Sandra came around and perched on the stool next to hers. 'You will no doubt find out, if you haven't already, that I started my career as an underage stripper. My sister and I were teenage runaways. The usual story, a stepfather who looked at us the wrong way and a mother who didn't want to know. So, what else is it you need from me?'

Sandra opened a bottle of sunscreen and squeezed some into her palm. She began applying a layer to her shoulders and arms. Clearly, she found it intrusive to have to talk about her past, which had been full of suffering.

'I'd like to understand more about Jade's adoption,' Tara said. 'I was wondering if it was a complicated time, for all of you?'

Sandra shrugged. 'I wouldn't say complicated, no.'

'Even though you were applying for custody of your sister's child?'

'Look,' Sandra said, 'Jade had already been in long-term foster care with us for over a year, and it was clear to everyone by that stage that Paula could not cope. Jade was always in and out of different placements, ever since she was tiny, and most of the time Paula couldn't even be bothered to turn up to visit her at the contact centres. Knowing my sister, she probably spent the transport money they gave her on drugs for her and her latest boyfriend. On one level, I actually think Paula was relieved when we took over. And yes, after a while, she'd start making noises about missing Jade and wanting her back. But she never followed through.'

Sandra still wasn't making eye contact, her gaze flitting around the roof terrace, but she was speaking more openly, and certainly in more detail than when her husband was around. Tara felt she was getting a far more nuanced picture of Jade's history. She wanted to ask how Jade had reacted after Paula's overdose, but she had a sense this question was premature. Sandra was doing her best to hide it, but her relationship with her sister was a source of pain.

'What about Jade's father?' Tara said.

'Your guess is as good as mine. No one was about to come forward and take responsibility for knocking up an underage stripper.'

Tara had the sensation that with each question, she was intruding on some intensely private space. Given that Sandra and Paula had both worked at Ray's club, and Ray was so protective of Jade, the obvious question was whether Ray Jameson was, in fact, Jade's biological father. It would be both insensitive and pointless to ask, though.

'I understand that Jade suffered extreme neglect,' Tara said, 'but do you know if she was also physically or sexually abused while living with Paula? I am trying to understand if there is anything in her past, any specific trauma, which could be linked to what happened in the Red Suite.'

Sandra pulled her shawl tighter around her shoulders. 'I don't know the full story. I'd see marks on Jade – bruises on her arms and legs. Paula would make up some bullshit about her slipping in the bath or falling in the playground, whatever. And it always bothered me that Paula would never let me change Jade's nappies or bath her. But Paula was her mother, and I was young too, trying to get on with my own life with Ray, so...' Sandra pursed her lips. She stopped talking.

'Did Jade ever disclose anything to you?'

Sandra shook her head. 'Jade was very quiet, very withdrawn when she first came to live with us. She barely spoke at all. The social workers advised us not to ask her about any of that. They said she would tell us when she was ready, in her own time. But she never did. She just seemed to move on. To forget.'

That was likely to be wishful thinking.

'I understand your sister died of an overdose?'

Sandra nodded. The muscles along her jaw stiffened. 'It wasn't the first time she'd tried. But the overdose, the final one, was a few months before the final adoption went through.'

Sandra's guilt was palpable. On some level she must feel she'd betrayed Paula, by taking her daughter away. Sandra had everything and Paula had nothing.

'I'm sorry,' Tara said.

Sandra packed the cream back in her bag. She took out a pair of large sunglasses and put them on.

Tara remembered her own vision of death in the Red Suite. She didn't believe in ghosts, but the hotel was built on the site of the old club, Diamonds. A place where countless women and girls had been abused and exploited. Perhaps their spirits were restless.

'Sandra, do you think it's possible that Carl Ress might have known Paula and Jade when they lived in Camden?'

Sandra gave a sigh of frustration. 'Don't you think the police have already asked me that? If there was a connection between them, they would have found it by now.'

Unless the only people who knew what that connection was were members of the Jameson family, and they weren't saying.

'You know, when Jade was little,' Sandra said, 'I had endless appointments with you people – so called professionals. Social workers, psychologists, police officers, God knows who else. And not a single one did *anything* to help my sister or Jade. It was like a joke, only it wasn't funny. Someone would make a report about what was going on in that flat in Camden, usually me or Ray, eventually the police would turn up with some useless social worker – a new one each time so we'd have to start from the beginning, trying to explain. Sometimes Jade would be removed and put in foster care, and then a few months later, they'd believe Paula's lies that she'd changed, and Jade would be sent back again. Over and over and over again. There was nothing we could do besides watch. Maybe if you lot had done something then—'

Sandra took her sunglasses off, rubbed at the skin under

eyes, then put them back on. Then she stood up. She was smiling and waving. 'Hello, you!'

A woman was walking towards them, wearing workout clothes and carrying a yoga mat. She must be Sandra's next client.

When she came closer, Tara saw that she had an eye patch over her right eye and the right side of her face was disfigured. It looked like she'd been in an acid attack.

TWENTY-ONE

The lobby of The Onyx was all white beaded chandeliers, limestone floors and guests in designer outfits. Before leaving the hotel, Tara went over to the reception desk where Jade's friend Lucy Moyo was on duty alongside another staff member. They were both dressed smartly in red waistcoats, white shirts and black trousers. Lucy made a point of looking down intently at her computer keyboard as Tara approached.

A tall man with tortoiseshell glasses frames and a warm smile greeted her. His name badge said Vincent. 'How may I help you?'

'I wondered if I could have a word with Lucy.'

Vincent looked across at Lucy, who was studiously ignoring Tara. His smile faded a little.

'Could I maybe help with something?' He swallowed, his Adam's apple rising and then falling.

'No, that's all right,' Tara said. 'I think I'll go and stand outside in the sunshine for a while.'

'Oh,' he said, confused. 'Well, that sounds nice.'

On the pavement, a couple of metres away from the sliding

glass doors, Tara waited a few minutes, closing her eyes to feel the warm rays on her skin. When she opened them, Lucy was standing beside her.

'I was wondering if you've seen Jade, since that night in the Red Suite?' Tara asked.

'No. She doesn't want me to visit.'

'That must be difficult.'

'Maybe she's ashamed,' Lucy said. 'Everything is so different for her now. She has to wear an electronic tag, and she can't go back to school. But I don't know why she would be ashamed in front of me.'

Or maybe, Tara thought, Jade was afraid she might end up telling Lucy the truth. Maybe Lucy was the one person she couldn't hide from. Presumably, Lucy could be interviewed again by the police at any time.

'I'm guessing that you're probably sick of people asking you questions,' Tara said. 'Would it be all right if I tell you what I'm thinking instead?'

The girl nodded. Her arms were crossed, she was all tensed up.

'I think you care about Jade very much, and that you want to help her. I also think you are the kind of person who likes to tell the truth. And I think all of that puts you in a tricky position.'

Lucy didn't respond, but she didn't leave, either. A black cab pulled up and the doorman rushed forwards to open the doors.

'From what I know about Jade,' Tara said, 'she would not take a strange man up to the Red Suite. Especially not with Risha Bassi and her father around to get wind of it. So, my guess is that Jade did know Carl.'

Lucy didn't deny it. Tara was cautiously optimistic that she might be making progress.

'And maybe you knew Carl too.'

The girl was stubbornly silent now. She'd made a point of coming outside to see Tara, but something was holding her back.

'I have to go back inside,' Lucy said. 'I shouldn't leave Vincent on his own at the desk.'

'I have one last question. If you were me, what would you do to help Jade?'

Lucy's answer came easily. 'I'd talk to Risha.'

'Risha, the hotel manager?'

Lucy nodded. 'Risha and Jade had a big fight that night, in Risha's office. I could hear Risha yelling, and Jade was crying, after. I helped her fix her make-up in the toilets.'

'What were they fighting about?'

'Jade wouldn't say, but I think it was because of what she was wearing. Risha has a mirror in her office so she can watch us in the lobby, and she must have seen Jade talking to me, wearing that sequin dress and heels and everything. She came out and hauled Jade back into her office and started yelling at her. She hates it when Jade flirts with Marco.'

'Because Jade and Marco are both employees of the hotel – is that not allowed?'

Lucy shook her head. 'Half the staff in this place are involved with each other.'

'So why would Risha tell Jade not to flirt with Marco?'

Lucy looked at her strangely. 'I suppose because she's her big sister.'

It took Tara a few seconds to put two and two together. Risha was the older daughter Ray had briefly mentioned. Funny how neither of them had mentioned the connection though.

Tara went back inside to the reception desk with Lucy, hoping she could set up another meeting with the hotel manager.

'Was it lovely outside?' Vincent asked her.

'Yes, very lovely. Thank you.'

But Risha was nowhere to be found and no one seemed to know when she'd be back. Tara left a message.

TWENTY-TWO

After she'd finished seeing patients back in Marylebone, it took Tara over an hour to drive across the city to meet with Carl Ress's widow at her home, a semi-detached Tudor-style house in Chiswick.

Penny Ress was an elegant woman, somewhere in her early fifties, with a Welsh accent. The first thing Tara noticed about her was how well she looked. Her pale-blonde hair was shot through with silver and looked as though it had been recently and professionally blow-dried. Her fingernails and toenails were painted in a matching shade of pale pink.

She asked Tara to please take off her shoes before she came inside the house. Tara took off her flats, leaving her black secret socks on, and followed into an open-plan kitchen and living room.

'Would you like some herbal tea?' Penny said. 'I've just made a fresh pot. Camomile with some fresh mint from the garden.'

'Thank you that would be lovely.' In the interests of rapport, Tara did not say that she would much prefer a very strong coffee.

While Penny was preparing the tea, Tara took a closer look at a series of portraits that hung above the sofa. The first photograph was of a newborn baby swaddled in a pink blanket, in the second picture she had become a toddler with pigtails, and finally she had grown into a schoolgirl in uniform with a gap-toothed smile. There didn't seem to be any other photos on display, no wedding photograph of Carl and Penny, or anything else showing them as a family.

Penny came to stand next to Tara, handing her a mug. Fresh mint leaves swirled about in pale green water.

'Freya is fourteen now,' Penny said. 'I can't persuade her to sit for a photographer anymore.'

'The portraits are lovely.'

'Carl was not her father, in case you were wondering. I met him four years ago, when I was forty-seven, so it was too late for us to have any children together. Shall we sit outside? It's a beautiful day.'

The back doors were wide open leading out onto an unruly garden. Tara and Penny sat in the sunshine at a small table with a mosaic top.

'My mother's picking up my daughter from school, and they'll be back in about forty-five minutes. Can we finish by then? I don't want Freya overhearing any of this.'

'Absolutely. Thank you again for meeting with me.' Tara took her laptop out of her bag. As time was short, it would be quicker to type everything up as they spoke rather than take handwritten notes. 'I'm trying to understand as much as I can about your husband's personality.'

'You mean, what was it about Carl's personality that led to him being in a hotel room with a seventeen-year-old girl?' Penny clasped both her hands around the steaming mug of herbal tea.

'Yes.'

'Honestly, your guess is as good as mine.' There was no trace of anger when Penny spoke.

Tara's fingers hovered over the keys. The reflection on the screen made it difficult to see what she was typing.

Penny took a deep inhale of her mint-scented tea. 'Carl's personality. Well, he was handsome, protective, and extremely charming. At first.'

Penny sipped her mint tea. Tara did the same as she waited for her to go on.

'I met Carl about two years after my divorce. Freya's father and I had been through many years of fertility treatment, and then he decided to leave me for his much younger personal assistant.' Penny said this in a matter-of-fact tone, and then smiled. 'But they are separated now, and I have full custody of Freya and a rather generous divorce settlement, so as my life coach always says, everything that happens is the exact thing that should have happened.'

This seemed a strange thing to say in light of her second husband's recent and violent death, but Penny didn't seem to notice. She was also unexpectedly friendly and forthcoming, given that Tara was working for the defence team. Essentially, Tara's report could help her husband's killer avoid a murder charge.

'I met Carl through a dating website,' Penny was saying. 'He is, or was, eight years younger than me. There I was, heading for menopause, a divorced, single mother, and the last thing I was expecting was a love affair. And then I met Carl, my dashing detective. It was the stuff of romance novels. But if something seems too good to be true, it usually is, right?'

Tara nodded in agreement. 'Can I ask what went wrong?'

Something darkened in Penny's face. She was feeling something, under her serene exterior, but Tara was pretty sure it wasn't grief. It looked more like anger.

'Carl told me had retired early, after being injured at work. He had a back injury which still affected him quite a bit. But when we first met, he had all these plans, he was going to open a private detective business and so on.' As she spoke, Penny scratched at her left forearm with the nails of her right hand. 'But after we got married and Carl moved in here with Freya and me, he became quite... well, dependent. He couldn't find work, because of the constant pain in his back, and he had problems sleeping.'

Again, the scratching. That could be a sign of anger. Or rage, even. 'I realised pretty quickly that my husband had serious problems. We definitely got married too soon, less than a year after we met, and within a few months, I knew I'd made a mistake.'

'You mentioned serious problems – was Carl ever violent towards you?'

'No, nothing like that. But I felt manipulated. Used. He was living in my house, sort of under false pretences, you know? He was so different to the man I thought I was marrying. But then we were married, in sickness and health and all of that, and I felt very guilty about asking him to leave. Even though, on the other hand, I believe he hid some of these problems from me in the beginning. So, I was back and forth in my own mind, like that. Anyway, to cut a long story short, I got some counselling and eventually I decided I was not such a monster for leaving him.' There was no sadness in Penny's expression. If anything, the main feeling Tara was picking up was something resembling relief. 'I've been open about all of this with the police. They know that I consulted a divorce lawyer six months ago.'

'Did Carl know you'd seen a lawyer?'

Penny nodded. 'I told him a few weeks before he was killed that I was going forward with divorce proceedings. I'd given him a deadline to move out.'

'How did he take the news?'

'I don't think it came as any great surprise. I think he was mainly concerned with money and stressed that he had to find somewhere else to live. I did have the good sense to make him sign a very good prenup.'

'As you said, I'm trying to understand how your husband came to be in that hotel room with a teenage girl. Did you ever suspect he might do something like that?'

'I really did not. But then I didn't suspect my first husband of sleeping with his assistant, either.'

For a moment, Tara felt that Penny Ress was looking straight through her. She felt embarrassed, an imposter, with her cheeks flushed from sun and shame.

'Would you like some more tea?' Penny said.

'I'm fine, thanks.'

Penny stood up and went back inside. Tara waited as she refilled her mug before returning to the garden to sit down.

'Do you think your husband might have known Jade Jameson before that night?'

Penny shook her head. 'I have no idea. The police took his computer and his mobile. I imagine they'll tell me if they find something, when they're ready. Look, Carl had his problems, but I can tell you that infidelity wasn't one of them.'

'I don't mean to be insensitive – but, are you sure?'

'I can't be one hundred per cent sure of anything. But I may as well tell you this, it never came up with the police, who did not ask as bluntly as you do – but because of the injury and the anxiety, he had some... let's say performance problems. That's why I really did not expect an affair.'

'Sexual performance problems?'

Penny nodded. 'I found out he'd been taking Viagra, you know in the beginning, to perform. And then after we married, his attraction to me dropped off pretty quickly. He said his back was bothering him. He didn't make much effort.'

Penny gave a deep sigh. Tara stayed silent a while. She had to wonder whether Carl's performance problems were not so much related to his back injury, as to his possible preference for much younger girls. Jade and Penny Ress's daughter were not dissimilar in age.

'Would it have been normal for Carl to stay away from home for the night?'

Penny shook her head. 'No, not at all. This was the first time I can remember. He'd told me he was going to some kind of police reunion in Leeds that day and said he'd be home late.'

The doorbell rang, interrupting them. Penny put her mug down on the table with a clunk and went to answer it. From where she sat, Tara watched as she took delivery of a large cardboard box.

Their forty-five minutes were almost up, and Tara had covered most of her questions. She packed her laptop away and went back into the kitchen, where Penny was opening the parcel.

'It's a cat carrier,' she said. 'We're going to pick up a kitten for Freya on the weekend. To make up for all of this.'

'Was Freya close to her stepfather?'

'She adored Carl. He had a lot of time for her.'

Tara looked back at those portraits. If Carl Ress's tastes had run to young girls, could he have been grooming Freya? Could it have been even worse than Penny suspected?

The front door swung open, and a teenage girl came into the house, followed by an older woman. Both were carrying shopping bags, which they deposited in the kitchen.

The girl gave Tara a curious look. Penny introduced Tara briefly, then quickly shepherded her towards the front door. It was clear Tara was not going to get the chance to talk to Freya, that was where Penny drew the line.

Penny waited as Tara slipped her shoes back on and then walked with her all the way down the front path and to her car, watching as Tara put her briefcase in the back and opened the driver's door.

'The police told me that the Jameson girl doesn't remember anything?' Penny said.

Tara nodded. It was striking that Penny had expressed no anger towards her husband's killer. If anything, her tone when she referred to Jade was quite sympathetic.

'You asked me if I knew what Carl was doing with that girl in a hotel room,' Penny said. 'What I said was true, I don't know. But if I've learned anything about Carl, then I think it could have been about money. The Jamesons are an incredibly wealthy family, aren't they?'

'Yes, they are.'

'I came to understand that the only thing that motivated Carl was money. And looking back, I think he used women to get it. I don't think I was the first, and I wouldn't have been the last, either.'

Back in the tiny kitchen of the mews house in Marylebone, Tara was waiting for her coffee to filter through into the pot below as she reflected on her interview with Carl Ress's widow.

Penny had given a frank picture of a Ress as a troubled man, but she had also been adamant that her late husband was not a sexual predator, which was not ideal for the defence's argument. But then there was no guarantee that Penny's view of her deceased husband was accurate. Denial was a powerful psychological mechanism.

What Penny had said about Carl being motivated by money was interesting. Given the situation Penny had described, with Carl Ress being out of work, his marriage breaking down and in need of a place to live, he may have been looking for a new way to fund his lifestyle. The Jameson family was certainly a wealthy target.

If Penny Ress's suspicion was right, could Carl have found a way to extort money out of either Jade or her father?

Tara's mind drifted through all the associations, all the disparate links so far that still did not form a coherent whole. The dress Jade was wearing the night Carl Ress was killed had belonged to her biological mother, Paula. Could Carl and Paula be connected in some way? Could Carl have told Jade he was her father? Could that be the reason she agreed to be alone with him?

Tara had to assume that DNA tests would have revealed if that were the case. Surely she would have been told about something that significant. She'd better check with Valerie though, just to be sure.

Olivia walked in and began filling the kettle at the sink. Lately, all she could keep down was weak black tea and the occasional salted cracker.

'I'm guessing from the expression on your face,' Olivia said, 'that this assessment is giving you a headache?'

'To put it mildly.' Tara took down two mugs, then put a teabag into one of them for Olivia. 'The client is avoiding me and her parents are pushing to have the rest of the interviews cancelled.'

Olivia poured boiling water over the teabag. 'Why?'

'I'm not entirely sure.' Tara hesitated. 'The thing is, I'm running out of time and I don't think the standard interview techniques are going to get me anywhere. I wanted to ask you more about the idea of ketamine.'

She handed Olivia a salted cracker. The morning sickness was a constant now and Olivia was cancelling a lot of clients.

'It's worth a try,' Olivia said. 'And even if it doesn't work, the advantage is that it could look good for your client, right? If she's willing to take drugs to help with her memory loss it means she genuinely wants to remember.'

'Exactly. Is it a complicated procedure?'

'Not at all. The drug comes in spray form – two squirts in each nostril, that's it.'

'What about risk?'

Olivia shrugged. 'Very unlikely to do any harm. I recommend medical supervision the first time though, and blood pressure monitoring. I could administer it with you present.'

Tara had her doubts. Both she and Olivia knew what was at stake in terms of the financial health of the practice and maybe that made them both too keen to make this case work. In any case, it wouldn't happen. Even if Jade wanted to go ahead, Tara could not imagine that Ray and Sandra Jameson would ever give permission for something so unorthodox. What would be interesting though, would be to see Jade's reaction.

'I'll float the idea with my client,' Tara said. 'But I doubt the parents will agree. In fact, they'll probably have a fit when they hear about it.'

'I'll order some in today and keep it here, just in case.' Olivia took a tentative bite of the cracker. 'I think I'm going to have to cancel my last patient.'

She put her mug down in the sink and then put a hand on her belly, where her bump was beginning to show. 'Only five more months of this to go.'

Tara was ambushed by an unexpected moment of sheer envy.

Tara and Olivia had been supposed to go to the gym together that evening, but Olivia had left work early, still feeling unwell. Tara decided she'd take the opportunity to skive off from the kettlebells class. She wasn't in the mood for grocery shopping or cooking either, so she stopped off at the Japanese place on her way home and headed for the usual table along the side wall.

'Hello again,' the owner said. 'Miso soup and assorted sushi?'

Tara nodded. She was reading up on ketamine treatment on her phone and checking her email. There was still no reply from Risha, the manager of The Onyx and Jade's newly discovered stepsister. Valerie had got back to her confirming that there was no indication of matching DNA between Jade and Carl Ress. Though that didn't mean that Ress hadn't floated the idea of paternity. But why would Jade be so desperate to keep that a secret?

'Tara, is that you?'

Tara looked up. For a second, she thought she was seeing a ghost. Daniel's wife was standing beside her table.

'Oh my God,' Sabine said. 'I thought so. It is you.'

Tara stood up and the two women embraced. Sabine was tiny, and Tara looked over the top of her head, wondering if Daniel was with her.

'How are you?' Sabine said. 'Do you live around here?'

'No, but my office is around the corner. How about you, what are you doing here?'

'Harrison has an orthodontist appointment on Harley Street, and I had a craving for sushi. The receptionist told me to come here, she said their sushi is the best...' Sabine tailed off, staring at her. 'This is so strange.'

It was an odd coincidence. Daniel and his family lived south of the river, so there was little danger they would ever cross paths.

'How many years has it been?' Sabine said.

'I don't know.' Tara had not seen Daniel's wife in person since their wedding, and then at a couple of the children's early birthdays, but Sabine had barely changed.

Sabine was a physiotherapist, she said she was running a small business from home. Their son getting braces was fourteen, she said, and their daughter, Charlotte, had just turned ten. Tara explained she'd left the hospital and gone into private practice.

Sabine was still holding on to Tara's hand. She squeezed tighter, looking into Tara's eyes with her own big brown ones. 'It's so strange, seeing you.'

Tara's mouth was dry. She had a bad feeling she might have

screwed up with that telephone call to Daniel. Did Sabine suspect something? That was so unlikely. She was paranoid, because of her own guilt.

'I think of you, you know,' Sabine said. 'Especially on your brother's birthday. I don't know why I've never called you.'

'I think about you too,' Tara said.

'There's no news, about Matthew?'

Tara shook her head.

Sabine had been Matthew's girlfriend in the year before he went missing, and Tara's brother had been crazy about her. Sabine had been such a stabilising influence; Matthew had been happy. And then all of their lives had changed course on one night.

Around two years after Matthew had been missing, Sabine and Daniel had got together. Maybe their joint sense of loss had drawn them closer. Or, more likely, Daniel had had a crush on Sabine all along. Sabine, half-French on her mother's side, was very beautiful. She had a certain vulnerability which seemed to make men want to take care of her. Tara remembered exactly how her brother had looked at her: with a sense of wonder, as though she was perfection, and he couldn't believe how lucky he was to be with her.

'I'm sorry we lost contact,' Sabine said. 'We should keep in touch, catch up properly.'

'That would be lovely.' Of course, Tara's words were empty.

'I have to dash back now, but let me have your number?'

Tara gave it to her.

After Sabine had left, she sat down again. Numb. Sick of herself. She had the urge to call Daniel, to tell him what had happened and to ask if he really thought it was possible that the chance meeting was pure coincidence. But something stopped her from making that call. Something inside of her felt that, one way or another, this was a sign. This was the beginning of the end, and she did not want to talk to him about that.

TWENTY-FOUR

It was Thursday and Tara had set the entire day aside to meet with Jade. She still hadn't had confirmation about the rescheduled appointment, but she hadn't received a message cancelling it either, so she decided to go to the Jameson house at the arranged time and hope for the best.

Her sense of unease grew the closer she got to the Jameson house. She was already anticipating being given a hard time about seeing Jade, and even if she succeeded, she was not looking forward to going down into that basement. Her dreams were full of knives and bloodstained pillows and Sabine. She had been thinking much more than usual about her brother, what he'd done and where he was. She could probably do with one of Sandra Jameson's tranquillisers herself to get a reasonable night's sleep.

Tara stood at the front door, aware now of the camera pointing down at her. When she rang the bell, there was no answer. The curtains on all floors were closed and there was no sign of the Bentley that sometimes waited outside.

She waited a couple of minutes and rang again. A few

seconds later, Sandra Jameson opened the door, dressed as usual from head to toe in Lycra.

'Morning,' Tara said. 'I have an appointment with Jade.'

She was half expecting Sandra to ask her to leave, but she didn't. If anything, Tara had the impression Sandra was more at ease as they walked through to the kitchen. The entire house felt brighter somehow and Tara suspected Ray Jameson might not be at home.

In the kitchen, Tara and Sandra paused at the kitchen island, both of them looking out towards the garden where Jade was playing with the dog.

'Jade looks like she's feeling better?' Tara said.

'She is.' Sandra reached for a glass containing her green drink.

Jade and Ziggy were engaged in an energetic game of fetch. Jade would throw the ball, with a powerful overarm swing, and the dog would bound off to fetch it and then bring it back and drop it right at her feet.

Sandra made no move to call her daughter inside. Instead, she watched her playing with the dog in the garden, taking small sips of her juice.

'After Jade came to live with us,' Sandra said, 'she never asked for her mother. Not once. Do you think that's strange?'

'It's hard to say.' But Tara very much doubted that at the age of nine it could have been so simple for Jade to adjust to her new life, or to leave the old one behind.

Sometimes, I miss her a lot.

Jade could only say those words when she was not in full control, when she was under the influence of sedatives. Jade was sensitive and smart. She had probably understood that Ray and Sandra couldn't deal with the fact that she still longed for her mother, and that she was struggling with complex feelings that were too much for any of them to bear.

And then, Jade had changed into Paula's dress the night she

had allegedly killed a man. There was something buried in this family, only Tara couldn't make out the shape of it yet.

Jade was walking slowly round the edges of the grass, encouraging Ziggy to sit and wait until she called him back to her. She was patient, encouraging and praising the dog.

It occurred to Tara that her client looked different. First of all, she looked much better than when Tara had seen her last up in her bedroom. She had good colour in her face and her hair was glossy and loose around her shoulders. For whatever reason, Jade was feeling less anxious.

'She won't talk to you today,' Sandra said.

'I'd like to ask her myself.'

'Go ahead.' Sandra went over to the sliding doors and opened them.

Tara stepped out onto the patio. Jade shaded her eyes and looked straight at her. Tara raised her hand and waved, but Jade ignored her and turned back to the dog.

'Come!' she called.

Sandra had been watching this exchange. 'It is Jade's choice. My husband and I don't think that you should force her. Ray has let Valerie know.'

Tara followed Sandra back into the kitchen. Sandra closed the sliding doors to the garden.

'Are you sure it's her choice?' Tara said. 'Or is she worried about talking to me because she doesn't want to upset you, or her father?'

'I'm sorry. There's nothing I can do.' Sandra gripped the empty glass on the counter.

Tara's eyes drifted to the knife block only a few inches away from her hand.

'Sandra, do you ever feel afraid of your daughter?'

'No. Never.' Sandra drew out one of the knives. Long and sharp. She laid it down flat on the marble surface. 'Everything is my fault. It's always been completely and utterly my fault.'

'How are you responsible?'

'I failed them both. Paula was my baby sister and I brought her to Soho, to that club. And then I let a bunch of predators destroy her, while I was chasing after Ray. And then I failed Jade. I left her with Paula, for much too long. I could see—'

Sandra fell silent.

'That's a heavy burden to carry,' Tara said.

'Ray loved Jade so much, right from the very beginning. Maybe I didn't love her enough. Maybe I was jealous of how much he worshipped her. If it weren't for Ray—' Sandra collected herself, as if she remembered she should not be saying any of this.

'You're wrong about being responsible,' Tara said. 'The decision to remove a child from their parents is huge, and it takes time. Too much time, often. You and Ray went to the authorities, over and over again. There's nothing more you could have done.'

Maybe too many people wanted to believe in parental love, Tara thought, and the power to change.

Outside, Jade retrieved the ball from the dog's jaws and threw it across the garden.

'There isn't much time left for me to finish this report,' Tara said, 'and I really believe it's in Jade's best interests to work with me. I think she deserves a chance to remember what happened in that hotel room. If she can't, the risk is that she can never move on.'

Sandra was staring at her daughter.

'Can you help me persuade Jade to talk to me?'

'You heard what my husband said. She didn't do anything. She doesn't need to talk to anyone.'

Who knew what life with Ray Jameson was really like behind closed doors? Even if Sandra was not at ease with Jade being released into their care and living at home, she would not feel free to say so in front of her husband. Maybe the safest thing for Sandra to do, even if she had her doubts about Jade's innocence, was to go along with whatever her husband wanted her to say.

Tara felt sad for them both. Jade had been trying so hard to be the perfect daughter, while Sandra was doing her best to be the perfect wife and mother.

'Do you really believe that Jade doesn't need to talk to anyone? Or is that what your husband thinks?'

'Jade and I have Ray to look after us.' Sandra turned her head so she was looking directly at Tara. 'You should worry about yourself.'

'Excuse me?'

'Ray knows how to find people's weaknesses. He breaks you down, when he needs to.' Sandra picked up her empty glass, went over to the sink and rinsed it out, before placing it out of sight in the dishwasher. 'I think it's better if you leave now. Please. I shouldn't have invited you in.'

TWENTY-FIVE

Tara was back in her car, frustrated at not being able to connect with Jade, but equally relieved to be out of that house. There had been something chilling in what Sandra had said.

She was not optimistic about being able to coax her reluctant client back for even one more interview, let alone the three she had wanted to complete before the deadline. Tara needed to get to the point where Jade not only *wanted* to talk to her but felt safe to do so. And at this point, Jade was under too much pressure, caught between her parents and the legal system, to be able to open up to anyone.

Tara thought again about Anthony Edwards, and wondered exactly how far he had got with the case before he had withdrawn. It seemed a little strange, and unprofessional, that he hadn't yet replied to her email. Tara had initially thought that his illness might have been serious, but when she'd looked at his website, it seemed like his practice was up and running as normal.

Desperate for a caffeine shot, Tara drove over to the station, parked, and popped into the Beatles Coffee Shop for a black

Americano. As she was about to start the drive back to Marylebone, her mobile rang with a number she didn't recognise.

She turned off the ignition. 'Doctor Black speaking.'

'This is Mary Crane, I'm a teacher at North End Secondary School.' The woman's voice had an authoritative edge. 'Valerie Bennett asked me to give you a call regarding one of my pupils, Jade Jameson?'

'That's right. Thank you for calling.'

'Is it convenient to talk now? I have around fifteen minutes before my next class.'

'Now would be great.' Tara manoeuvred her laptop out of her bag and put it on her lap, opening a blank document.

'The solicitor didn't give me much information, I presume this is about Jade's withdrawal from school, the parents informed us she won't be returning next term—'

'I'm very restricted in what I can say, I hope you understand.'

'Of course.' But Mary Crane sounded a little peeved. 'Well, the parents have given the school permission to share information with you, so how can I help?'

'Can I start by asking how long you've known Jade?'

'I've been her form teacher right through secondary school, so I first met her when she would have been around eleven. She's also in my A-level biology class at the moment. Or was.'

'How would you describe Jade's behaviour at school?'

'I'd say she's a model student. You know, the girl at the front of the class, excellent concentration and engagement with lessons, taking meticulous notes, never late with an assignment, always does well in exams. Highly intelligent and mature for her age. Very polite, good manners. I'm not sure what more I can add. Jade would have been the last one of my students I'd have guessed would end up dropping out of school and needing a solicitor.'

'How about socially?' Tara asked.

'Jade is a reserved girl, but she does have a small circle of friends. She's confident in social situations. Not one of those girls who needs make-up or short skirts to attract attention, if you know what I mean.'

'Right.' Tara reflected that she herself would have been described by teachers as 'one of those girls' when she'd been at school. She had been desperate for any scrap of affection wherever she could find it.

'Did you ever pick up any emotional problems?'

There was a pause. 'No.'

There was a chance the police had got it wrong. History was always the best predictor of behaviour, and there were simply no previous reports of Jade ever being violent. Or even mildly troublesome. Which made it even more frustrating that Tara had no access to Jade and could not help her retrieve the memories of that night which could support her innocence.

But her gut instinct was that this could not be the whole story. Someone must have seen something different.

'Is there anything else you can tell me,' Tara said, 'even something small that doesn't seem important, but that comes to mind?'

'Well, it's ancient history now, but I do remember having concerns when Jade first started secondary school. Even at the time, there was nothing specific I could put my finger on, it was more that we knew Jade had a very difficult history – she'd been in foster care, her biological mother had died of a drug overdose and then she was adopted by relatives, not long before she started with us. So we were expecting a traumatised child. And what bothered me, frankly, was that there was simply never any sign of distress. In the beginning, Jade was so quiet, she barely spoke. When she did, she was always impeccably polite. Now I'm no psychologist but I always wondered, when would all this trauma she'd been through show up? If you ask me, a little rebellion is healthy in the teenage years. But Jade was just so compliant. I don't remember her ever being angry, or making a fuss, about anything.'

Tara had her laptop on her lap and her phone propped between her chin and her shoulder as she typed. 'Did you ever have any contact with Jade's parents, did you speak to them about your concerns?'

There was a longer, pregnant pause. 'In the early days I did try to set up a meeting with them. My recollection is that they were determined to maintain this "everything is perfect, Jade is a happy child", scenario. I seem to remember I suggested that Jade see a counsellor, and that went down like a lead balloon.'

That was interesting. Jade's parents were certainly consistent in their avoidant behaviour. Although in fairness, they had also experienced a period of several years where they felt that social workers and psychologists had done nothing to help Jade at a time when she desperately needed it. 'Can you remember any more details about that meeting?'

'I'm afraid not. As I say, this was years ago. What I do remember is that the Jameson family was not open to outside help. In my experience, that can be a red flag. And I would say that Mr Jameson can be quite... reactive. But on the other hand, Jade clearly adores him and, frankly, he is more involved than a lot of other fathers. Never misses a sports day or a parents' evening, that sort of thing. And Jade's done so well since then, she's really come out of herself. And then out of the blue – this – whatever this is? I suppose we'll find out in due course?'

'Thank you again,' Tara said. 'It's been very helpful talking to you. If you remember anything else, please feel free to contact me again.'

After saying goodbye to Mrs Crane, Tara closed the document, put her laptop back in her bag and secured her seat belt. She was thinking about Valerie's warning: to keep the assessment tightly focused on Jade's memories of the night in question, and not dig too deep into wider family dynamics. But the more Tara looked into this case, the more vital she thought it was to understand the Jamesons as a unit. This approach would certainly not make her at all popular with Ray Jameson.

She finished off her coffee, cold now. As Tara was about to start the car, a familiar figure walked past on the opposite side of the street. At first, Tara thought she was mistaken. The way this girl carried herself was different, but she was wearing a familiar pink hoodie. And she was heading into the underground station.

TWENTY-SIX

Tara left her car and dashed across the road. She entered the station building in time to see the girl touch her phone to the card reader and then step through the electronic gates.

It was Jade Jameson.

Tara's own phone was already in her right hand. Without thinking, she tapped it and the barriers opened and she followed Jade onto the escalator leading down towards the trains. There were a couple of people between Tara and her client. She wanted to call out to Jade, but didn't want to risk causing a scene or alarming her. She decided to wait until they reached the bottom.

When Jade stepped off the escalator, Tara found herself following the girl towards the trains. Given the determined way Jade was walking, it looked like she had somewhere she needed to be. Even her posture was more confident than Tara remembered.

This was a girl who had supposedly been too fragile to attend an interview with Tara, and who also, according to her solicitor, hardly ever left the house. But the person Tara was following did not look anxious. Her head was high, her hands tucked in her pockets and her pace fast as she headed towards the platform for southbound trains.

Tara wasn't sure about the ethics of following her client, but she needed to know what was going on. Time was growing shorter and shorter. She had other patient commitments, and she couldn't keep rescheduling at Jade's convenience. This was their allocated interview time and Tara decided to make the most of it.

Jade now stood among a smattering of people along the platform. Tara was about two metres away. Jade stared straight ahead, seemingly unaware of anyone around her. The train arrived and the doors opened. Jade entered the half-empty carriage, and so did Tara. She sat down in the seat next to her client.

'Hi, Jade.'

Jade turned her head, shocked to see her. 'What's going on?'

'I saw you go into the station. I wanted a chance to talk to you.'

'You followed me?' Jade's voice was louder than expected, carrying over the loud drone of the train. At home, she was more timid.

The man across from them, sitting with a backpack on his lap, was staring at them.

'I'm running out of time, for the report,' Tara said. 'Our appointment today was important.'

After the initial shock of seeing her, Jade seemed to calm down. 'I don't mean to mess you around. But there's no point. I don't want any more interviews.'

'I think there is a point, and so does your solicitor.' Jade had been fairly co-operative, right up until the direct questions about the night of the killing.

The train had reached the next stop on the line and jerked to a stop. The man opposite them had lost interest and was scrolling through his phone. Tara wasn't sure how long she'd have with Jade before she bolted. The doors opened, letting in a rush of fresh air. They closed again and the train hurtled down the tunnels.

Jade was staring straight ahead again.

Tara kept her voice low as she leaned towards her. 'Jade, I think you know how important this assessment is for your case. Can I ask why you've changed your mind?'

'I've spent hours and hours answering questions. With the police, and my solicitor, and the other psychologist they sent, before you. It doesn't work. Answering the same bunch of questions, over and over again, doesn't bring my memory back. I don't want to go on repeating the same stuff, over and over. I feel like I'm getting more confused, not less.'

'Okay. I understand.'

Jade turned to look at Tara, surprised by her response.

'Where are you going?' Tara said.

'I don't know. I needed to get out of the house.'

'I can understand that.' Tara had to raise her voice, so Jade could hear her over the sound of the train. 'Are you meeting up with Lucy? She's lovely. She cares about you a lot.'

Jade shook her head. She pulled her hood down further over her face and pushed her hands deeper into the pockets of her hoodie. 'Lucy's got enough problems. I don't want her anywhere around me. It was bad luck she was the first person to find me in the hotel room. Because of me, she also ended up having a million police interviews.'

It was interesting that Jade had empathy for what Lucy had gone through, but that she had never shown any concern about the victim in that hotel room. In fact, Jade had never once referred to Carl Ress. She had shown no curiosity about him, no regret about his death, and no pity for his family left behind.

One interpretation could be that Jade wasn't sorry he was dead. Interestingly, his wife seemed to feel much the same way.

Tara wanted to press on with more questions while Jade

was relaxed and away from her parents, but she knew she was taking a risk. They were on public transport and they could be overheard. This was hardly good practice. But it might be this conversation or nothing because her report was due next week.

'I know you had a really rough time before Ray and Sandra adopted you,' Tara said.

'I don't remember much about it.'

'Forgetting is one way our minds try to cope with pain.' Tara hoped the noise of the train would make it impossible for anyone to make out what they were saying, but she couldn't be completely sure. 'The problem is, those buried memories can find a way to come back. Sometimes in ways we don't understand.'

They were passing several stations, the doors opening and closing, people trickling on and off. The carriage was filling up. Jade leaned down to adjust the hem of her jeans, making sure it was pulled down over the electronic tag. She was showing no sign of leaving the train. Maybe she did just need to get out of the house.

'Jade, do you want to remember what happened in that hotel?'

Jade looked directly into Tara's eyes. 'The police say I killed someone. They say I stabbed a man eleven times. Why would I want to remember something like that?'

In their first interview, Jade had told Tara she couldn't harm a fly. Now she seemed less certain. Tara wondered if something had changed.

'If you do want to remember, I have an idea. There is a drug that can help bring your memory back.' Tara kept talking. This might be her last chance. 'I work with a doctor who would help you take it, at my office. I'll stay with you the whole time, to make sure you're okay.'

Jade was silent but she was listening. Tara felt a spark of hope, and she sensed Jade did too.

'I can set up an appointment if you decide to go ahead,' Tara said. 'Soon. Tomorrow morning, if possible.'

The train stopped. The doors opened, and a group of schoolchildren got on, rowdy and laughing. Jade had withdrawn again, looking straight ahead of her with the hood covering her face so Tara couldn't read her expression. Jade seemed a world away from her peers, so much older and more burdened.

The doors closed and they were moving again. There were people in the seats on either side of them now.

'There is one thing, though,' Tara said. 'Because of your age, you need permission from at least one of your parents.'

'They will never let me.'

'Why?'

'Nobody wants to know the truth anyway.'

The train was pulling into Waterloo Station and Jade stood up and went to stand at the doors. Tara followed her. 'Jade, what do you mean? Who doesn't want to know the truth?'

'Don't follow me. I'm serious.' There was a note of fear in the girl's voice.

The doors opened and Jade stepped out. The platform was crowded, people thronging in all directions, into the tunnels and up the stairs. From the train, Tara watched Jade as she walked away, her head down, swallowed up by the people around her.

TWENTY-SEVEN

SEVEN YEARS EARLIER

That first night in the strange house, Jade fell into a deep, deep sleep. Later, she was woken by the sound of footsteps on the gravel outside her window. She got up and went to peek out of the curtains. There was a man with a gun outside and he was walking up and down. Past her window and back again.

When Jade woke again, light washed in through the half-open curtains. Everything was a white blur. She pushed aside the mosquito netting that had been draped around her bed and looked around the room. She remembered where she was. She remembered the man with the gun. Maybe he wasn't real. Maybe he was part of those strange dreams she'd been having.

The house they were staying in was spooky. Sky-high ceilings painted with images of half-dressed angels, in pink and gold, looking down on her, cold brick floors, and walls thicker than she'd ever seen before.

She got up and tried her door. This time, it was unlocked.

The corridors were dark and silent. Ray and Sandra must still be asleep. Their door was always closed; Sandra hardly came out of that room. Ray would play board games with her or swim in the pool, but his eyes were sad.

This did not feel like a holiday at all. She didn't understand why they had taken her out of school in the middle of term. She was worried about all the work she'd have to catch up on when she got back.

In the kitchen, a woman was sitting at a table and cutting up fruit. She looked like someone's grandmother with grey frizzy hair and glasses on a chain. When she saw Jade, she shook her head and wagged her finger. Jade wasn't allowed to go in the kitchen.

In the living room, she tried the door to the outside. That one was open too. *See*, Jade said to herself, *this is not a jail*.

Outside, the sun was half-risen in an orange sky. She found a frog hiding in the shade under a bush, and watched him for a while, to see if he would hop away. The frog's eyes were wide open. His neck bulged, in and out, in and out. He was frightened of her.

Jade walked down to the swimming pool even though she wasn't supposed to go down there alone. She sat on the edge, legs dangling in the water. Birds were making a racket in the trees. It was hot and she was itchy. Mosquitoes had got at her in the night even under the nets. She dug her nails into the raised bumps on her legs.

Jade watched her legs make ripples in the water as she kicked back and forth. Away and back. Away and back. After a while, she got up and went over to one of the trees, stretched up on tiptoes and pulled down a ripe orange.

When she looked down at the bricks again, she saw a small knife. She didn't understand where that had come from. She was sure it wasn't there before. She wasn't allowed to go in the kitchen.

Did she remember? Jade was confused. Somewhere, she thought she did.

She put the fruit down on the ground. She picked up the

knife and held it high above her head with both hands, and then she brought the sharp tip down, right into the belly of the orange.

Before she went back inside, she went to find the frog.

TWENTY-EIGHT

Daniel's car was parked outside her cottage when Tara got home. She felt a jolt of happiness.

He was waiting for her in the garden, with an open bottle of wine. He poured them each a glass. It was so peaceful, sitting with him under the cherry tree. Tara wished it could feel like this, always. Daniel was quieter than usual though, and this visit was unexpectedly soon after the last one.

Tara took a sip of the wine. It was chilled and fruity. 'Sabine told you she saw me?'

Daniel nodded.

'It was such a strange coincidence.' Tara was going to ask what exactly Sabine had said, but decided not to. It wasn't her business. 'Did Harrison really have an orthodontist appointment in Harley Street?'

'He did,' Daniel said.

'I had this feeling, that she knew. It wasn't anything she said, and she was very warm and friendly. It's probably my own conscience.'

'You're not the one who's married. I should be the one with

the guilty conscience.' Daniel was more than halfway through the glass of wine. He never drank in the week.

He and Sabine must have had an argument. Daniel said she was volatile lately. She'd recently started on new medication, which didn't appear to be helping. Maybe somewhere, Sabine did know, and the pain of living with a man who didn't really love her was eating away at her.

'Sabine was always kind to me, when she was with my brother,' Tara said. 'Ever since I saw her, I haven't been able to stop thinking about Matthew. All those questions going round and round in my head again. *Is he alive? Does he not want to see me because of what he did? Is he suffering?* Usually I can kind of compartmentalise them.'

'Did Sabine ask about him?'

Tara nodded.

'She never mentions him to me. Matthew was the love of her life, she thinks it would hurt me to know.'

'Does it?'

'Not anymore. Not for a long time.' Daniel put his wine glass down and reached for her hand. 'It's getting harder and harder for me to stay in that house. But I feel like the older the children get, the more they need me. You must be sick of hearing this.'

Nothing would change, Tara thought. This was the way it was. The way it had always been between them. She should end it.

Daniel pulled his hand away from hers as he checked his watch. Expensive gold casing and a black face. A gift from Sabine. 'Sorry, I can't stay. I just needed to see you.'

'We never go out,' Tara said. 'We hide in this cottage.'

'Please, let's not do this now.'

'When should we do it then?'

Daniel left. He turned his back on her and walked out of

the garden and out of the front door. They'd never left it like that before. Tara felt bereft. And angry. Mainly at herself.

She sat alone in her kitchen, finishing her notes about the Jameson case from earlier that day. She was writing in her notebook, using a fountain pen with purple ink. The luxury of it made the chore of writing up notes less tedious, sometimes. Not tonight though. Tara kept checking her messages, hoping for something from Jade, saying she wanted to go ahead with the next appointment, but nothing came. There had been nothing from Risha at the hotel, either.

Tara wasn't finding it easy to focus. Solitude had never bothered her before, but suddenly, she was acutely aware of feeling lonely.

Daniel had never promised her anything different and she did not want to be the reason he abandoned his family. But seeing Sabine had brought home the reality of what the two of them were doing. Their relationship had started in the wrong way, with dishonesty, and the rational part of her knew it could only end in pain.

The problem was, she loved Daniel. He was her closest friend. He was all she had left of her old self.

She didn't want to think about the way he had walked out, and how maybe that was the best thing, for both of them.

Tara forced her mind back to her notes. She detailed her observations of Jade earlier that day as she had entered the underground station and travelled to Waterloo. She wrote up as much as she could recall of their conversation, including the discussion around medication that might help to recover her memory. Following Jade had been unorthodox and could be questioned if the case ever went to court. But she did not regret it.

Jade was hiding something.

Nobody wants to know the truth anyway.

Tara had lied to Sabine without saying anything untruthful.

All the fragments of information she'd collected so far would not fit together into a whole. She was restless, dissatisfied.

When Daniel called, she did not pick up the phone.

Instead, Tara went upstairs to her bedroom, opened her cupboard and searched through her clothes for something different. Practical trousers and shirts, jeans and casual blouses for weekends. It was all so boring. Right at the back though, she found a black velvet dress, short and fitted. She hadn't worn it in a very long time.

She slipped it on, with a pair of nude heels. She put on red lipstick. Then she ordered a cab to take her to The Onyx.

TWENTY-NINE

Tara crossed the vanilla-scented lobby, her heels echoing against the limestone floor. She passed the table full of orchids as she headed to the polished concrete staircase leading down to the basement bar. The same staircase Jade would have used, wearing her emerald dress and stilettos, on the night she met Carl Ress.

Tara paused on the landing, looking down over the room below, a rectangular space with fluorescent lighting and a long pewter counter. Crammed and loud. She descended into the sea of bodies, weaving her way through them. As she stood at the bar, waiting to be served, music pulsed in the background, drowning out the conversations around her.

'What can I get for you tonight?' The bartender leaned in close. His tight white T-shirt shone pink under the neon lights. Perhaps this was Marco, the object of Jade's crush.

'An Apple Martini,' Tara said.

According to the police report, that was the drink Jade had ordered that night.

'Apple Martini coming up.'

How are you feeling, Jade?

Nervous? Excited?

Did you arrange to meet Carl Ress down here?

Or does he see you first, young and beautiful and defenceless in your sequins and high heels?

Jade's emerald dress gave Tara some of the answers to her questions. Jade's friend Lucy had confirmed it was out of character. When Jade had chosen that outfit, she had wanted to look older and more seductive. She had been intending to meet someone that night. An older man.

The bartender placed a bright green drink down on a coaster in front of her. He smiled at Tara a moment before slipping a slice of apple onto the edge of her glass and moving on.

Had Jade and Carl Ress been planning to meet all along? According to his widow, Carl Ress might have been interested in her money.

Perhaps Jade had left the bar with Ress because she hoped to make Marco jealous?

Tara's drink was a strange combination of sour-sweet. Bodies crowded in from all sides; everyone seemed so young and so beautiful. She felt so much older, and out of place. A man caught her eye. He was standing with his back to her. Tall and well built, his shoulder-length brown hair was tinged with ginger. He wore a denim shirt and black jeans and he was drinking a beer, tipping the bottle to his lips with his left hand.

Tara walked towards him. She had to see his face. 'Matthew?'

He turned around. He was far older than twenty-three and his face was all wrong. He wasn't her brother. Of course he wasn't. Matthew was gone.

'I'm so sorry.' The bartender had been generous with the vodka, she was already light-headed.

Tara made her way over to an empty chair in the corner. She had downed the drink too fast. She found herself staring again at the man in the denim shirt and feeling a deep sense of longing. The fluorescent light on the wall behind him was in the shape of a heart, pierced by an arrow.

It was autumn soon, Matthew's birthday. If her brother was still alive, he would be forty-five years old. *Do you miss me, Matt?*

A haze of alcohol settled across her thoughts. She was no longer in the bar, she was sixteen again and she was back at home in the house on Wildway Close.

She walks into the kitchen where she finds her brother in a clinch with Sabine, their tongues down each other's throats. As usual.

'Don't mind me, lovebirds,' Tara says as she passes them on the way to the fridge.

'Hey, cutie,' Sabine says in her French accent. She only reaches up to Matthew's chest. She has huge brown eyes and curls to her waist. Matthew is crazy about her.

Several bottles of beer and vodka have appeared on the kitchen counter.

'What's going on?' Tara says.

Matthew is supposed to have stopped drinking. He promised.

'A few mates are coming over.' Her brother says this casually, as if it's no big deal.

'Is that a good idea?' Their parents are away for the weekend. Her father will be furious.

'Daniel's coming.' Sabine looks up at Matthew and winks.

Matthew laughs. He and Sabine have worked out Tara's secret crush on her brother's best friend.

Tara gives him a light punch on the shoulder and he pretends to be in pain before he puts an arm around her and kisses her head.

Matthew is happy, which is rare. He is happy because Sabine is there. He is happy because their parents are away. Matthew is a different person when he's not around their father.

'*My two favourite people.*' *Matthew pours himself a healthy shot of vodka.* '*Let's drink to how much I love you both.*'

He lifts his glass. He's already on his way to being drunk and Tara has a bad feeling about all of this. But she soon forgets about her brother, because Sabine is right, she is dying to see Daniel.

He arrives late. Tara is wearing a soft jumper over white jeans, hoping this outfit makes her look more sophisticated. She's borrowed the jumper from Sabine, who has an envy-inducing natural French style. Tara bites her bottom lip as she goes to the door. She tastes strawberry lip gloss.

Daniel is standing in front of her with his crooked smile. He's wearing her brother's denim shirt, the one he borrowed and never gave back. He's holding a six-pack of beer. Tara gets a whiff of his aftershave, clean and spicy.

'*Hi, little sister,*' *he says.*

She wishes he wouldn't call her that. She's tongue-tied.

'*Matthew and Sabine are in the kitchen,*' *she says, eventually.*

Tara knows from police reports that there were around thirty people at Matthew's party that night, and that drugs were found all around the house. Sabine, Tara and Daniel gave them all the names they could remember, and everyone who could be traced was interviewed. All of them denied knowing where the drugs came from.

According to the statements of others at the party, her parents had come home unexpectedly. Her mother had gone straight up to her bedroom. Her father had been furious and had laid into her brother, humiliating him in front of everyone.

And then Tara woke up at eleven the next morning.

She had never been able to explain why, but she had heard nothing. She had slept through the screaming. There must have been screaming. She had gone downstairs to get some orange juice and that was when she had found her father's body.

Tara believed she must have been drugged, given a roofie, which was why she ended up fast asleep upstairs, with no memory of the events of the night before. The toxicology screen was done too late though, so she would never know for sure. The police, and many family members, believed her brother was the killer. There were other suspicions too, that Tara had been complicit. That she was lying. She had been interviewed, several times.

Now, in the basement bar of The Onyx, Tara was still watching the young man in the denim shirt drinking his beer. He caught her staring, and when she smiled at him, he turned away.

Let's drink to how much I love you both.

Tara had not known that would be the last thing she would ever remember her brother saying.

THIRTY

Tara was walking across the too-bright lobby, head still buzzing, wiping away the smudges of mascara from under her eyes, when someone grabbed her arm.

'What are you doing here?' Jameson spoke through gritted teeth as he looked her up and down.

'I wanted to have a look at the bar.'

'Dressed like that?' He was taking in the dress, the heels, what was left of her lipstick.

'Let go of my arm.' Tara shrugged herself loose.

The lobby was mostly empty, but a couple of guests and staff members behind the reception desk were staring. Jameson's hand was on her back, forcing her towards the glass doors. When they stepped outside, the Bentley with the tinted windows was idling right in front of the hotel.

'I'll take you home,' Jameson said.

His hand was still heavy on her lower back, making her flesh crawl.

'I can get a cab.'

'Get in.' He opened the back door of his car with his free hand, blocking any attempt at escape with his bulky frame. 'We need to talk about what happened on the Jubilee Line this morning.'

'I'd be happy to make an appointment to meet in my office—'

'Either we talk now, or I can take my concerns up directly with Valerie Bennett. Your choice.' Jameson was seething.

Tara wished she hadn't drunk that awful Apple Martini. She was feeling queasy now, as well as light-headed. She needed to sit down. The easiest course of action seemed to be to co-operate, to get into the car.

Jameson got into the back seat next to her and the locks clicked into place. The driver pulled out and began driving, though Jameson hadn't given him any instructions about where to go.

'What did you want to discuss?' Tara said.

'Let me have your phone.'

'Excuse me?'

'I need to see your phone. I wouldn't want this conversation recorded.' Jameson held out his hand. 'Neither would you, frankly.'

There was no point resisting. Tara reached into her clutch bag for her mobile phone and handed it to him. He checked the screen, turned the phone off and slipped it into the breast pocket of his jacket.

'Is it normal practice for you to go through clients' private property?' he said.

'I don't understand.'

'In my kitchen, you looked through the drawers. Examined our knives. I let it go, I thought I'd overlook it.'

'You have cameras in the kitchen?'

'We have a very comprehensive home security system.'

Did he have cameras in the basement snug? In Jade's room? Was that how he knew the exact moment to walk in, as she had her hand on Jade's shoulder?

Tara was sure Jameson had monitored her interviews with Jade. He had listened in to every word said between them. That was the real reason Jade had refused to come into her office: Jameson wanted to control the process.

And now he was livid that Tara had managed to talk to Jade outside the house, without his knowledge.

The back of the car smelt strongly of new leather. Tara rolled her window down a little. She needed to feel air on her face, to breathe.

'Then we have the incident where you insisted on going into Jade's room when she was half asleep and took the opportunity to touch her. And to top it all off, today you followed my daughter into an underground station, pursued her on public transport halfway across London, and harassed her in public. When you put all of this together, it's concerning, if not downright bizarre.'

Jameson spoke in a low voice full of threat. The back of the car shrank around him, stocky and squat, in his pinstripe suit.

Tara was so thirsty. There was a bottle of water in the netting of the seat in front of her, but she could not bring herself to reach for it. She wasn't feeling good at all. She was aware of how much power Jameson held. He would find a way to torpedo her career if he chose to do so.

'Jade left the house when she was supposed to be meeting with me, and as you know it wasn't the first appointment she'd missed.' She sounded defensive, weak. She tried to shift her tone. 'Look, I've been having difficulty setting up appointments with Jade. The report deadline is—'

'You offered my daughter drugs to get her memory back? What if your conversation on the train was overheard? Recorded? What if it ends up on YouTube? She's facing a murder charge, for Christ's sake. What kind of professional are you?' His voice was rising.

Tara was rubbing the palm of her right hand with her left

thumb, distracting herself to keep her rising anxiety under control. Laid out like that, she could see how her sequence of actions might look if Jameson went to Jade's solicitor to complain. She had been too driven to succeed in this case. She had wanted to impress Valerie Bennett as much as she'd wanted to understand her client. She'd gone too far.

She still wasn't sure she regretted it, though. Yes, she had walked a fine line, but in her mind, she had not crossed over it. Everything she'd done had been in the best interests of the client. And if she hadn't done everything she could, it would have meant she had given up on Jade Jameson.

When Jameson next spoke, his voice was calmer. 'And then, as if that wasn't enough for one day, I was contacted by a member of staff, in the middle of the night, to let me know that the psychologist working on Jade's case is drinking up a storm in my hotel bar.' He paused for breath, pushing his hair back from his forehead. 'The crime scene, for God's sake.'

The driver was looking at her in the rear-view mirror. He was separated from them by a thick pane of glass, and Tara wasn't sure if he could overhear their conversation. She was sure he was a different driver to the one that had been waiting outside the Jameson house a couple of days before. That man had been older, with grey hair. This one was young, dark-haired with big brown eyes and a close-cropped beard. He was in a white T-shirt.

Tara checked out of the window. They'd left the congestion and lights of Soho behind and were coming up to the Baker Street area. The route they were taking seemed to be the right one to take her home.

She reached for the bottle of water in the seat in front of her, taking a long drink. She took a moment, to think, to breathe, before answering. 'If I have made Jade uncomfortable, I'd like to talk to her about it.'

'I can assure you that you won't be getting anywhere near my daughter ever again.'

What if Jameson was threatened because Tara would not give up on Jade? What if he was abusing Jade in some way? A history of abuse by her adoptive father, on top of her earlier trauma, might go some way to unravelling Jade's reactions in that hotel suite.

'I could have gone directly to Valerie Bennett with my concerns.' Jameson paused for effect.

'But you didn't.'

Her professional reputation was on the line. The thing was though, Jameson was nervous too. She could see it in his eyes. His breathing had become heavier.

'I'd hate to damage your reputation if I don't need to,' he said.

How thoughtful.

'Do you want to know why I didn't go to Valerie?'

Tara nodded. Her thumb pushed hard into her palm and she began to feel a throbbing pain. She was agitating the half-healed cut.

'I want to give you one more chance. I believe you have enough information to reach a conclusion about Jade's memory loss. You don't need another appointment.'

Tara knew exactly what he was saying, and why he didn't want their conversation recorded. Jameson was threatening her, and he wasn't being as subtle about it as he had been when he'd let her know he'd accessed her mortgage documents. Either Tara wrote a report stating that Jade's amnesia was genuine, or he would find a way to discredit her.

'I can't draw any conclusions, I don't have enough information yet. I need to interview Jade again.'

'Right. Let me explain this more clearly then.' In a smooth motion, Jameson brushed his fringe back off his face. His back teeth clenched. 'When Valerie Bennett came to me, to tell me that the initial expert we'd hired had withdrawn, she gave me a fresh list of experts with the relevant experience who could take over at short notice. I'm sure I don't need to tell you that medico-legal experts are thick on the ground in London?'

Tara didn't answer. She was seriously beginning to doubt whether illness was the real reason Anthony Edwards had withdrawn from the case. He had made a surprisingly swift recovery for one thing. And given the pressure Jameson was putting on her, Tara had to wonder if something similar had happened to Edwards. That could explain why he was refusing to answer her messages. He'd passed on a poisoned chalice.

Jameson's tense body was angled towards hers, his legs crossed. Tara was conscious of his hands, large and powerful, one gripping the handle above the door, the other on his thigh. 'Valerie had helpfully narrowed down this new list of hers to a shortlist of ten. You were number ten, Doctor Black. The weakest contender. You only made it on there because you were available at short notice, and you'd written a research paper on amnesia, but you had the least experience in criminal cases. I had the final say in whom to hire and Valerie was, I think it's safe to say, surprised at my choice. She tried to persuade me to pick someone else.'

The car was smooth and silent. They were still driving in the direction of her cottage. She was halfway home. Rationally, Tara did not think that Jameson would harm her, but her racing heartbeat said otherwise.

'I am not the kind of man who believes in leaving anything to chance.'

'I can see that now.'

'A sense of humour goes a long way when times are tough.' Jameson smiled, and it was disconcerting because he looked almost friendly.

Tara took another swig of water. The car was too warm and she was still fighting the nausea.

'Before I instructed Valerie to go ahead and hire you. I did some due diligence of my own. I came across Mr Daniel Franks, in Mergers and Acquisitions. The two of you have remained – let's say – close throughout his marriage?'

Tara placed the water bottle back in the net behind the front seat.

'Do you ever think about his wife?' Jameson said.

Tara's thumb was rubbing against her palm again. The cut was beginning to reopen, a trace of blood left on her palm. Jameson had seen it, in the same way he saw her every weakness.

'I have never been able to understand people who have affairs,' he said. 'Do they not think about the people they are hurting?'

Tara looked at him with silent loathing. The worst part was the truth in what he was saying.

'Then there is the more serious matter of your name change.'

For a second, Tara closed her eyes. She didn't want him to see his victory.

Tara Black is not the name I was born with.

I changed my name by deed poll when I was eighteen.

How could Jameson know all of this? He must have had a private detective looking into her background. Had he also got hold of the police reports?

She looked him directly in the eyes. 'Nothing I have done is illegal.'

'It really is a very sad situation, I have a tremendous amount of sympathy for you.' Jameson seemed sincere, even his eyes were warm. Psychopaths could be so charming. 'First your parents were killed and then your brother went missing, under somewhat of a cloud as I understand it.'

Tara couldn't look at him any longer. She stared straight ahead at the back of the driver's skull. He caught her eyes in the mirror again. She was sure now that he was listening to every word.

'I don't hold any of this against you,' Jameson said. 'In fact, when I found out about all of this, I had hope. I believed that with everything you had gone through, at the same age as Jade, and having been under suspicion yourself, unjustly I'm sure – I thought that all of this would help you empathise with my daughter.'

So he had seen the police reports. He knew.

Jameson clasped his thick-fingered hands on his lap. 'My concern now though, is that your personal issues are getting in the way of your professional judgement. The way you've been behaving is a clear sign. And this whole sordid mess in your past would of course explain your strange behaviour and also affect your credibility if it came out in court, or heaven forbid, in the media. I'm afraid that changing your name does make it look as though you have something to hide.'

Reputation was everything in her work. Tara knew that many solicitors carried out an internet search before hiring expert witnesses. She sometimes searched for her own name, to make sure her profile was clean. So far, it always had been. She had made sure to stay clear of social media. The only traces of herself she could find online were related to her work, first at the hospital, and now the Marylebone mews house. There was nothing about a double murder or a missing brother under suspicion for double murder. Nothing about the accusations of complicity the police had made against her.

Tara had not allowed her life to be defined by loss or victimhood, or even suspicion. This case had the power to change all that. If she defied Ray Jameson, he would find a way to destroy her career.

'Now,' he said, 'please don't look so worried. There is a way out of this situation, a good outcome for all of us. An excellent outcome.'

Tara pressed herself against the door. 'Despite what you may think, I am not unethical. I don't have enough information to know whether Jade's amnesia is genuine. I can't do what you're asking of me.'

'I would never have allowed Valerie to instruct you if I believed that were true. I think you can give me exactly what I want. And I'm going to give you a chance to do that. One chance.'

Jameson had never had any intention of co-operating with the psychological assessment. To him, this was a chess game, and he had always been several moves ahead of her.

'You know, I have always believed in using the carrot rather than the stick,' Jameson said. 'What if instead of worrying about all of this, you could turn everything to your advantage? I am a very powerful man. It could be life changing to have me on your side.'

'Are you afraid that Jade might trust me?' Tara said. 'That she might tell me the truth?'

'You misunderstand. I'm not afraid of anything.'

Yes, you are. You're afraid your daughter is lying. You're afraid she's guilty.

The car had pulled up alongside the pavement outside Tara's cottage. She tried to open her door, but it wouldn't budge. 'Unlock my door, please.'

Jameson was silent. The driver did not move or turn around. The door stayed locked.

Tara took a deep breath. She tried one last time to appeal to any shred of rational thinking, decency or honesty that Ray Jameson might have. 'Aren't you worried about what Jade might do in the future if we don't understand what happened in that hotel room? She may be a risk to other people. And she may be a risk to herself.'

'My wife and I have identified an excellent private treatment facility in Germany. I have full confidence my daughter will get all the help she needs.'

'Jade deserves the chance to understand what happened to her that night. She should be able to make her own choice, you don't have the right to decide for her.'

The locks clicked open.

'Jade does not belong in jail. I am going to ensure that she doesn't end up there.'

There was a pause as they looked at each other.

When Tara reached out her hand, it trembled. Her voice didn't sound quite right, either. 'I'd like my phone back, please.'

Jameson took it out of his pocket but held on to it. Tara tried to keep her hand steady.

'You didn't answer my question,' he said. 'Are we to be allies?'

She shook her head.

'I see.' Jameson placed the phone into her palm. 'I have full confidence in you. I'm sure that after a good night's sleep, after that Martini's out of your system, you'll be thinking more clearly. We all have a lot at stake here. We can all be winners.'

THIRTY-ONE

Tara closed her eyes, relishing the cool night air on her face. The conversation with Jameson had left her completely sober.

She opened the latch on her low front gate and walked along the uneven paving stones towards her front door. Halfway down the path, she stopped. She always left a light on in the hallway inside when she went out at night, but her cottage was in complete darkness.

Maybe she'd forgotten to turn that light on before she left. But that would be very unlike her.

She had a look around, to see if she'd missed Daniel's car. There was no sign of it. She took out her phone and called him, but his phone went straight to voicemail.

She left a message. 'Did you by any chance come by the cottage and turn the lights out?'

Seconds later a text came through: *No. Can't talk now, will call tomorrow.*

She must have forgotten. Or maybe the hallway bulb had blown.

Tara went back to her front door. Using the light from her

phone, she inserted her key into the lock. Once she was inside, she tried the light switch. The bulb was working fine.

Tara checked every room, on the ground and first floors. The cottage seemed to be exactly as she'd left it. Only one thing had been disturbed.

Her red notebook was lying open on the kitchen table, where she'd left it next to her laptop. Her interviews and notes on the Jameson case were all in there. Leaving the book out on the table was a serious data protection fail. Those notes should have been locked in her filing cabinet in the study. More ammunition for Ray Jameson if he'd known about it.

And Tara had the strongest suspicion that Jameson did know, because she was one hundred per cent certain she had closed that notebook when she got up from the table. Out of habit, she always closed it and secured the elastic around the cover, placing her fountain pen on top of it. She remembered doing that earlier that night. She could picture the exact way the table had looked when she'd stood up and abandoned her notes.

Jameson knew where she lived. He had known about Daniel's comings and goings, so he probably also knew she lived alone. He had known she was out, and that she was at the hotel.

Tara picked the book up and looked through it. None of the pages had been removed or damaged. Her heart was hammering away. Someone had been in the cottage and had read her notes, including her private thoughts on the case and the conclusions she'd reached so far, as well as her frank observations of the behaviour of the Jameson family. Whoever it was may have made copies.

Jameson wanted her to know he had access to those notes. That's why he – or whomever he had sent to do his dirty work – had turned that light in the hall off and left the notebook open.

Tara checked the back door was locked and bolted. She put the security chain on the front door. She went around the cottage making sure all the windows were securely closed and the curtains were drawn. Upstairs in her bedroom, she looked out through a crack in the curtains. The street was empty, but she had the sensation she was being watched.

Could he have put cameras in her house?

He had really got to her.

Jameson could access her home anytime and do whatever he liked.

She was not going to be able to sleep alone. Downstairs, back in the kitchen with all the lights on, she texted Daniel and said she needed him to come over.

The alcohol and the adrenaline from earlier had worn off, leaving Tara feeling shattered, but clear-headed. Curled up next to Daniel on the couch, she told him everything. Her reckless actions, the way her client's father had tried to bribe and threaten her to influence her report findings, the suspected break-in. Daniel's face was more and more grave as she spoke.

'It gets worse,' she said. 'It turns out there was a reason I was chosen for this case in the first place. The client knows about my name change. And he knows about us. I'm sorry.'

Daniel pulled away from her and sat up. 'I need to know the client's name.'

Tara hesitated.

'I need to know.'

'Ray Jameson. His daughter is accused of killing an ex-policeman in one of his hotels. Have you heard of him?'

Daniel nodded.

'And?'

'If I'd known, I would have told you not to take the case. Not that you would have listened.'

'I read up on him online, there was stuff about a murky past, rumours of involvement with organised crime? Is that true?'

'And a lot more. I doubt it was by chance that a police officer was murdered in one of his hotels.' Daniel was rubbing his temple, as though he had a headache coming on. 'Why didn't you tell me what was going on?'

'It's my job, I was handling it. It only came to a head tonight.'

Daniel stood up and walked over to the window. He looked out of the curtains, the same way Tara had done earlier in the upstairs bedroom, then he made sure they were shut tight.

'You said they can't find any connection between Jameson's daughter and the victim. Is that right?'

She nodded.

'Maybe that's because there isn't one. Maybe this isn't about the daughter at all. Maybe Jameson was taking care of some business, and somehow the daughter got in the way. Or, someone put a hit out on Jameson and his daughter got in the way. Whichever way round, I'd put money on it that Ray Jameson is at the centre of whatever happened in that hotel room.'

Could Jameson be such a monster as to let his daughter take the fall for a crime he committed? All the while pretending to be her protector?

According to their statements, Ray and Sandra had been out for dinner in Mayfair on the night of the killing. This had been confirmed by friends they were with, and staff at the restaurant. They'd left the place around midnight. But Ray Jameson would know how to bribe any number of staff at the restaurant or at very least call in a few favours from his friends to provide alibis. And, in any case, Mayfair wasn't that far from Soho.

Daniel was still on the other side of the room, in front of the window, arms crossed and knuckles pressed against his mouth, thinking.

She shouldn't have asked him to come over in the middle of the night. She wondered what he had told Sabine.

'I'm sorry you've been dragged into this,' Tara said.

'You're not responsible for this thug. Bennett hired you with Jameson's dirty money, you couldn't have known what you were getting into. It could happen to any of us. We'll work it out. It'll be all right, I promise you.'

But Tara was thinking about that strange coincidence, bumping into Daniel's wife. Jameson knew about the affair; Sabine knew about Tara's past. She didn't want to go there.

Tara stood up. She needed to move so she could think, so she could get rid of the build-up of anxious energy inside her body. 'I need a coffee.'

Daniel followed her into the kitchen. 'Tell me exactly what Jameson wants from you.'

His left hand, the one with the thin wedding band, rested on the countertop.

She spooned a generous amount of espresso blend into the cafetière. 'He won't allow me to meet with his daughter again. And he wants me to write a report confirming that her amnesia is genuine.'

When he next spoke, Daniel's voice was calm and measured, but deadly serious. He never used that tone with her, it was the voice he used on the phone, for work calls. 'I know you don't want to hear this, and you know I would never presume to tell you what to do in one of your cases, but please, walk away from this one. Please. I have a bad feeling about this.'

Tara turned on the gas cooker. The flame burned bright blue under the coffee pot. 'I have a responsibility to my client. She's a minor. And I'm starting to think she's as much a victim in this as the dead man.'

'Have you found out anything so far that contradicts the amnesia theory?'

'It's complicated. But in summary, no. The client has been

evasive, probably because of pressure from her father, and I'm sure she knows that our interviews are being recorded on the home surveillance system. Whether or not the amnesia is genuine, she and her mother could be in a situation of coercive control in that family. I won't write a false report for Ray Jameson.'

'And you don't have to,' Daniel said. 'The critical thing is that you don't have any further contact with his daughter. But if you have another meeting with her and end up in possession of information Jameson doesn't want you to have, then you potentially have a huge problem.'

Tara poured the coffee into a mug.

'Are you listening? If you meet with that girl again, you risk uncovering something that you have to disclose to the solicitor or worse, to the police.'

'The last psychologist on the case claimed he was ill and withdrew.'

'Smart move.'

'But if it's safe for Valerie Bennett to be working with Jameson,' Tara said, 'then it must be safe for me, right? She's so high profile, so well respected—'

'Valerie Bennett is working *for* the Jamesons. She's hired to come up with a defence. Your problem is you're looking for the truth.'

She took a sip of coffee. It was bitter. She no longer wanted it.

'You told me that there is nothing so far that proves your client is lying about the memory loss?'

Tara nodded.

'So, write an inconclusive report, submit it tomorrow and end this. Say that there is nothing to contradict the client's claim of amnesia, which is true. Then send Valerie the report and your invoice, confirming your involvement in the case is over. With any luck, she'll read between the lines, maybe rein in her client. And you walk away.'

'Is it that simple? Jameson can still use what he knows to shred my reputation if I don't give him the conclusions he wants.'

Daniel shook his head. 'If you're no longer a risk to him, he won't bother. You're small fry to him. You're okay.'

'So all I have to do is compromise my integrity and give up on everything that matters to me about my work.' Tara turned away. She poured herself a glass of water from the tap and drank it down, trying to settle her stomach. Half nausea, half anger.

'Do you understand that this is a chance for you to save yourself a whole lot of pain?'

'Is it my pain you're worried about? Or yours?'

'That isn't fair.'

'I know.' She hated this. The sense of being powerless. Her own cowardice.

Daniel came up close behind her, reaching for her hand, intertwining his fingers with hers. 'It makes no difference what you do or don't write in that report. Remember that the defence is perfectly entitled to bury your findings if they don't like them so, frankly, nothing you write will make a difference anyway. The police are entitled to appoint their own expert witness and they probably will. Let this be someone else's problem.'

She turned to face him. Daniel traced his fingers over the cut on her thumb and then the lines on her palm. 'For once in your life, please don't be stubborn. You don't need to risk your entire career for this one girl.'

He pressed her hand to his lips.

'What do I have left, Dan? If I don't have ethics and my responsibility to my clients. What exactly do I have left?'

Her eyes pricked with tears. It had been a long and crazy

day and all she wanted was to lie down and escape into sleep. 'Do you need to go?'

'I'll stay tonight.'

'And Sabine?'

'I'll stay as long as you need me.'

They were silent a few moments. When she looked into his blue eyes, she felt so much better. As if everything could be all right again. He pulled her close, his arms wrapped tight around her. Daniel was right. She was out of her depth. Maybe she was allowed to give up, to take the easy way out. Just this once.

THIRTY-TWO

Tara was always up early. Usually, summer dawn was her favourite time of day, with the sun half up in the sky and the city peaceful. Not today though. Daniel had left while she was still asleep. She had woken up feeling vulnerable in her own home, and knowing she had to finish writing a report she didn't believe in.

She made a pot of coffee, sat down at her kitchen table and stared out at the cherry tree. The night before seemed surreal. The crowded bar, the back seat of Ray Jameson's car, the darkened cottage. Her red notebook lying open on the kitchen table.

She wished she could convince herself she'd overreacted. It was possible she'd forgotten to turn the light on in the hall, and possible she'd forgotten to close the notebook. She could not be certain someone had been in the cottage. In her gut though, she knew someone had.

She had to follow Daniel's advice. He was right. Any report not to Jameson's liking would never see the light of day anyway, because Valerie would bury it, so she would be putting herself in the firing line for nothing. She hated to let her client down, and equally, she hated to admit defeat. But she also had to face reality and there was too much that could be lost.

Both Tara and Jade were stuck. Trapped by their own actions and Ray Jameson's need to control them.

She would take Daniel's advice. And yet she wasn't moving from her kitchen table.

She had woken up with unwelcome clarity of mind, and not only about the Jameson report.

Do you ever think about his wife?

The irony of Jameson preaching morality wasn't lost on her, but Tara could not get his words out of her head.

She had bought this cottage and clung on to Daniel because she was desperate to keep her last links to her brother and her parents. But in clinging to what was left of her old family, she had left it too late to have one of her own. She was alone.

It was as though a light had been switched on inside of her brain, illuminating all the wrong turns, and she couldn't turn it off.

To clear her head, Tara went to an early morning class at the gym. The small, no-frills place along the high street, was run by Louis, an ex-accountant turned martial arts expert. Tara had come to realise that lifting weights and working up a sweat had the same effect on her mental health, if not better, than a therapy session. By the time she'd showered and changed there, she felt almost normal.

At the office, she sat at her desk and finalised her report with inconclusive findings. She composed an email to Valerie Bennett, in which she submitted it and ended her involvement in the case. Then she filed this email in her drafts folder.

She thought again of Dr Anthony Edwards, pretty sure now that his reason for withdrawing was very possibly more sinister than she'd initially been led to believe. Impulsively, she sent him a third email. This time, she said it was urgent she speak to him.

Oksana, the woman who cleaned their building once a week, knocked on the door, carrying the vacuum cleaner.

'Do you need me to get out of your way?' Tara said.

'Yes, please. And this is for you, a messenger just dropped it off at the front door.' She handed Tara an envelope. Her name and address were on the front in impeccably neat handwriting. Inside was a white card with The Onyx logo on the top and a handwritten message in the same handwriting. *Risha Bassi, Penthouse, Saffron House, Berwick Street. I'm free all day today if you still need to meet. Text me a time.*

Risha's phone number was written at the bottom.

The address was in Soho, only a few blocks walk from The Onyx. Tara stood up, gathering up her laptop and briefcase.

'Before you go.' Oksana took a folded piece of paper out of her overall pocket. 'Can you have a look at this one?'

Oksana would often ask Tara for her thoughts about the pictures her daughter drew, though Tara kept telling her she didn't have any experience with younger children or interpretation of drawings. The last picture had been rather alarming, showing the child's teacher as a witch-like figure with fangs, dressed all in black with red eyes. Tara was hoping the situation at school might be more cheerful this time.

The page held a drawing of a family, a little girl with dark hair standing in between her mother and father. The mother had short, dark hair, just like Oksana's, and was holding a flower. The father wore a white uniform; Tara knew Oksana's husband worked as a chef. All three of them were smiling and holding hands. Behind them was a house with windows and a door and a tree growing in front of it. A bright sun was shining up in the sky.

'This shows a happy family,' Tara said.

'Yes!' Oksana said. 'That's exactly what I told my husband.'

Tara's hand shook a little as she handed the drawing back. Either the universe was conspiring against her, or she was particularly sensitive these last days.

Tara's curiosity, and her defiant streak, had got the better of her. One more meeting for the Jameson case couldn't hurt, she told herself. The address on Risha's handwritten card directed her to a new development of apartments inside a former Victorian factory. The concierge in the lobby was expecting her, and told her to go straight up to the penthouse. On the fourth floor, the lift opened directly into a capacious, industrial-style apartment, all glass and exposed brick walls. Risha was waiting right in front of the lift doors with her arms folded and her gloss-black hair reaching her waist. She was wearing her usual silk shirt, bright blue on this occasion with a bow at the neck.

'I thought it was better to talk here,' she said. 'I didn't want the staff being unsettled. Or eavesdropping.'

Risha led Tara through into the living room, which had wraparound windows and heart-stopping views over the rooftops and red chimneys of Soho. The apartment was quite something. Risha's salary must be generous.

There was a L-shaped sofa facing the windows, but Risha did not invite Tara to sit down. Tara put her bag on the floor, instinctively reaching inside it to take out her pen and notebook, then remembering she was no longer officially working on the case. All she had to do was click send on the email to Valerie as soon as she got back to the office.

Risha's eyes fixed on the notebook. 'I won't say anything unless you guarantee I won't be quoted. You can't even say we met. And if you can't promise me that, then I have nothing to say.'

'No problem.' This meeting was a selfish one. Tara had come because she was angry at Ray Jameson who had prevented her from doing her job. 'I won't quote you in the report.'

'I'll deny everything if you do.'

'I understand. You have my word.' Tara put the notebook and pen back in her bag. 'You're Jade's stepsister, is that right?'

Risha nodded. 'Ray Jameson is my father.'

'May I ask why you didn't mention that when we first met?'

'I don't know. Or, I suppose I do know. I thought it was better not to get involved.'

'Why is that?'

'I saw you last night at the hotel,' Risha said, 'with my father.'

Daniel's warnings were still ringing in Tara's ears. 'Did you tell him I was there?'

'I told you, I don't get involved. But I'm sure he has several staff members acting as his eyes and ears.' Risha paced up and down along the panoramic glass windows, her heels clicking against the wooden floor. 'You know you're the first person from Jade's team who's bothered to contact me. I suppose her solicitor doesn't particularly want to hear what I've got to say.'

'I understand that you and Jade had an argument on the night Carl Ress was killed?'

'Lucy told you?'

'Lucy is young, and very vulnerable, and she's desperate to help Jade. I hope this won't impact her job in any way.'

'What do you take me for? I'm not my father.'

'Right.' Tara hoped for Lucy's sake that was true. And it was interesting that Risha would hint at her father's ruthlessness. 'So the argument had something to do with Marco, the bartender?'

Risha nodded. 'This is why you can't say this came from me. I swear Jade has an instinct for trouble, she makes a beeline for these people. I didn't want Marco anywhere near the hotel, but Ray forced the issue.'

'I'm not following. What is the problem with Marco exactly?'

Risha's speech was fast and pressured as she walked back and forth. 'Marco is the grandson of Ray's old boss at the club, who himself happens to be stuck in jail. Marco has some kind of – shall we say – interesting past back in Italy. He's come over here all ridiculously good-looking with his tail between his legs and promising to be a good boy and the first thing he does is make eyes at Jade. What a piece of work.'

Tara remembered the driver of the Bentley the night before. His deep-brown eyes. She had a strong suspicion that might have been Marco. Someone Ray trusted not to leak their conversation.

'I was trying to do Jade a favour,' Risha was saying, 'but of course she thinks I'm trying to keep her away from her one true love. All Romeo and Juliet. The more I tried to warn her, the more interested she was. In fairness though, every woman that crosses Marco's path pretty much goes weak at the knees.'

Could it have been Marco in that hotel room? And if so, how far would Ray go to protect him?

Daniel believed that Jade had been caught in the middle of something that had nothing to do with her. Maybe losing her memory was the safest option.

'Since this is entirely off the record,' Tara said, 'are you saying that Marco had something to do with what happened to Carl Ress?'

Risha looked confused. 'No. God, no. No, you don't understand.'

Finally, Risha stopped pacing and turned to face her, her arms folded. 'I'm trying to tell you that if your report gets the charges dropped, then someone else could get hurt. Because this isn't the first time Jade has tried to kill someone.'

THIRTY-THREE

Risha had begun moving again, up and down along the vast windows, looking out at the view, as if trying to calm herself down. Tara sat down on the sofa, her fingers itching to write notes.

'After my parents split, I lived with my mum,' Risha was saying, 'but I was still close to my dad. I used to stay over at Ray and Sandra's place every second weekend, and sometimes I'd go away with them in school holidays. I loved it, I'd always get spoiled rotten and Sandra treated me like I was her own daughter. She's a good person. But then, when Jade came to live with them, things changed. I used to beg my mum not to send me.'

'How did things change?'

'Jade was really disturbed. She barely said a word. Sandra couldn't get her to stay in her bed at night, she'd get up and wander around the house. She wouldn't wake Ray and Sandra, or anything like that, but she'd steal stuff from around the house and then she'd hide. In the morning, there would be this panic, and then we'd find her eventually, usually in one of the cupboards, with a screwdriver, or knives from the kitchen, or whatever dangerous objects she could get her hands on. I started locking my door at night, and stacking things in front of it in case she tried to get in. Honestly it was like something out of a horror movie.'

What was striking was the extent to which Ray and Sandra Jameson had lied, and whitewashed Jade's history. Maybe they had never been able to face the degree to which Jade had been traumatised in her early life. If Risha's memory was correct though, Jade had a pattern of troubled behaviour, and a preoccupation with sharp objects.

'Jade had a very difficult start in life,' Tara said. 'So it makes sense that she'd be showing some signs of that. But are you saying she actually hurt someone?'

Risha still hadn't got around to telling Tara what she'd meant when she said Jade had tried to kill someone.

'I know she had a rough time with Paula,' Risha said, 'and I know it's not her fault she's screwed up. And most of the time Jade is kind and loving, but something is also very wrong. And no one is allowed to talk about it.'

Risha went over to her handbag, which was lying on the kitchen counter, and took out a vaper. 'Tell me something, do you feel safe when you're around Jade?'

Tara remembered that moment of intense fear, when she had been desperate to get out of the basement, away from Jade and her dog. She didn't answer. Risha was staring at her, inhaling deeply.

'Risha, did Jade ever hurt you?'

She shook her head. 'No. Never. Not me, and not Ray or Sandra either. But I'm telling you, there were a lot of times when Sandra and I were scared of her. Jade is not a bad person. But she needs serious help, and she won't get it if my father keeps protecting her.'

There were a few moments of silence. Risha turned her back, looking out of the window. She was still avoiding talking directly about the accusation she had made earlier.

'Risha, you said Jade had tried to kill someone before. Are you sure about that?'

'Not exactly, no.' Risha came over to sit near Tara on the sofa. 'But there was this one time, Jade was around ten, and she had some kind of mental breakdown after a visit to her mother's place. Something happened there, but it was all kept very hush hush. As usual. Ray and Sandra suddenly took her out of school and whisked her off on holiday to Spain, for like a month. Then the three of them came back and pretended nothing had ever happened. That was when Ray got her that nightmare rescue dog.'

Risha was puffing away anxiously and the air in the apartment filled with the scent of menthol. 'I was a nosy teenager. I'm still like that, actually. I like to know everyone's business, that's why I love hotels. Anyway, I used to eavesdrop on my mother when she was talking to Sandra, and I heard Sandra say that one of Paula's boyfriends had ended up in hospital half dead with stab wounds. She said Ray had paid both Paula and this boyfriend of hers off to keep quiet. I knew it was Jade who'd attacked him. It explained everything about that bizarre holiday of theirs. I'd been jealous the whole time because I wasn't invited.'

Risha's words poured out. She had been waiting a long time to say all of this out loud.

'But you can't be sure that it was Jade who attacked this man?'

Risha put her vaper down on the coffee table. In motion again, she stood up and went to pace along the glass window. 'I'm right. I know I am.'

'Okay, let's say you are,' Tara said. 'I don't understand why Ray and Sandra would cover it up and go off on holiday, as opposed to getting Jade help? She was very young, she had a history of abuse, she wouldn't have faced criminal charges.'

'You don't understand. They were terrified of losing her.

Ray and Sandra always tried to hide how bad things really were in that house. They knew the adoption would fall through unless social services believed that living with them was a safe environment for Jade. And that meant her behaviour had to appear to be normal. I say *they*, but really, I mean my father. He always thinks he knows better than anyone else.'

Tara was processing all of this new information which painted a very different picture from everything she'd heard before. There seemed to have been a massive family collusion going on, where they had all been under pressure to lie and pretend.

'Sandra used to beg Ray, literally beg him, to let her take Jade to see someone. I used to hear them fighting about it, all those mornings when we'd be frantically searching around the house for her, terrified she'd done herself harm. But Ray would never in a million years voluntarily get involved with social services, or psychologists, or anything like that. As far as he's concerned, police are the worst kind of criminals, he hates them like absolute poison, and social workers and psychiatrists and psychologists come a close second. I think they were pretty much all involved in his childhood, and that didn't go too well either.'

No wonder Ray didn't want Jade anywhere near a psychologist's office. It must have taken all of his acting powers to welcome her into his home that first day. 'So Ray and Sandra took Jade on this trip, and then what happened?'

'I have to admit she did settle down afterwards. That dog was like some kind of security blanket, or therapist. And then Paula died a few months later – and, to be honest, I think everyone was just relieved and we all thought maybe that was the end of it. Until now.'

Tara got up and went to stand next to Risha at the window. There was so much glass, she had the sensation she was floating.

There was something magical about the view of grey slate-tiled roofs and red chimney breasts.

'I hope you can do something,' Risha said. 'Jade needs to face the truth. For everyone's sake.'

'I don't think that's going to happen.'

In the same way as he controlled his wife and daughters, Ray Jameson had found a way to control Tara. He was determined to stop her from understanding the way Jade's mind really worked. That also meant that Tara could not know what help Jade might need to heal.

'My father got to you, didn't he? I saw you get into his car last night.'

Tara didn't answer. The two of them were silent a while, side by side, looking out across the city.

'This view is gorgeous, isn't it?' Risha said.

'It's stunning.'

'My father bought this place for me, off plan about three years ago. A fourteen-million-pound gift. Lucky girl, right?' Risha smiled, bitterly.

'Is that how he controls you?' Tara said. 'With money? Or is there more?'

'If you're asking if he's ever been violent, then no. But I am afraid of him. My father likes to control everything. And he knows everything. He probably knows I'm talking to you right now.'

'You're taking a big risk then.' Tara felt a twisting in her belly.

Daniel had warned her, practically begged her, not to put herself in a position where she found out something incriminating that would provoke Ray Jameson into taking more drastic action.

'I must be mad.' Risha wiped away her tears. 'You know, Jade has always been my father's favourite. I think Ray knows exactly what Jade did in that hotel. And he still loves her. He's always loved her more.'

Tara felt for her. And for Sandra and Jade. All these women caught up in Ray Jameson's charismatic, corrosive control, that appeared, on the surface, like love and protection.

'Family loyalty is everything to my father. If he finds out I've betrayed Jade, I'll pay the price. I'll lose my job. He'll cut me off. And I'll be honest with you, I love my job and I need his money and I deserve my inheritance. And besides that, I love him. He's my dad.'

Risha walked over to the dining table, picked up her bag and hoisted it over her shoulder. 'I don't sleep much anymore. I'm scared of what Jade's going to do next and I'm scared of what my father will do if I speak out. I'm stuck.'

Ray Jameson had a way of doing that to people. Tying them up in their own minds.

'If it makes you feel better,' Tara said, 'I'm not sure how much you could do. I wouldn't have included what you've told me in my report, even if you had given me your permission. I couldn't base my conclusions on your suspicions about Jade.'

'It's actually a relief to just tell someone. Even though opening my mouth about all of this was probably a terrible mistake.'

'It wasn't a mistake. I'm glad it gives you some relief.'

Risha's relief might be the one thing Tara achieved in this case. She thought about the resignation email sitting in her draft folder. She hated that she was giving in to Jameson's toxic pressure.

Risha checked her phone, which had been clutched in her left hand for most of the time they'd been talking. 'Sorry I'll need to show you out. I need to get back to the hotel.'

'One last thing. Do you know of any connection between Carl Ress and your family?'

Risha shook her head.

'So, if the police are right, why would Jade attack him?'

'I was hoping you could tell me.'

'You really have no idea?'

Risha shrugged. 'Maybe he made a move on her. I suppose she was defending herself.'

'His wife doesn't think he'd do that.'

'The wives never do.'

THIRTY-FOUR

SEVEN YEARS EARLIER

Even before she opened her eyes, Jade knew Ruby was there. She struggled her way out of sleep, feeling the space where the other girl slipped in.

The bed next to hers was empty, but it had been slept in. The mosquito net was pushed to one side, the sheets were rumpled. Ruby was crouched down in the corner. When Jade went closer, she saw that Ruby was staring at the small frog squatting underneath the chair.

'What did you bring him inside for?' Ruby said.

'I don't know. I like him. He eats the mosquitoes.'

Ruby reached out and touched the frog's head with her finger. 'He'll bring snakes into our room. Snakes love to eat frogs. And after they eat him, they'll slither into our beds. So we have to get rid of him.'

Jade shuddered. 'Don't hurt him. Please.'

'Don't be a crybaby,' Ruby said.

A strange blackness blossomed in Jade's chest. 'Don't you dare touch him.'

'Stop crying.'

Jade took a deep breath and then another. She tried to stop the tears.

Ray and Sandra were sitting in silence in the kitchen. Fruit and pastries were spread out on the table and the smell of coffee filled the room.

'I had a dream about Ruby,' Jade said, breathless.

Sandra didn't even turn her head to look at her. 'Sit down and eat something.'

Ray reached over and gave her hand a squeeze as she sat down. 'Eat your breakfast and then we'll go for a swim.'

The feeling in the room was all wrong.

'Graziella says there are knives missing.' Sandra's face was like thunder.

Inside, Jade was afraid. Confused. 'I didn't take them.'

'You promised us you'd stop this,' Sandra said. 'Why do you lie?'

Ray reached out his hand out and put it on Sandra's arm. He gave her a look.

Jade didn't know what to say. She didn't want them to be angry. She kept thinking about Hansel and Gretel.

'Are we going to talk about what happened at Paula's place?' Sandra said.

Jade knew something bad had happened. Only, she wasn't sure what. A stench of sweat; Paula screaming. Sometimes Jade didn't remember which of these things came first, and which came after.

'Sandra, please,' Ray said.

Sandra pushed her chair back and stood up. 'I can't do this anymore.'

Ray and Jade watched her as she left the room. For a while, there was an empty silence.

'Why did you bring us here?' Jade said. 'Sandra hates this place. And I need to go back to school, I'm missing too much work. And you've been in the sun too much. You look like a lobster.'

Ray laughed, a big loud, belly sound. Jade's sadness lifted a little. If Ray was happy, maybe he could work his magic and make them a family again.

'Give Sandra some time. She'll come around.' Ray was scrolling through the photos on his phone. 'And in the meantime, I have a surprise for you. Here we go, look at this little fella.'

He handed her his phone. It was a photo of a teeny grey puppy with a white stripe on his forehead.

'Aww!' Jade said.

Ray put his arm around her shoulders. 'He's lonely. He's waiting for someone to come and get him out of his cage. If you like him, he's yours.'

'Really?' Jade had tears in her eyes again. She couldn't help it. She was a crybaby.

'He's going to grow big,' Ray said. 'He's a real brute. And if you train him well, he'll look after you. When we get home, we'll go straight from the airport to fetch him.'

She flung her arms round his neck, holding him tight. 'I love you so much.'

'When we go back, you don't have to go see Paula again if you don't want to.'

'I do want to.' She clung to him.

Ray sighed. 'Well maybe you can take Ziggy with you.'

'Who's Ziggy?'

'Your pup. Isn't Ziggy a good name for a dog?'

Jade giggled. 'Maybe. But sometimes Ruby comes with me, and I don't know if she likes dogs.'

Ray sighed.

'Sandra doesn't like it when I talk about Ruby.' Jade was

chewing the skin on her bottom lip; Sandra told her off when she did that, but Ray didn't notice.

'Sandra thinks old Ruby might be a bit of a bad influence. Your Ruby is a bit of a drama queen, isn't she? She likes to make up stories.'

Jade nodded.

'And those stories are sometimes not true, right?'

Jade wasn't sure what to say.

'I was thinking, maybe Ruby should stay here,' Ray said 'Maybe we could leave her behind. Just for a while, until the puppy gets a bit bigger. What do you think?'

Like Hansel and Gretel.

'She won't stay without me,' Jade said.

Ray sighed again. 'I had a feeling you might say that.'

THIRTY-FIVE

Tara and Risha were waiting for the lift to arrive. It was down on the ground floor and taking forever to reach the penthouse. Risha pressed the call button repeatedly. When the doors finally opened, Tara recognised the woman standing inside. She was Sandra's client from the rooftop, the one with severe scarring on her face.

'Mum this is Doctor Black,' Risha said. 'The psychologist working with Jade. Doctor Black, meet my mother. Noor Bassi.'

Noor shook Tara's hand. Her hair was loose, long grey curls almost to her waist, falling forwards over the right half of her face and almost covering the eye patch.

Risha kissed her mother's cheek. 'We were just leaving, Mum.'

'No, no, you can't go, I just got home. Stay a little.'

'I can't, I have a VIP check-in to sort out, but I'll be back for dinner. Don't cook okay, we'll go out?'

Noor turned her attention to Tara. 'What about you, Doctor Black?'

'She's busy, Mum,' Risha said. 'She's working.'

Noor ignored her daughter, giving Tara a charismatic smile.

Tara was thinking that Risha's mother must have known Ray Jameson even longer than Sandra. And she might be less loyal to him. 'I wouldn't mind staying for a chat,' Tara said.

'Fantastic!'

Risha stepped into the empty lift, holding the door open. 'This is your last chance of escape. She will show you my baby pictures. There are a lot of them.'

Tara smiled. 'I don't mind.'

'And she is going to grill you about Jade's case. If anyone can get you to crack it's my mum. Don't say I didn't warn you.' Despite her jokes, Risha looked nervous about leaving the two of them alone. With some hesitation, she let the lift door close.

Noor tossed her tote bag down in the lobby area and went ahead into the kitchen. 'Risha is very beautiful, isn't she?'

'She is.'

'She got nothing of Ray's looks, thank God!' Noor was humming as she moved around the kitchen. She seemed very much at home in the penthouse.

'Do you live here with Risha?'

'I do.' Noor had her back to Tara as she opened the fridge and took out a jug of creamy, thick liquid. 'Have you ever tasted Shardaayi?'

'No, I haven't.'

'It's a nut-milk, very good for you. Full of protein.' Noor took out a silver tray and set it with two glasses. She filled both from the jug. 'Can you carry these over to the sofa for me? Thank you, my darling.'

Tara did as she was asked. She found herself sitting on the sofa again, facing the lovely view of the London skyline.

'I sometimes wish I had studied psychology instead of accountancy. Your job must be so fascinating.'

'It is.' Tara took a sip of her drink. 'This is delicious.'

'Good.' Noor looked pleased as she sipped from her own

glass. She was observing Tara quietly. 'My daughter has been filling your head with stories. I can see it in your eyes.'

The drink was cold and refreshing, redolent of cardamom and saffron. Rich, too. Tara wasn't sure she could make her way through the entire glass.

'It was very difficult for Risha when her father left us and started a new family. My daughter was left with a lot of pain in her heart. She has always believed that Jade is her father's favourite, even though it isn't true. I know it eats away at her. Jealousy is so destructive, isn't it?'

Could Risha be so intensely jealous that she would lie about Jade attacking a man with a knife as a ten-year-old child? That would mean that Risha herself was quite disturbed.

'And Jade was such a gorgeous little girl,' Noor said. 'It's so terrible what's happening.'

'Did you feel there were any warning signs, that Jade might be violent?'

'No, no, no.' Noor shook her head. 'Nothing at all.'

Which was odd, because according to Risha, she had told her mother about her fears about Jade and begged her not to send her for sleepovers to Ray and Sandra's place. One of them was lying.

Tara had believed Risha was sincere, she was clearly distressed and anxious about what she'd disclosed. Noor, Tara wasn't so sure about.

'Did you know Jade when she was still living with her biological mother?'

Noor shook her head. 'The first time I met her was when she was visiting Ray and Sandra, I suppose she was around five already. Such a quiet little thing. I'm telling you, Sandra has got a heart of gold. It wasn't easy on her marriage.'

'In what way?'

'I think she never really got to explore her own path, you know? Her sister had so many problems with drugs and pimps, Ray was always rushing out in the middle of the night to sort them out. Then Ray and Sandra took Jade in, and soon afterwards, Paula died. There was constant stress in their lives for so many years. And now this crazy business at the hotel.'

'Risha mentioned you might have some photographs, from when Jade was little?'

Noor reached into a drawer that slid out from under the coffee table and took out a rectangular, blue photo album. The photographs were in plastic sleeves, the images turning slightly yellowish-brown with age.

Noor moved over to sit closer to Tara. 'See, there's Sandra and Paula.'

She pointed out two women in a group, all of whom were sitting around a table at a pavement bar. Tara bent down to take a closer look. Sandra and her sister Paula looked very much alike, only Paula was emaciated and had the haunted look of an addict.

'Paula was a sad girl, that's really all I can say. She started at the club too young, she was offered drugs, men took advantage of her. Then she disappeared after she got pregnant. You don't see too many pregnant pole dancers, do you?' Noor sipped her drink, holding it on her lap where it left a damp patch on her jeans. 'And that's me, when I was nineteen.'

In the photograph, Noor was standing on what looked like a Soho street, her hands in the pockets of a winter coat, smiling. She wasn't wearing an eye patch and the skin of her face was smooth and unscarred.

'How did you meet Ray, if you don't mind me asking?'

'I don't mind at all. I had a lot of problems at home – my father died, and my mother married again too soon, because she was really struggling with children to look after on her own, and then they both started drinking and fighting. So anyway, I moved to London to live with my cousins and I loved music and

I thought it would be fun, working at the club. I wanted to be a singer. I was quite good!'

'The club Ray Jameson was managing?'

Noor nodded. 'I had the looks for it, and I had quite an advantage too. Asian girls were exotic. But I wasn't a dancer, I had no rhythm whatsoever and worse, I could never take my clothes off in front of all those strange men without crying. So Ray took pity on me and gave me a job as a cleaner.'

'What was he like, back then?'

'He was a good man. Exactly the same as he is now.'

Tara was not expecting that answer. 'A good man?'

'Ray never took advantage of the girls, if that's what you're thinking. He wasn't like that. He hated that the club employed underage dancers, but he couldn't control everything. There were many others involved. He did his best for us.'

Noor seemed to be as loyal to Ray as Sandra. With the expensive apartment and her daughter's job, she might feel she owed Ray a lot.

'How long were you and Ray together?'

'Three years. Here, I'll show you.' Noor took the photograph album from Tara's lap and searched through the photographs. She handed it back, open to a photograph of a much younger and very muscular Ray Jameson lying next to Noor on a beach. They were both propped up on their elbows, in swimsuits and sunglasses, smiling.

'Three happy years,' Noor said. 'And now I have my Risha.'

Tara took a while to examine the photo. While Noor was looking at the camera, Ray was looking at Noor. His expression was one of intense adoration, as though he could not believe his luck. Noor had been stunningly beautiful.

'Do you want to ask me about the scars?' Noor said.

Tara nodded, handing the album back. Noor held it open on her lap.

'One night as I was leaving the club after my shift, a man threw acid in my face.'

'I can't imagine how horrific that was.'

'No, you can't. The pain was beyond anything.'

'Did you know this man?'

'No, and they never caught him.'

In the pause, Tara sensed something more.

'Did this man know Ray?'

'There was a lot going on to keep that club running. All these lowlifes needing to be paid off. From drug dealers and pimps to policemen, Ray had to manage everything, all of them. I was collateral damage. They got to him through me, because he was in love with me. Ray has always blamed himself.'

Noor was smiling at Tara now, with sad eyes. 'You mustn't think Ray left me because of my face. Because if you think that, you don't understand him at all. He took care of me and Risha, for a year, while I was in and out of hospital. But as soon as I was back on my feet, I left him. He begged me not to go. Begged me.'

'Why did you leave?'

'Because of Risha. I had to protect my daughter, and so I could not be involved in the life Ray was involved in. Do you understand?'

Tara nodded.

'That was one reason. But the second reason I left was because I was too strong for him. Ray is a rescuer, and I never wanted to be anyone's rescue project.'

Noor closed the photograph album. 'Like I said, when Ray and I first met I was working as a cleaner at the club, and I may have come to London with nothing, but I did have ambition. When Risha was two years old, I put her in day care so I could finish my degree. That's when Sandra came along. She needed him more. Sandra was happy to be rescued – or to let Ray think he was rescuing her.' Noor winked and smiled. She did not seem at all bitter. 'Sandra was seventeen and Paula was fifteen when they arrived. Two little wounded birds. Ray thinks he took them under his wing, but I can tell you, Sandra had her eye on him from day one. She knew exactly what she wanted, that one.'

Given that Sandra was her fitness instructor, the two women seemed to have made their peace. But Ray and Noor did seem to have stayed in rather close proximity to each other, and Tara had to wonder how Sandra felt about her husband's ex being ensconced in an expensive penthouse. Noor had a warm and dynamic personality, while Sandra was so passive and restrained. And Ray did not look at Sandra the way he looked at Noor in that photograph.

'How are you enjoying the drink?' Noor asked.

'Delicious.' Tara was halfway through the glass. There was something addictive about the taste.

Noor was easy to like and fascinating to talk to. Tara could have happily stayed talking to her and delving into Jade's family history for the entire afternoon, but she had to be back in the office in half an hour for an appointment with a client. And she had to send that email to Valerie Bennett.

Tara took the envelope with the crime-scene photos out of her bag. She slipped the top of the first picture out, so that Carl Ress's face was visible, but not his injuries.

'Do you recognise this man?'

'That's the man who died?' When Noor looked at the photograph, Tara couldn't see any sign of recognition.

'Yes. Carl Ress, a retired police officer.'

All these lowlifes needing to be paid off. Everyone. From drug dealers and pimps to policemen.

Noor shook her head. 'No, doesn't look familiar at all. And if you are wondering if I might recognise the man who threw acid in my face – the answer is no. He was wearing a balaclava.'

But Ray might well know who had attacked Noor. And he

was not the kind of man to let that go. Maybe Daniel was right, and Ress's death was some kind of hit gone wrong. Maybe Ray had been settling an old score in the Red Suite. But why do it in his own hotel, leaving his daughter to take the fallout?

Noor closed the photograph album, which had been lying on the sofa between them. She put it back safely into the drawer that slid out from under the coffee table.

Tara was startled when Noor reached out and laid a hand over hers. Her skin was like silk. She gave Tara's hand a few pats, then drew back. 'May I ask you one question, as a professional?'

'Sure.'

'One moment.' Noor got up and went into the kitchen area, opening one of the drawers and taking out a piece of paper. She came back and handed it to Tara.

'Can you tell me what this medicine is for?'

The paper had one word written on it in capitals: QUETIAPINE.

'It's an anti-psychotic medication,' Tara said.

'You mean for things like schizophrenia, hearing voices, those kinds of terrible problems?'

'Possibly, but not always. Sometimes it can be prescribed in low doses to treat depression.'

Behind the bubbly, optimistic personality, it was clear that Noor was troubled.

'Has this been prescribed for you?' Tara said.

Noor shook her head. 'I saw a box of pills with that label in Risha's room. She doesn't know I found it.'

Tara handed the piece of paper back.

'Now,' Noor said, her cheery mask back in place, 'I'm giving you some Shardaayi to take home with you. No arguments.'

THIRTY-SIX

During the drive back to her office, sitting in the back of a black cab, Tara reflected on the conversations she'd had with Risha and her mother. The habit of keeping notes was too difficult to break, and she wrote up a brief summary on her laptop.

Risha's description of Jade's troubled behaviour was in stark contrast to what every other person Tara had interviewed had said. But there was no way to know if what Risha had reported was true, especially if, as Noor had hinted, Risha had some serious mental health problems. Also, the problems Risha had described were several years earlier, and Jade could well have stabilised in her new home.

Risha was the outlier. Her allegations about Jade having killed before did seem far-fetched, and speculative. There was no actual evidence. Even so, Risha's version of Jade's history seemed more credible than the sanitised one Ray and Sandra had tried to convey. Jade must have been affected by her early experiences with Paula. She may have been far more disturbed than Ray or Sandra wanted to acknowledge. Jade's teacher had been concerned about this too, unconvinced by the too-perfect, compliant façade.

Tara had specifically asked Jade's parents about any disturbed or aggressive behaviour, and they had denied everything. Given the way Carl Ress had been killed, the fact that Jade had a habit of hoarding sharp items hardly seemed like something they might forget to mention.

Under the circumstances, Tara had no intention of going back to confront Ray and Sandra about what Risha had told her. Instead she googled Ray Jameson's strip club, Diamonds. Everything had started there.

Both Jade's biological and adoptive mothers had worked there as underage strippers. Noor had been attacked there. It was at the club that Sandra had first set her sights on Ray Jameson. Then, almost two decades later, Carl Ress had been killed there.

Photographs came up of an Edwardian mansion house, with most of the windows bricked up. The building was painted black, with a white dancer's silhouette stencilled down the side. According to Wikipedia, the club had been open from 1967 until 2009. At first it had been a gambling venue, and afterwards a 'home of erotic dancing'. Diamonds had eventually closed after a scandal involving drug dealing, and the Italian owner was imprisoned and then deported. Former employee, Ray Jameson, had somehow raised the finance to buy the condemned building, and over several years had had it demolished and then rebuilt as a luxury hotel that he named The Onyx.

Tara closed her laptop.

Tell me something, do you feel safe when you're around Jade?

There was another possibility in this case she hadn't considered. Maybe there was no complex motive behind the death of Carl Ress. Maybe Jade had killed for pleasure and she knew that with her father's protection, she could get away with it. Like father like daughter.

In her gut, Tara did not find this a convincing argument. But some of the signs were there: evasiveness, lying, even a fascination with weapons, if Risha was to be believed.

Was Jade a vulnerable victim who needed her help? Or a cold-blooded killer? Or both?

If she sent that email to Valerie, she would never know.

She held her bag tightly as she got out of the cab in front of her office. *He probably knows I'm talking to you right now. My father knows everything.*

Ray had admitted to having had Tara under investigation. He knew about her past and about Daniel's visits. He had most probably broken into her cottage, or if not him personally, then one of his henchmen. Marco, perhaps, if Risha's doubts about the bartender were accurate.

Tara looked around, wondering if she was being watched. A black SUV cruised past with the windows blacked out.

She got back into the cab. 'I've changed my mind,' she said. 'Can you take me over to Royal University Hospital?'

Tara traced the familiar route from the entrance of the hospital, past the kiosk which sold terrible coffee, and through labyrinthine passages to the Neurology Department.

When she arrived at the unit, Neil was busy in a late-running ward round. After a catch up with the receptionist, Tara waited in his office where it was so reassuring that everything was exactly the same: piles of books stacked around the room; half-empty mugs from his endless cups of tea; the frayed Persian rug; the armchairs covered in peach faux leather.

She still missed the place.

'This is a surprise.' Neil was exceptionally tall and had to mind his head as he came through the doorframe. There was an undercurrent of worry in his voice, like a parent whose child has returned unexpectedly from their first week at university. He knew her well and she wasn't the kind of person to turn up on a whim.

Tara stood up to give him a kiss hello, catching the familiar whiff of cigarette smoke in his tweed jacket. Her old boss was a clandestine smoker when under stress. Tara and his wife had nagged him about it for several years, but both had finally accepted that at sixty-eight, he was never going to give up.

Neil sat down in the armchair opposite hers, his long legs stretched out in front of him, crossed at the ankles. Even his worn-out trainers gave her a pang of nostalgia. The Jameson case had made her feel very exposed, acutely out on a limb.

'Thank you for referring Melanie Davis to see me,' Tara said.

'Ah, I'm glad she made contact. I thought the prognosis was good?'

Tara nodded. 'The physical pain she's having is all about guilt, right? She's punishing herself for what happened to her sister.'

Neil nodded. There were a few moments of silence.

'I'm in a... situation,' Tara said. 'I've been working on an assessment report for a criminal case and it's not been straight-forward. To say the least.'

'Go on.'

'The client is a seventeen-year-old girl. She's accused of stabbing a man to death in a hotel room, but she claims to have no memory of it. It triggered my own stuff, at first. When I went to have a look at the crime scene, I had this vision of a blood-soaked pillow on the bed.' Tara blinked the image away. 'And then while I was interviewing her, I felt afraid. As if I was really in danger.'

'It makes sense that your fear system was activated. She's violent. She killed someone.'

'Allegedly killed someone. And I do think I lost some objectivity. She's the same age I was when my life imploded.'

'It's understandable. You're only human.'

Tara nodded. From the moment she'd met Neil, she had been deeply affected by his kindness. He was one of the few people who knew about her history, she had told him everything when she'd accepted the job.

'I've found my feet now,' she said, 'but the bigger problem is that the client's family is pressuring me to step down. Her father has threatened to expose me if I insist on seeing her again.'

Neil cleared his throat. 'Expose you?'

'He knows. About my parents, and about the name change. He'll go after my credibility and my reputation.'

'So what?' The simplicity of Neil's answer was a surprise. A relief. 'You have nothing to be ashamed of, you aren't responsible for what happened to your parents. And if necessary, you have several colleagues who will testify to both your expertise and ethics.'

'I stepped over a line. I followed the client onto a train.'

'Whatever you did was, in your opinion, in her best interests, is that right?'

'I believe so.'

Neil adjusted his position. There was never enough space in any of the hospital chairs to accommodate his long limbs. 'What is your clinical judgement telling you now?'

'I think my client needs this assessment. Whatever did or didn't happen in that hotel room, she has been in need of professional help for years, but her father keeps blocking it. If they don't get to the bottom of it now, I don't think she has much of a future. And also, I want to finish this piece of work.'

Neil said hmm and then was quiet a while. Tara was used to the silences. He always took time to assemble his thoughts.

His office faced out onto a high brick wall which blocked out most of the natural light. Tara used to have the exact same view from her old office, a few doors down. She remembered how much she hated the harsh overhead lights and how the long days sitting underneath them left her eyes and her head aching. She thought fondly of the soft recessed lighting in her new office that she controlled with a dimmer switch.

'I don't want to admit defeat,' Tara said. 'But I don't know if that's a good thing.'

'You know that if you start ignoring your instincts and acting from a place of fear, you'll regret it.'

'I know.'

But then Neil hadn't met Ray Jameson. And Daniel was equally astute, and he took a very different position.

'Having said that,' Neil said, 'don't rush this decision. Come back and see me in a couple of days. We should talk again.'

'Thank you. I will.' She could tell he was worried, but that he didn't want to undermine her confidence by showing it.

He looked at his watch. 'Are you in the mood for apple crumble?'

'Always.'

'We should get going then. They always run out after lunch.'

They met up with the rest of the team in the canteen. No one seemed surprised to see Tara back and it was almost like old times for a while, only Tara kept reaching around her neck, missing the comforting feel of her lanyard.

THIRTY-SEVEN

By the time she left her office much later that afternoon, London was clogged with early evening traffic, all the way from Marylebone back to the suburb. There was no chance Tara was going to make it back in time for the kettlebells class, which she very much needed to clear her head. Despite this frustrating end to a long day, Tara was feeling lighter.

She had been half-waiting all day for a message from Jade, in case she agreed to come in to the office for an appointment. Olivia had the medication ready. But there had been no word. And even if Jade's mother might support her daughter's choice to take psychedelics to trigger her memory, Sandra would no doubt feel obliged to tell Ray, and Ray would put an end to it.

The choice seemed to be out of Tara's hands and maybe that was for the best. Her involvement with the Jameson family had become a constant, corrosive pressure. She was beginning to look forward to her freedom.

She'd been driving for almost forty-five minutes and had finally reached Golders Green; the traffic was still stop-start. As she passed the Italian place opposite the underground station, a parking space opened up and on impulse, she pulled in, feeling a sudden craving for pizza.

The restaurant smelled of garlic and fresh bread and was full of people talking and eating. Tara found a quiet table in the back corner. A teenage waiter handed her a menu. She enjoyed her solitude and the sense she was invisible.

She still hadn't drawn a line under her involvement in the Jameson case. She hadn't yet sent that email. It was unlikely that Valerie Bennett would be inclined to use her services again given that Tara had not even managed to see much of the client, and as a result the report was underwhelming and not particularly conclusive or helpful. That was a gloomy thought. On the other hand, if Valerie couldn't put the pieces of the puzzle together, and didn't see how problematic her client was, then maybe she wasn't someone Tara wanted to work for.

The place was filling up and there was a queue at the door. The waiter had not reappeared to take her order. A message came through on her phone from Daniel.

Let me take you out to dinner. Pick you up at 7.30?

It was exactly what she needed. It was also an unusual offer, because it was Friday night. A family night. Although it was the middle of the school holidays, so maybe Sabine had taken the children to see her parents in France.

Tara texted back a simple *Yes*. She got up and abandoned her table.

By the time she got back to her car though, another message had come through. This one was even more unexpected than the last.

Hi, Dr Black, it's Jade Jameson. I want to take the medicine if it will help me remember. My mum has given permission. She can bring me to your office tomorrow morning, if that's okay?

THIRTY-EIGHT

The place Daniel had chosen was almost an hour's drive north of the city, in a small village. He said it was a gastropub he'd heard about, that he had wanted to try for ages, but Tara thought it more likely he was nervous about bumping into someone he knew in London.

She was preoccupied as they drove, excited that she might crack this case, but knowing she may be risking her entire career in the process. In her mind, she was trying to justify what she was going to do. Jade was the client. Tara's responsibility was to her, not to Jade's father. She had to give this process one last chance before she gave up.

You know that if you start ignoring your instincts and acting from a place of fear, you'll regret it.

Ultimately, it was Jade who had made the choice. But as Tara had texted her back earlier, to confirm their appointment, she kept hearing Daniel's warning. *Please, walk away from this one. I have a very bad feeling.*

Jade would come to her office at ten o'clock the next morning. Olivia would be there to support the procedure. Tara had no idea whether Ray knew about the appointment, but she hoped that Sandra could keep her husband in check.

Tara hadn't told Daniel about the appointment. When he'd asked about the case, she said she didn't want to talk about work. This evening was for the two of them.

There would be this one last appointment with Jade and then Tara would finish her report and go directly to Valerie Bennett's office and tell her everything, including the details of her conversation with Jameson in the back of his Bentley.

If the procedure worked, Tara might succeed where Dr Anthony Edwards, London's top medico-legal expert, had failed. That was not an unappealing thought.

She had to finish this case. Because really, what else did she have besides her integrity? Her work was her life.

After the last, hair-raising part of the drive down narrow country lanes, Tara and Daniel were finally sitting opposite each other in candlelight.

'Everything okay?' he said. 'You're very quiet.'

'I'm happy being with you.'

Tara was thinking that Daniel was the most beautiful man she'd ever seen. Blue eyes behind wire-framed glasses. His hair was receding now over his high forehead, but for her, he never aged. He was always twenty-three, smiling awkwardly at her, with his hands pushed into his back pockets and his shoulders up around his ears.

Once, when Tara was in her twenties, when Daniel wasn't her lover yet only her missing brother's oldest friend, he had visited her out of pity and a sense of duty. Tara had asked him what his aftershave was called. The question had slipped out, exposing the way she'd felt. Maybe he'd looked at her a little differently after that day, but by then he was already engaged to a pregnant Sabine. Tara had bought that aftershave for other men over the years, but it didn't have the same effect.

They ended up ordering the same thing: butternut soup to start and salmon as their main course. Tara looked at him over the top of her glass as she took a long sip of red wine.

Do you ever think about his wife?

Suddenly, she knew she was going to end this. Tonight.

It was time to do what she asked her patients to do every day. She had to face her own reality. She was clinging to a hopeless relationship for reasons related to her past.

'I was so relieved Sabine was alone when I bumped into her,' Tara said, 'because I could not bear to see your children's faces.'

The waitress arrived with the bread and soup.

'Anything else I can get you guys?' She hovered next to the table nervously, the tension between them was obvious.

'No. Thank you,' Daniel said.

Once she'd left, Daniel sighed. He took off his glasses and rubbed his eyes.

Tara reached for his hand across the table. 'We have to end this, Dan.'

'The other night, before I came over to your place, I told Sabine the truth. Or part of it anyway. I said I had to leave for the night, and that I had a lot to think about. I said I was unhappy.'

'How did she take it?'

They were still holding on to each other's hands.

'She already knew. We're both unhappy. I'm going to ask her for a divorce and I'm going to try for custody of the children. I'll make sure she's taken care of, but I can't stay.'

'Please don't leave because of me. I don't want that responsibility. In the end, the betrayal is going to destroy us too. I still think we need to end this.'

Tara stood up. She tried not to look at anyone as she walked through the packed restaurant, with low beams and jazz standards playing in the background, down a passageway to the toilets. She locked herself in one of the cubicles, put the toilet seat down and sat there a while. The walls were painted an indigo blue so it was like being underwater. Floating.

There was a knock on the door. 'Tara?'

It had taken Daniel a while to get used to calling her that name.

'All the other diners think I'm a jerk for making you cry,' he said.

She laughed through the tears.

'I shouldn't be in here, but I'm not leaving until you open the door.'

Tara stood up and unlocked it. She reached her arms around his neck, found his mouth.

'I love you,' she said.

One last time. This is goodbye.

Tara and Daniel left the restaurant hand in hand, walking in peaceful silence back towards his car, along the village road, slick and deserted after the rain. The church across the way was lit up with a string of coloured light bulbs.

Tara heard a car in the distance. A quiet hum at the edges of her awareness. Daniel's arm was heavy across her shoulder, hers tight around his waist; they held each other close for those last few seconds.

There were no headlights, only the sound of an engine picking up speed. They stopped to look up, still with their arms around each other. And then everything in Tara's world went dark.

THIRTY-NINE

Thames Valley Police are appealing for witnesses following a road accident in the early hours of this morning (September 7). At around 12.19 a.m., a white minivan collided with two pedestrians, a woman and a man in their 40s.

The incident happened on Upper Street in Penn. One of the victims died at the scene and the other was taken to hospital and remains in a serious but stable condition.

Investigating officer Detective Sergeant Lisa Lee, based at Whielden Police Station, said: 'I would like to appeal to any witnesses, or any person who may have information about what happened, to please come forward, including those who might have CCTV or dashcam footage from the area around the time of the incident.'

FORTY

Tara lay on her back with her eyes closed, needles poking at the back of her hands, trying to be still. If she moved there was an axe waiting, ready to crack open what was left of her skull.

She was completely focused on the pain. Behind her eyes, sharp and deep, splitting her brain right in two and building until she screamed. Nurses would come put something in her drip. For a while, she'd float.

Can you tell me your name?

And your address?

Do you know your date of birth?

Her words erupted in a strange, garbled way and didn't make sense and they were not the words she was thinking of. Hampstead Lane. Plate. Blank. Chimpanzee. Blank. Science. Blank. Axe. Blank. Blank. Key.

Losing her balance. The sound of metal on flesh. Blue flashing lights.

She could not see Daniel, only the starry sky.

Faces peering down at her.

Why can't I breathe?

Someone stroking her hair. Blue flashing lights.

Crack, crack, crack.

She was panicking inside. When they asked her questions, her brain was scrambled like eggs, runny, yellow, oozing out of the cracks in the bone. Time bent and stretched and stopped, fading to black, and she had no idea how long she'd been in that bed.

Then, everything became calm. Tara knew her name, her address, the year she was born. Her words settled down into sentences, short ones, with everything in the right order.

Can you tell me what year it is now?

Do you know where you are?

What's the last thing you remember?

Now she was alone in a room, her neck in a brace, her shoulder strapped. Whatever they were putting in that drip was good stuff. She was floating, above the hospital bed and even her own body, or sinking, under a thick and soundless sea. Most of all, she was asleep. There comings and goings, whispering. Nurses. Ghosts.

Neil, sitting quietly in a chair.

Olivia, holding her hand. 'Don't worry about anything. I'm handling everything. We have insurance.'

Tara wasn't worried. She didn't care.

Daniel. Walking down a silent lane, coloured light bulbs.

She wanted to ask where Daniel was, but she didn't want to know the answer.

They sat her up and the room came into focus. She was alone and she saw the way the nurses looked at her with nervous eyes. After a few days, she could tell them apart. Some were softer, while others had sharp edges. She could read their name tags now her eyes were working again.

Come on, Tara, try harder for me. There's no reason you shouldn't be able to walk. Your muscles are a little out of prac-tice, that's all. Let's trying standing up, shall we?

They forced her to walk to the toilet and back, holding her up.

You're going to need to start dressing yourself soon.

You're lucky, the doctor said. *Your neck is perfectly healthy but the clavicle is fractured. We expect a complete recovery. Eight weeks and you'll be out of that sling.*

She was always the lucky one. The one left alive.

The different parts of her body were working fine. She sat up. She walked without help. She fed herself. The axe still came, sometimes, without warning. The nurses still looked at her in that strange way, perhaps because she had so few visitors and no one to go home to. She counted the hours until they gave her a sleeping tablet each night.

The hospital might have discharged Tara earlier if she'd had someone at home to help her. The clavicle was healing well, apparently, and the concussion had lifted. But, as things were, they kept her in for ten days.

On the day she went home, she was dressed, sitting in a chair next to her hospital bed, her arm in a sling, waiting until a taxi arrived to fetch her and take her home.

FORTY-ONE

Tara woke at the usual time each morning. Early, as if she was going to go to work. She showered and went downstairs to get her first coffee. She stared at the cherry tree as she sipped from her favourite mug. Every time the doorbell rang, her first thought was that it would be Daniel. She still had the urge to call him several times a day.

Neil and his wife visited, bringing her dishes filled with chicken and rice. Olivia came over in the evenings and they went through case files; some clients had to be referred on, others wanted to wait until Tara was back at the office. She warned Olivia not to ask her about Daniel. The driver of the vehicle that killed him was never apprehended.

There was a sense of emptiness inside, where her old self used to be. This vacuum wasn't new, it had been there for years, only it had not troubled her as much before, when Daniel was still in her life. Decades before, she had wanted to leave her old life behind, dead and buried. Now the new one she had constructed was hollow too.

Tara didn't trust the police to help her. They would dismiss her fears about the hit-and-run being deliberate, and she didn't want Sabine and the children to have to go through any more suffering or revelations. She did not believe the police would ever find any evidence against Ray Jameson. Neither did she believe the police would be able to protect her against him.

One day, she opened her front door and Sabine was there. Face washed out from crying. Eyes wild and red. 'You were together, the night Daniel died,' she said.

Tara nodded.

'My husband spent his last night with you.'

'Do you want to come inside?'

Sabine didn't move. Her hair hung lank and oily around her face. Her baggy trench coat had mud stains all the way along the hem. The weather was chilly, but she wore flip-flops on her feet. 'How long were the two of you together?'

'I'm sorry,' Tara said. 'Please come inside.'

'Answer my question.'

'On and off, since I was twenty-five. Seventeen years.'

Sabine tucked her hands deeper into the pockets of her coat, hunching her shoulders. Tara was sure she wanted to lash out. She didn't blame her.

'You know,' Sabine said, 'I used to be so jealous of you because Matthew loved you more than anyone in the world. And then, when Matthew was gone, you took Daniel from me too.'

'I'm sorry.'

'I always knew something was wrong. I tried so hard, but he was never really with me. With us. With our family.'

If she had not made that appointment with Jade, Daniel would still be alive. If she had listened to him, Daniel would still be alive. His children would still have their father.

'Don't come to the funeral,' Sabine said.

According to his wishes, Daniel was cremated. There was

no grave for Tara to visit. Instead, she planted a bottle of their favourite wine under the cherry tree and marked it with a pile of stones. The thought that she would never touch him or hear his voice again was unbearable.

FORTY-TWO

Valerie Bennett had been in touch with Tara by email, first with brief condolences and then to request that all of her notes on the Jameson case should be disposed of immediately.

Tara unlocked her filing cabinet. She hauled out her notebook with its pages and pages of handwritten interview notes. Before she tore them out and fed them through the shredder though, she scanned them and stored them in a folder buried in her computer. Afterwards, the sound of metal teeth crunching through paper was grimly satisfying.

She opened her laptop, but again, instead of deleting her report, she renamed it and saved it in an unrelated folder. She could not let go of the belief that the Jameson case was linked to Daniel's death. One day, she might need those files.

Tara sent an email to Valerie Bennett. She lied, confirming that she had disposed of all documents in the Jameson case. There was no way Valerie Bennett could be oblivious to what was going on. Valerie must know who her client really was, and what he was capable of.

Without wasting any time, Valerie had hired a new psychiatrist to complete Jade Jameson's assessment. Tara did not recognise the person's name. As a professional courtesy, Tara requested a copy of the final report, though she wasn't expecting to get one. She was surprised when Valerie did send her a copy, but she was not surprised to see that the report concluded that Jade's memory loss was genuine.

Tara didn't necessarily disagree with this finding. Jade had wanted to engage with the assessment; she had even been willing to take medication to try to uncover her memory of what had really happened in that hotel room. The psychiatrist went on to suggest a diagnosis of Dissociative Amnesia. Essentially, she believed that a threatening experience with Ress had triggered Jade's memory of past trauma, and Jade had then entered an extreme state of fear and dissociated from reality. In other words, if Jade did stab Ress, she was essentially not in her right mind.

Third time lucky, Tara thought. Finally, Ray Jameson had got the exact opinion he was paying for. He had never had any intention of allowing Jade to delve any further into her lost memories.

Tara could see Jade so clearly on that first day she'd met her. Pale faced and soft spoken. *I could never kill anyone. I couldn't harm a fly. Literally.*

She would never get a chance to prove that now.

Daniel had believed there was a connection between Carl Ress and Ray Jameson, perhaps some old score to be settled. Tara no longer had any doubt that Jameson was monstrous enough to let his daughter take the blame for his own crime.

Her night-time walks to Wildway Close became more frequent, until she was there most nights, at around ten o'clock. She began walking further, some way onto the Heath, before returning to sit on the grass opposite the house once the light was gone.

Did you know your brother was violent?

You must have heard something.

Do you expect us to believe you slept through a violent double murder?

Why were you the only one spared?

Why did you wait so long before calling emergency services?

Tell us where we should look for your brother.

You stand to inherit a great deal of money, don't you?

You know where Matthew has gone.

Why did you stay in bed when you heard the screaming?

Tara's thumb was rubbing against her palm.

I don't know.

I don't remember.

She was sitting on the grass verge opposite her old house, her knees pulled up in a foetal position, allowing the images of that last night to drift through her mind.

A car pulled up in front of the house and it took her a few seconds to realise that it was the police. A young female officer was standing in front of her. 'Is everything all right?'

'Yes.'

The front door of the house was open, and a man was standing on the porch. He must be the husband of the woman Tara sometimes saw at the kitchen window. They must have been watching her too.

'I used to live here,' Tara said.

'Is that so?' From her condescending tone of voice, Tara could tell the officer thought she was drunk. 'Where do you live now?'

'A short walk away.'

'Shall we give you a lift home then?'

FORTY-THREE

THE NIGHT OF THE KILLING

Lucy left the Red Suite, making sure to take the key card and then to close the door behind her. She turned right, heading down the passage to the emergency exit, letting herself out and then climbing the external staircase. The roof terrace was three flights up.

It was dead quiet up there. The rooftop bar closed at eleven thirty and the staff had long since tidied up and left. Spotlights lit up the silver-tipped olive trees. She went to stand right at the edge of the roof.

Lucy unwrapped the knife from the hotel hand towel, took one last look at it, then wrapped it back up again. She was going to get rid of it by throwing it off the side of the building. She leaned forwards, peering down. She couldn't see much of anything down on the ground, she could only just make out the row of massive bins that took up most of the narrow alleyway. Those were emptied early every Saturday morning, so in about four hours' time the knife would be gone forever. If she got her aim right.

But it was no good. She couldn't be sure the knife would land inside one of the bins. And even if it did, for all she knew, the police might stop the council collection and search them. She needed another plan. She couldn't think straight. She had to get back down to the hotel room to check on Jade. She wasn't happy about leaving her alone.

Something caught her attention, a sound behind her. Lucy turned around and scanned the rooftop.

'Hello? Who's there?'

Someone was standing in front of the service lift. The figure moved. The sound of those heels was familiar. 'I think it would be best if you gave that to me, don't you?'

Risha held out her hand.

FORTY-FOUR

Lucy Moyo was sitting opposite DS Barbara Fuller in an all-white interview room with no windows. A little red light flickered in the fisheye camera in the ceiling above the desk. On-off. On-off. Lucy stared at the detective from behind her large tortoiseshell glasses' frames. She did not need the glasses, because she had excellent vision, but the lenses were tinted and this made it easier for her to look people in the eyes.

The police would notice if she did not make eye contact. That was the sort of thing they looked for, to decide if she was lying.

Lucy had come to the station straight from work and she was still wearing her uniform of white shirt, red waistcoat, and black trousers. Jade would not have been allowed to keep her own clothes. She would have had to undress in front of a police officer, which gave Lucy the total creeps thinking about it. Jade would probably have had to put on one of those grey prison tracksuits, like you saw them wearing on television, while her beautiful green sequined dress was sealed up in a bag, never to be seen again. And Jade loved that dress.

DS Fuller was sitting opposite her, asking the questions.

Doctor Black was sitting quietly in the chair beside her. Lucy was kind of surprised that the psychologist had agreed to come to the police station, especially since Jade's father wasn't paying her anymore. Lucy had heard she'd had to resign because she was in a car accident. Dr Black looked okay now, no broken bones or anything like that, but something had changed behind her eyes. They had gone dull.

The police officer was watching her and so was Dr Black. Lucy was watching them right back from behind her glasses. She had come in voluntarily. If she hadn't, she supposed she might have been arrested, which she supposed might still happen by the end of the interview. Then she would have to get a solicitor. Not one of those free ones, though. She would ask Mr Jameson to pay. She didn't like asking for favours, but sometimes a person had no choice. He'd say yes, that's for sure.

Lucy sat with her back straight and her hands loosely folded in her lap. It was hard to know what to do with your hands when you were nervous. She picked up her glass of water and took a sip. It had white stuff swirling in it and it was too warm.

The officer started with the easy questions, working up to the main event. Lucy confirmed that yes, she'd been working at The Onyx Hotel over the summer, on reception, and that she also worked some shifts on housekeeping if the hotel was short of cleaners. She was happy to take the extra shifts, she always needed the money.

'And how did you come to be working at the hotel?' DS Fuller asks, as if she didn't already know.

'My friend Jade Jameson put in a word with her dad. You'll probably also want to know that at Christmas time I go on holiday to the Bahamas with Jade and her family, which is a very luxurious experience.'

'Right. Thank you.'

DS Fuller looked more like someone's mum, or a dinner lady, than a police officer. Her wedding ring was too tight; she had probably been wearing it for years and years. That reminded Lucy of her foster carer, Mrs Martin, and how the flesh on her finger spilled out along the sides of her wedding ring in the same way, and how Mrs Martin always gave good advice, when she was still alive.

'Lucy, the officers on my team have been going through the CCTV in the area around The Onyx Hotel.' DS Fuller sighed as if she was about to ask a very difficult question. 'I have some footage which I would like to show you. Is that all right?'

Lucy nodded. Her thoughts kept wanting to go off in tangents. She knew it would come to this, at some point. She was nervous. DS Fuller seemed like a kind person. Mrs Martin was a big believer that kindness was the most important personality trait. Lucy was still deciding.

DS Fuller opened her laptop and turned the screen so it was facing Lucy and Dr Black. The video was grainy, taken at night. Lucy didn't need to watch it, she already knew what would happen. Dr Black leaned forwards so she could see better.

'Do you recognise the individual in the video?' DS Fuller asked.

'The individual in the video is me.' Lucy's glasses slid down her nose. She pushed them back up again.

'You are throwing something off the side of the roof terrace of the hotel. Can you tell me what that object is?'

'A towel. With a knife wrapped inside.'

Out of the corner of her eye, Lucy could see Dr Black was surprised. Her legs were crossed one way, and now she changed them over to the other side. She cleared her throat.

'Lucy, where did that knife come from?'

'I pulled it out of Carl Ress's chest. I checked that he was dead first before I pulled it out. In case that's relevant.'

The police officer frowned. She rubbed her forehead.

'Before we go any further, she said, 'I need to caution you. You do not have to say anything—'

Lucy's ears were playing up, all she could hear was a low ringing sound. Soon that sound would get terribly loud, until it was a screeching that would make it impossible for her to think at all.

Anything you do say may be given in evidence.

DS Fuller was asking her for about the hundredth time if she wanted a solicitor, and saying that one would be provided for her, blah-blah. Lucy said she didn't want one, she just wanted this over with.

'Lucy, did you stab Carl Ress with that knife?'

'No.' Lucy looked up at the camera on the ceiling. She was sweating. It was a strain, having to keep making good eye contact with the police officer.

'Your colleagues have confirmed you were at the reception desk from eight o'clock that evening until midnight. And by the time the paramedics arrived, indications were that Mr Ress had already been dead for at least two hours.'

Lucy nodded. She was thinking about whether DS Fuller had any children, and if she was a good mother, and how she had never met her own mother. Her ears were ringing and her mind was wandering in wider circles and it was getting more and more difficult to bring herself back to the desk and the room.

'What I'm saying is, we believe you. We know you didn't stab Mr Ress. So why did you decide to dispose of the weapon before the police arrived?'

'I was worried about my friend Jade. I hoped that if you didn't have the murder weapon, it would be harder to convict her. There are big bins down the side of the building, in the alley, that get collected early on a Saturday morning. I thought that was a good plan.'

'You must have very good aim. It's a long way down to those bins.'

Lucy nodded.

'The thing is, we searched all of those bins and the alley-way. But there was no sign of that knife. Why do you think that is?'

Lucy shrugged. Leaving things out isn't lying, she told herself. The small room was filling up with a high-pitched whine.

'Don't you think Jade should be held responsible for killing Mr Ress?'

'She didn't kill him.'

'How do you know?'

'I've known Jade since she was five. She could never kill anyone.'

The police officer sighed. 'You can't know that.'

'I can. Everything I said in my statement was true. I just left out the part about the knife.'

'Are you sure you didn't leave anything else out?'

Lucy pushed her hands against her ears.

Dr Black put a hand on her shoulder. 'Take a couple of deep breaths.'

She couldn't stay in this room much longer.

'She needs a break,' Dr Black said.

'Could we carry on just a little longer? I have a few more things I'd like to ask you.'

Lucy took her glasses off and put them down on the table. She looked down at her lap. That helped.

'Lucy, I know that you understand you have done some-thing very serious to interfere in the police investigation.'

'I am sorry. Jade is the only friend I've ever had. I wanted to help her.'

'I think there might be other reasons for what you did.' The detective was sweating too. The greying curls around her temples were damp. 'You live on your own, in a flat in Swiss Cottage, right?'

Lucy nodded.

'Now I know you have a part-time job while studying for your A-levels, but I'm wondering how you manage to pay your rent?'

It was annoying when they asked questions that they already knew the answers to, but Lucy knew this was standard procedure. 'Mr Jameson pays my rent. I'm a care leaver and I can't afford it on my own.'

'Mr Jameson pays your rent. Now why would Mr Jameson do that?'

'Because they have plenty of money, and Jade asked him to.'

'I see.'

'Maybe you already know this, but when children in care turn eighteen, we are alone in the world, with no one to help us. It's scary. The Jameson family literally saved my life.' The tinnitus had settled down a little. Lucy put her fake glasses back on. It didn't matter much now because her eyes were so blurry she couldn't see the officer's face anyway.

The DS leaned forwards, perking up, her elbows on the table. 'So, because Jade is such a good friend, and you have so much gratitude towards the Jameson family, maybe that's why you agreed to dispose of the knife when Jade asked you to help her?'

'Jade didn't ask me to help her. It was my idea and my dumb decision.'

'Are you one hundred per cent sure about that? You are a very loyal person. And given how intelligent you are, I doubt you make many dumb decisions.'

Lucy sighed. 'I'm one hundred per cent sure. No one asked me to do anything.'

'You have an interview at Cambridge, don't you?'

Lucy nodded.

'And I'm guessing that if you get in, you will get assistance in funding from the Jameson family?'

'I hope so.'

'Ms Moyo, please listen to me carefully. You are in a lot of trouble here and there may be charges against you. That means that right now, you need to look after yourself. I understand you are very loyal to the whole Jameson family, but we need to apprehend the person who killed Carl Ress before other people get hurt. Don't you agree?'

She nodded.

'I'll ask you one more time. Did Jade Jameson ask you to dispose of that knife?'

Lucy shook her head. The officer kept talking but the tinnitus was so loud again she could barely hear the words.

'She really does not look well.' Dr Black pushed her chair back and stood up. 'I think we need to end this interview now. I'd like a chance to speak to her—'

DS Fuller stood up too. 'One last question, please. What did the knife look like?'

Dr Black was standing behind her chair.

'Small. Like you'd use in a kitchen to peel vegetables.'

'Was there anything special about it?'

A small, sharp knife with a black wooden handle. A monogram on the blade. The letters R and S and J, intertwined.

Lucy shook her head. The word 'special' was open to interpretation after all.

Leaving things out isn't lying.

'That knife going missing is very convenient for Jade Jameson.' DS Fuller was no fool.

Lucy felt sorry for the detective, she was only trying to do her job. Money, especially the amount of money the Jamesons had, made everything easier.

She knew she would probably have to come back to this

room again, but for now, it was over. Dr Black was guiding her to the door.

'I do hope we won't find a large sum of money suddenly dropping into your bank account,' DS Fuller said.

'Don't worry, you won't.'

Dr Black stood aside and let Lucy leave the room first. The detective was still following behind them. 'Lucy, if you know something, please tell me now, before someone else gets hurt.'

But Lucy was finished answering questions.

FORTY-FIVE

The call from DS Fuller had come through while Tara was standing at her kitchen window, looking out at the cherry tree and the pile of stones on top of the wine-bottle grave. It felt as though she had been there for days, if not weeks.

If Tara had not felt so guilty about Daniel, maybe she would have been less reckless. Maybe she would have refused to go to that police station. But somehow it had felt inevitable she should be drawn back in. She couldn't get off so lightly, with only a broken clavicle and her career intact. The police might claim Daniel's death was a random hit-and-run, but she knew Ray Jameson had killed him, and that she had been the real target. She was responsible for Daniel's death.

The police officer had said that they were interviewing a vulnerable young witness, Lucy Moyo, who had requested that Tara sit in as a responsible adult. Maybe, she thought, Lucy had information that could incriminate Ray Jameson. Maybe what she was really looking for was revenge. So she said yes, she would go.

Getting herself dressed to go out at short notice had been a challenge. In the end she'd taken off the sling, she couldn't be bothered with it, but she had to be careful with that arm. She was already taking more painkillers than the doctors were entirely happy with.

As they exited the station after the interview, Lucy thanked Tara politely as they stood on the pavement.

'You were very confident in there,' Tara said. 'But the officer was right, you need to look after yourself. You should absolutely have had a solicitor with you. You must never waive that right.'

Lucy was surely bright enough and had watched enough television to know this. But she was also naïve, and Tara could see how she could become a pawn for the Jameson family. As the officer had pointed out, it was difficult to believe that Jade Jameson had not asked for Lucy's help in that hotel room. Lucy was financially and emotionally indebted to the Jamesons. Given what she'd done with that knife, it was also hard to believe it was a coincidence that she had been the first person to walk into that scene in the Red Suite.

'I'm going back to the hotel now,' Lucy said. 'My shift starts in twenty minutes. There's this place on the way where they make really good hot chocolate. I can't afford to pay your fees, but could I buy you one, as a thank you for your time?'

'Sure.'

They wound through the streets of Soho under grey skies. Walking was awkward, Tara had to be careful not to turn her head too fast and her peripheral vision was restricted. The discomfort in her neck and shoulder made her impatient.

They came to a small café and Lucy went inside to order, while Tara stayed on the pavement. Through the glass, she saw Lucy smiling and talking to the young man at the counter. She didn't seem unsettled by her brush with the police.

There was a reason Lucy had wanted Tara in that interview, and it wasn't only for moral or emotional support. Something was weighing on her conscience.

Tara should have left it there. Maybe if she kept telling herself Daniel's death was a random crime, one day, she might even believe it.

Lucy came out with two takeaway cups and handed Tara her coffee. They stayed outside the café a while. Lucy sipped her hot chocolate while staring at Tara from behind her oversized, tinted glasses. When she put the cup down, she had a white line of whipped cream along her upper lip.

'I think there's something you want me to know,' Tara said. 'Something you didn't tell the police officer.'

'You don't work for Mr Jameson anymore, do you?' Lucy said.

'No, I don't.' Tara sipped the coffee. It tasted good. She had missed takeaway coffee and the grungy streets of the city.

Lucy wiped the cream from her top lip with the back of her hand. 'I'd better not be late for my shift.'

They began walking again. Lucy stopped on a corner and tossed her cup into an overflowing dustbin. Tara could see the hotel from where they stood. Glass doors swishing open and closed. The question on her mind was always the same one: why would Jade go up to a hotel room with a stranger?

Tara had a strong feeling that Lucy had the answer. But Lucy was trapped. She was young, alone in the world and totally dependent on the Jameson family. She was also desperately loyal to her friend.

'You did the right thing, calling me today,' Tara said.

Lucy was looking over at the hotel.

'You have my mobile number, if you need to talk again.'

'You should be careful with your bag,' Lucy said. 'There are pickpockets around here.'

'I will be.' Tara felt for the strap across her chest, it was quite secure.

Lucy turned and walked away without saying goodbye.

FORTY-SIX

Since she was already dressed and in the city, Tara decided to go over to the office in Marylebone. She let herself in with her key, feeling like a stranger.

Reception on the ground floor was empty. Olivia's consulting room door was closed and Tara could hear a faint burble of voices coming from inside. The sound of the vacuum cleaner was going overhead. She followed it upstairs to her own office.

'Can I give you a hug?' Oksana said, when she saw her.

Tara stood awkwardly as the woman embraced her. She had a mother's touch, warm and solid.

Oksana let go of her and stepped back, pointing to Tara's desk. 'Katya made something specially for you.'

It was a drawing of a teddy bear with a big red heart on his chest.

'It's beautiful. Please tell her I said thank you.'

Tara stood at the window, pushing it wide open and feeling the chill, damp air against her face as she looked across at the park. The benches, the gravestones, the pots were all still there though the flowers were dying down now. The sky was steel-grey.

After her patient had left, Olivia came rushing upstairs. She hugged Tara too. Tara still had that strange sensation of being not quite present, as though she was observing her life from a distance. They stood together in the kitchen, drinking coffee and herbal tea. Olivia was no longer nauseous as she rested her hand on her growing belly.

Tara stayed in the office a couple of hours. She spent some time checking her neglected email. She found a reply from Dr Anthony Edwards, the psychologist who had preceded her in the Jameson case. He apologised for taking so long to get back to her and offered to set up a time to talk. Tara deleted the message without replying.

She went through her case files and looked at re-booking patients. If she was going to stay sane, she had to go back to work sometime soon.

Later, though it was drizzling, Tara walked up the Finchley Road instead of taking the bus for the last leg of her journey home. She was in no rush to get back to the empty cottage. She had the urge to call Daniel's mobile so she could hear his voice. But that was a consolation for his wife, not for her.

Her cottage was set back from the main road. There were no streetlights, only the glow from inside her neighbours' houses seeping out through the cracks in their curtains. A dog barked somewhere in the distance.

By the time Tara reached her front door, her hair and blouse were damp and her shoulder was aching. Inside, she dropped her bag on the floor and turned on the hallway light. She needed a hot bath and a couple of painkillers, and she needed to get her sling back on. First though, she needed a cup of tea. Daniel would have suggested a cup of tea. She wanted to tell him about the meeting with Lucy. She knew he wouldn't approve; he would want her to stay safe.

The rain drummed down harder outside. The kettle boiled. She took her favourite mug down from the shelf and placed it on the kitchen table. Something made her look up, out of the back window.

A movement in the darkness.

Feeling exposed, Tara switched off the kitchen light. Then she flicked the switch that lit up the garden. Jade Jameson was standing underneath the cherry tree, staring at the house.

FORTY-SEVEN

Jade was wearing her pale pink jumper, with the hood pulled up. She was sheltering under the cherry tree, her arms wrapped tight around her chest.

Tara opened the kitchen window, shouting so she could be heard above the sound of the rain. 'You shouldn't be here.'

'Please can I talk to you? I've been waiting for hours.'

Tara lived in a row of terraced cottages and there was a narrow path running along the back of the gardens that led out to the street. Jade had somehow got hold of Tara's home address, found that back path and climbed over the back gate. This might not be the first time Jade had been to her home. Maybe it had been Jade who had broken into the cottage and read her notebook. Like father, like daughter.

Jade walked closer to the house. She stopped halfway between the tree and the window. 'Lucy says I can trust you. She said I should ask you for help.'

Tara spoke from behind the open window, rain blowing in against her face. 'What kind of help?'

'My solicitor says I can take a charge of manslaughter by diminished responsibility and then there won't be any court case and I won't have to go to jail. They'll send me to this special clinic. I don't know what to do.' Jade was soaking wet. She looked sad and desperate. 'What if I didn't do it?'

Tara could not let her in. That would be insane.

But Jade was a vulnerable child who had, in one way or another, been failed by the most important adults in her life. Her mother; her absent, unknown father; her adoptive parents, who for whatever reason stood between their daughter and the truth.

Jade was right on the other side of the window now. Her lips were pale with cold; her fingers gripped the sill. 'I don't want to live like this – not knowing and scared it will happen again. I have to remember. You said you could help me.'

'It's too late.'

Daniel died. He was murdered.

'I know you were doing your job and you were being paid, but I felt like you were trying to help me. The psychiatrist they sent after you left only came to the house once, for two hours. She asked most of the same questions you did, but she didn't mind when I gave short answers. And then Ziggy growled at her, and she nearly had a heart attack.'

Tara laughed. She realised she wasn't really afraid. Suspicious, for sure, but not afraid. She had not felt any real fear since the night she'd lost Daniel.

Maybe Jade was offering her the possibility of closure. The girl standing in her garden was the reason Daniel had died. There was a chance for both of them to uncover the truth.

'I think you lied to me,' Tara said. 'I think you or someone in your family knew Carl Ress. If you want me to help you, then I need you to tell me the whole truth. Otherwise don't waste my time.'

Jade bit her bottom lip. She nodded.

Tara unlocked the back door.

FORTY-EIGHT

FOUR WEEKS BEFORE THE KILLING

Jade took Ziggy for a walk every morning before school because if she didn't, he'd end up chewing shoes, handbags, or some bit of Sandra's furniture, and Sandra would go ballistic. She had a twenty-minute route worked out, past the tube station, down the high street to the entrance of the park, and then home again. Once that was done, the dog would settle down in his basket in front of the kitchen window and hopefully not destroy anything until she got home from school and gave him some attention.

As Jade passed the tube station, she noticed a man leaning against the wall outside, watching her. Men often looked at Jade. She ignored them. She had her AirPods in and her music playing. Her dad hated it when she walked round like that, he said it wasn't safe. He said she had to be aware of her environment. Jade took the headphones out and the everyday sounds came rushing back in. The hum of traffic in the distance; cars zipping past. With a dog like Ziggy at her side, it was unlikely anyone would mess with her. Still, something about the man had unsettled her.

When she glanced back, he was following her. He was much older than she was, probably around her dad's age. He was tall, with short dark hair and a strong build. Casually dressed in jeans, a T-shirt and a bomber jacket. He was wearing sunglasses even though the morning was cloudy. He gave her the total creeps.

It was all right. It was daylight. There were people around, not that many but some, walking to and from the tube. Usually, at this point, she'd turn right and head down towards Regent's Park. Maybe it would be a better idea to turn into one of the houses and ring the bell. Only they probably wouldn't open up for her and then she'd be trapped.

Jade leaned down and patted Ziggy's head. He looked up at her and whimpered. He could always tell when she wasn't feeling good. She turned around. The man was behind her, a few steps away. He was staring, his hands in the pockets of his jeans. She took out her phone, nervous and fumbling. Before she could dial, he said her name.

'Jade? Is that you?' He was standing still, a safe distance away. 'My name is Carl. I used to know your mum, Paula.'

The man didn't look familiar to her at all.

He took his sunglasses off. 'I knew you when you were very little. You always loved dogs.'

She did not have a good feeling. She should ignore him. Walk away. Call her dad. But she couldn't resist. 'You said you knew Paula?'

He had her full attention as he came a few steps closer. 'Paula and I were good friends when she lived in Camden.'

Jade wanted to believe him. Ziggy didn't like him. He kept whining.

'I used to be a police officer,' he said. 'I tried to help her. She was very young, and always in a lot of trouble. So much scum in London looking to take advantage of women like your mum.'

The whole time he didn't take his eyes off her and the way he was looking at her wasn't right. Jade felt like she was a piece of chocolate cake and he was about to take a huge bite out of her.

'You look so much like her.'

'Really?'

He nodded. 'I have videos I can show you, if you'd like. Of you and Paula together, when you were a baby.'

She knew in her heart this man was after something else. 'What do you want in exchange?'

'I'll come and find you again, okay? But only if you don't tell your parents about this. It has to stay strictly between us.'

'Why?'

'Because otherwise you won't see me again.'

Her father had warned her things like this could happen, they were a wealthy family and people would try to take advantage. But he'd found her weak spot. Paula.

She nodded.

He hadn't taken his hands out of his pockets the whole time. 'Next time I'll bring the video. I'll make you a copy.'

'Wait—'

But he'd turned and was walking away.

She knew she should go straight home and tell her father. But she didn't.

FORTY-NINE

Jade sat on Tara's sofa with a woollen throw wrapped around her shoulders while she described her first meeting with Carl Ress. By the time she'd come inside from the garden, her hoodie had been soaked through. That was now in the tumble dryer, and in the meantime she was wearing one of Tara's jumpers. Her jeans were pretty damp too, but she had not wanted to accept Tara's offer of a pair of leggings.

Tara did not sit down. She stood in the doorway of her living room, where she would easily be able to reach the front door through the short hallway. She wasn't convinced she'd done the right thing by letting Jade Jameson back into her life.

'Why did you lie to everyone about knowing Carl Ress?'

'I don't know.' Jade bit her bottom lip, rolling the gold chain around her neck between her fingers.

'I think you do know. You said you were ready to tell me the truth.' Tara's shoulder was aching and her patience was limited.

'Well, in the beginning, I knew my parents would freak out. They would never have allowed me to meet him again. My father would have made me get a bodyguard. I knew there was something creepy about him, something wrong. But Carl said he had videos of Paula and me together and I really wanted to see them. My parents never talk about Paula. And then when everything happened, I felt so guilty that I'd been lying to them. I wanted to tell my dad what happened, but I was too ashamed, and he would have been so angry. I should never have taken Carl up to that hotel room. So I just said nothing. And then it was all too late.'

'Did you see Carl again, after that first time he followed you?'

Jade pulled the blanket tighter around her shoulders. 'About a week later he was waiting for me outside the staff entrance of the restaurant when I finished my shift.'

She paused as she leaned forward and picked up the mug of hot tea Tara had made for her. She took a sip before carefully putting it down again on the coaster. 'That time we talked for a while. He told me he used to work in Camden, when Paula and Sandra were living there in a flat together. He said he tried to help them out, like when they got into trouble with drugs, and stuff.'

'And the video?'

'He said there was one special video my mum had made for me, and some stuff she wanted me to know. He said if we could go somewhere quiet together, he'd show it to me. I'm not stupid, I knew something wasn't right. I thought sooner or later he was going to ask me for money. With my dad's money, people are always trying, you know – or maybe it was sex or something he wanted, but I also knew he wasn't lying about knowing my mum, because he knew stuff about that flat in Camden, and me and Sandra and Ray. I was so happy there was this video. I would have given him money, if he'd asked.'

'What did he want from you?'

'I still don't know. I thought, if we met at the hotel, it would be safe. Lucy knew everything. She was keeping an eye on me in the Red Suite.'

'Right.' So it wasn't really by accident that Lucy was first on the scene.

'It's not Lucy's fault. She begged me not to meet him. She's always right. I wish so much I had listened to her.'

'Did you tell anyone besides Lucy that you were meeting Carl Ress?'

Jade shook her head.

'Are you sure?'

'Totally. I swear. I'm telling you the truth now. I mean, the whole truth.' Jade took a breath. She leaned back into the sofa, pulling the throw over her body so she was completely covered from her neck to her ankles. 'I remember seeing Carl in the bar, waiting for me, and then it all goes blank.'

As they'd been talking, Tara's sense of being on high alert had lessened. She sat down in the armchair, her legs folded underneath her.

'What if I come to your office and take that drug, like we said?'

The girl was still a minor, and her eighteenth birthday was months away. Tara could not take her on as a patient without her parents' consent. And in any case, there was no way Tara could have Jade at her office building. After what happened to Daniel, she would never get Olivia involved in this case. Defying Jameson could be fatal.

'I'm sorry,' Tara said, 'I can't help you. You'll have to ask your parents to set up an appointment with a psychiatrist.'

Jade's eyes welled up with tears. 'You know they won't let me.'

She stood up and the blanket fell away. The electronic tag bulged around her ankle, under the skinny jeans. Sooner or later, Ray Jameson would find out where she was.

'Please, don't say no. Please.' Jade came closer, kneeling down on the floor in front of Tara's chair. 'I'm begging you. No one else can help me.'

The small bottle of ketamine was no longer at the office. It was upstairs, sitting in Tara's medicine cabinet. After the hit-and-run, she had taken it from Olivia's drug cabinet and kept it. On those many walks to Wildway Close, Tara had often thought about using the drug herself, but she hadn't yet worked up the courage.

Jade took hold of Tara's hand, which had been resting on her knee. The girl's skin was still ice cold. 'Don't you think I deserve to know if I killed him?'

FIFTY

The rain had stopped by the time Tara and Jade walked down to the high street. Jade was wearing her hoodie again and had it pulled up over her head. They had not spoken since leaving Tara's cottage.

A black cab was coming towards them, yellow light on. Tara flagged it down and they both got into the back. Jade gave the driver the address for the hotel.

Tara was having massive second thoughts. She had set up reconstructions before, but those had been with patients who had suffered brain injuries or illness, never with a client accused of killing another human being. Going back to the hotel with Jade was too much of a risk.

Tara could not be sure that Jade was ready to remember. The girl's psyche may not be strong enough to bear the lost memories, and if she entered a dissociated or psychotic state, she could be dangerous, both to herself and to others around her.

And not only that, but Jade's memories could reveal something which implicated Ray Jameson in the murder, exactly as Daniel had predicted.

The cab was skirting St John's Wood, heading towards Soho.

'There's still time to change your mind,' Tara said.

'I want to do this.'

'Are you one hundred per cent sure?'

Jade nodded.

At some point, Tara knew she would face Ray Jameson's wrath for what she was about to do. He would find a way to destroy her career or her life, or both. But this was payback as much as anything else. A goodbye to Daniel. She was in pain. She was enraged. She wanted vengeance and this was a chance to make Ray Jameson pay the price.

The cab reached The Onyx a few minutes before ten o'clock.

Risha was waiting for them in her office, leaning back against her large desk with her arms folded. The room smelled strongly of her menthol vape cigarettes. A large one-way mirror on the wall gave a view through to the reception desk, and the lobby beyond. The staff must know they could be constantly observed by their manager.

Tara had called Risha earlier and asked if they could meet at the hotel. She said it was urgent, and that she would explain in person.

'You're sure this reconstruction is a good idea?' Risha said.

Tara was about to speak, but Jade interrupted. 'It's my deci-sion, Rish,' she said.

They needed Risha's support, not only to get access to the Red Suite but also because it was inevitable that one of the staff members would alert her to Jade's presence in the hotel. It was also possible the police might turn up at some point, given that Jade was both past her curfew and in an area that breached her bail conditions.

'There are risks,' Tara said. 'We don't know how Jade will react if the memories do come back.'

If those memories did resurface, and shattered her unstable state of mind, Tara would be to blame.

'How safe is this medication you're using?' Risha said.

'It's prescribed by a psychiatrist.' That churning was back in Tara's stomach. The original plan was for Olivia to have been with them. It was not ethical or safe to administer the drug for the first time without a doctor present. But Tara was absolutely certain that if they waited and tried to set this reconstruction up properly, it would never happen.

Jade went over to Risha, put her arms around her neck and hugged her. 'Please don't call Dad. Please, please, please. I need to do this one thing by myself.'

Risha was looking at Tara over Jade's shoulder, trying to work out whether she should give in to her sister and trust Tara, or call for help. After a while, she said, 'Maybe you're the only one crazy enough to help her.'

The alert on Tara's phone sounded. The video she had asked Penny Ress to send her had arrived. Jade had unwound herself from Risha's neck but they were standing side by side, holding hands.

'Half an hour,' Risha said. 'That's it. I can let you have half an hour in the hotel and then I have to let my father know she's here or he'll know I was involved. Jade is still wearing that tag, and sooner or later the police are going to come looking for her.'

'Thank you, thank you, thank you,' Jade said.

'Good luck,' Risha said. 'You'll need it when Dad finds out.'

Tara made Jade comfortable on the sofa in Risha's office, tucking her under a duvet that Risha had provided. She took a baseline reading of Jade's blood pressure with her portable monitor. It was normal.

Tara held the small spray bottle in her hand. 'We don't have to do this.'

Jade held out her hand and Tara placed it in her palm. Her face was pale and her skin was cold despite the duvet.

'One spray in each nostril,' Tara said. That was half the recommended dose, but Jade didn't need to know that. 'Lean your head back. That's right.'

Jade went ahead without hesitation, one puff in each nostril. She handed the bottle back and Tara slipped it into her pocket.

'It takes a few minutes to start working. Try to relax. You can put your music on now. I'll be here with you the whole time.'

Jade took out her phone and put in her earbuds. She leaned her head back and closed her eyes. On the surface she seemed calm. But, after ten minutes, when Tara took her blood pressure again it was slightly elevated. And Jade's eyes had changed too. They were glassy, as if she wasn't looking at Tara but through her.

FIFTY-ONE

The glass doors swished open and closed as guests entered and left the lobby of The Onyx Hotel. Glossy hair, tanned skin. Silk and gold. Heels. Perfume scents mingling. Laughter. Outside, the evening was slick and traces of rain lingered on the pavement.

Jade stood in front of the oval table full of orchids, resting one hand against it for support. Her outfit was borrowed from Risha. A short black dress, high heels, black eyeliner and pink lip gloss. Her hair was loose around her shoulders.

The electronic tag on her ankle was now in plain sight but Jade insisted she didn't care; she wanted to feel the same way she did on the night she had met Carl Ress.

Jade was looking towards the reception desk, searching for her friend Lucy, maybe, but tonight there was no sign of her. Risha would be watching through the mirror behind the reception desk. Tara realised that Risha could have seen Jade with Carl Ress in the lobby that night, as they passed through on their way up to the second floor. She may have called her father to let him know. Jameson may have been right there at the hotel, after all.

Jade crossed the lobby, walking in the direction of the stair-case in the corner that would take her down to the bar. She seemed oblivious to the people she passed. When she reached the stairs, she gripped the banister. She wasn't used to walking in heels.

The bar was heaving once again. Music was blaring, an upbeat, bluesy rhythm. So much noise, so many people. Tara was concerned Jade might be overwhelmed, given that she had spent months alone at home, but she didn't seem to be fazed. In the heart of that crowded bar, Tara felt the weight of the respon-sibility she had taken on for the teenager. She was risking Jade's physical and emotional safety, not to mention her own, and possibly that of everyone else in the hotel.

Jade once again moved easily through the throng of people, as though none of them existed. The colour in her face was coming back. When she reached the counter, it was obvious the bartender knew her and was shocked to see her standing in front of him.

Quickly, he hid his reaction behind a charming smile. 'What can I get you tonight?'

From the way he looked at Jade, it was also obvious he was infatuated. This must be Marco. Tara recognised him as the man who had been driving the car the night Ray Jameson had intercepted her visit to the hotel. She felt a rising sense of urgency. Marco might contact Ray, to tell him he'd seen Jade at the hotel. They might not have much time.

Jade smiled back at Marco as she ordered an Apple Martini. Her mood had shifted. The way she stood was different, as if in the bartender's gaze, she was aware of her beauty in a way Tara had not seen before. Her hand was quite steady as she lifted her drink.

Tara stayed a few steps behind Jade, keeping an eye on her but interfering as little as possible in the process. A reconstruc-tion was about tapping into right brain activity, like dreaming while awake, allowing memories to re-enter the conscious mind. So far, it seemed to be working. As far as Tara could tell, Jade was retracing her movements from the night she'd met Carl Ress.

Jade had walked across the bar, and she was now standing in front of a pair of armchairs in the far corner. Several people, including the bartender, Marco, had seen Jade talking to Carl Ress in that exact spot, before they had left together to go up to the suite on the second floor. A young couple were sitting there, leaning in close to each other, unaware of the young woman staring down at them. Jade took a sip of her drink, then leaned forward and placed the glass down on the low table in front of the armchairs. The young couple looked up at her, bemused, then lost interest and turned back to each other.

Jade headed back towards the stairs leading up to the lobby. At the foot of the staircase, she leaned against the wall and took off her heels.

FIFTY-TWO

THE NIGHT OF THE KILLING

Jade is happy to see Marco on duty behind the bar, with those gorgeous dark eyes and that tight white T-shirt.

'The usual, Ms Jameson?' His hands are splayed on the counter.

At first, she feels self-conscious in the skimpy dress, but for once, Marco is really looking at her and she doesn't feel like Risha's kid sister.

'I'll have an Apple Martini,' she says.

'Good choice.' Marco grins at her and raises his eyebrows.

Carl had told her that Apple Martini was Paula's favourite drink.

'Are you and Lucy coming to the Cocktail Club later?' he says.

'Will you be there?'

'For sure. Midnight to four a.m. shift.' With delicate fingers, he wedges a thin slice of apple onto the edge of the glass. The drink is a strange, bright green.

She takes the first sip. It's horribly sour. Bodies crowd in on her from both sides. It's hot down in the bar. And loud, too. Music thudding against her ears. Marco is gone, busy serving other people. Jade places the glass back down on the bar counter and turns around, scanning the room. When she thinks about seeing Carl, she has a sinking feeling, a closing down in her chest. She half-hopes he won't be there, half-hopes he will. She wonders if he will recognise Paula's dress.

He is there. He is sitting in the leather armchair in the far corner, underneath the fluorescent pink mermaid, waiting. Jade picks up her drink and walks towards him, taking care in those heels.

'Hey, beautiful,' he says. 'Look at you. All grown up.'

Carl is somewhere short of handsome. His features don't quite hang together in the right way. His hair is cut even shorter now, like he's in the army.

'Did you bring the video?'

'You look so much like Paula,' he says. 'You even move like her. You'll see, soon.'

His smile disturbs her. It is not kind.

'Where is the video?' she says.

'You said there was a room where we could go? Somewhere quiet?'

The heels are killing her. Before they climb the stairs, she slips them off. The floor is a cold shock under her bare feet.

It's much brighter up in the lobby. Carl is behind her, right up close as they wait for the lift to arrive. He rests a hand around her waist. She wants to shove him away. When she looks up, Lucy is staring at the two of them from behind the reception desk. She looks scared.

When the lift doors open, Jade sees herself reflected in the mirror at the back. She is a child, dressed up in her mother's clothes. Carl Ress is the wolf.

Up on the second floor, the quiet in the corridor presses in against Jade's eardrums. The scent of vanilla blasts through the air conditioning vents, filling the air. The carpet is soft beneath her bare feet; the straps of Paula's shoes dangle from her hand.

She slips the key card into the door of the Red Suite.

Carl whistles as he steps inside. 'This is a long way from Paula's place in Camden Town,' he says.

The bed has a red leather headboard. The sheets are turned down and there is a chocolate in a red-foil wrapper placed on each pillow. On the coffee table, there is a bottle of wine, two wine glasses, and a plate of square pastries covered in red icing.

'Where's the video?' Jade asks him.

Carl is more interested in the bottle of wine. He opens it, pours two glasses and hands her one. He takes a big gulp. She doesn't touch hers.

'Is it on your phone?'

He's no longer smiling. He refills his glass. Delaying. He keeps looking at the door of the suite, as if he's expecting it to open.

Jade knows then that there is no video. This is something else. 'Why are you looking at the door?'

'Bitch,' he says.

She's not sure if he's talking to her anymore because he's not looking at her. He has his real face on now, ugly and violent. He swigs down the whole glass of wine, reaches for the bottle again.

'You lied to me about the video.'

He turns to her now and takes a step towards her. He stinks of sweat and lies.

Carl is between her and the door. She can't escape.

Someone else is coming. She can't defend herself against two men.

She can't get past him to reach the door.

He's angry and half-drunk and she knows he will hurt her.

First the blinking starts. Jade closes her eyes, trying to stop the dizziness. Before she opens them again, she can feel that

Ruby is there. She gives up, sinking down, letting Ruby take over.

Ruby is not afraid. The knife presses against her thigh, comforting her underneath Paula's sequined dress. She took it from the kitchen at home, just in case. If it wasn't for that knife, she'd be in real trouble. That's why she always carries one.

'I remember you,' she says. 'I remember your face.'

'Since when? You were only a tiny kid.'

'You were there when they'd force Jade to visit Paula. But Paula made Jade promise never to tell. Jade always wanted to go and see Paula, even though she was terrified. That's why I had to go with her. To keep her safe.'

'What the hell are you talking about?' He looks away, at the door again. 'Where the fuck are you?'

A sugar craving sets in with a vengeance and Ruby picks up one of the square pastries and bites into the thick icing. Sweetness explodes in her mouth.

'You were always evil,' she says. 'I remember how you hurt Paula. How you looked at Jade.'

'You're as nuts as Paula. Paula and Sandra both. Crazy bitches.' He's sweating now, it's pouring down the sides of his face, there are big wet patches under his arms. He takes another long drink from his second glass of wine. He's watching the door, half turned away from her.

He should be more careful. He shouldn't underestimate her.

Ruby's fingers slide under the hem of her dress. The knife is tied to her leg with one of Sandra's stretchy gym bands. She grasps the handle and slips it out. She is not afraid of him. That's not why she does it. She does it because she wants to.

She steps forward and drives the small, pointed blade as hard as she can into his shoulder.

He staggers, grabbing onto the edge of the sofa, dropping the wine glass. It falls softly to the carpet. Ruby smiles. Risha won't be pleased about the stains. Blood and wine.

He's trying to stand up, turning around. The surface of her skin prickles with anticipation. She should run, get out of there. But she wants to stab him again, and again and again.

Then, the door opens.

FIFTY-THREE

Tara and Jade were inside the Red Suite. The lights were dimmed. A wine bottle and two glasses had been placed on the coffee table, next to a plate of bite-sized pastries covered in red icing.

'I don't know what happens now,' Jade said. 'There's nothing more.'

Tara sensed that something had shifted inside her. Jade was pulling back, both mentally and physically. She was edging closer and closer to the killing and she was fearful of going deeper into those memories.

Tara could have ended it there. She could have taken Jade home right then, safe and sound. But they were so close. So close to the secret Ray Jameson was desperate to keep buried.

'See if any images come up. Let them float into your mind.'

Jade was still and silent, staring at objects on the coffee table.

They were running out of time. Soon, Risha would call Ray Jameson, if Marco hadn't done so already. Another minute passed and Jade stayed frozen.

When Tara looked into the mirror that hung on the wall

behind the sofa, she saw Daniel's face. Gentle blue eyes behind wire-rimmed glasses. Behind her, she saw a blood-soaked pillow on the bed. She felt quite calm.

She took her phone out of her bag, opened Penny Ress's email and clicked on the video file. She took a few steps forward, holding the screen up so Jade could see it play.

Hey, beautiful. Carl Ress was alive. He was outdoors, under a blue sky. *I wanted to tell you I'm thinking of you. I'm missing you so much.*

Jade began blinking rapidly.

I'm so lucky to have you both in my life. I can't wait to put my arms around you. Carl held out his arms. *Come here, my beautiful girls.*

Jade literally changed colour. Her eyes brightened and her cheeks flushed red, as if a volcano was erupting inside of her. The high heels she'd been clutching in her right hand dropped to the floor. She turned to Tara. 'Go. You have to get out of this room.'

'What's wrong?'

Jade slid the right side of her dress upwards. Tara saw the knife, tied to her thigh with a latex band. In a second, her mouth went dry.

'I'm not leaving you in here alone.' Tara had brought Jade here, to this point. She was responsible for whatever was about to happen.

Jade slid the knife out of its latex sheath. It was small, with a black handle, ordinary except for the engraving on the blade. It was part of the set that belonged in the kitchen of the Jameson house in St John's Wood.

'Jade, can you hear me?' Tara's muscles were turning to jelly. 'I'm staying here, with you.'

Jade had brought that knife with her, she'd been carrying it all along. And Tara was sure she had brought it with her the last time too, on the night Carl Ress had died.

Risha had tried to warn her that Jade was dangerous.

Jade seemed to have grown taller. Her movements were more confident and more assertive as she took a few steps forward until she and Tara were only inches apart. 'Jade isn't here.'

'I don't understand?'

'My name is Ruby.'

Jade's dissociation was far more extreme than Tara had understood. The psychiatrist who had written the report had misdiagnosed her too. Jade's escape from reality went much further than memory loss. She had taken on a whole different persona.

'Ruby, were you in this room with Jade and Carl Ress on the night he died?'

'Jade is too trusting. I knew he was going to do something bad.'

'Did Carl hurt Jade?' Tara said.

'He would have hurt her. He kept looking at the door, like he was waiting for someone. If there were two of them, I couldn't have—' She held the knife close to her thigh, the tip pointing down at the carpet. 'He would have hurt her if I hadn't had the knife.'

'So you came to protect her?'

'No shit, Sherlock.' When she looked up at Tara, her eyes were cold. Jade's eyes had always been soft. 'I had to stop him.'

Jade's arm was so steady. The knife was perfectly still as she took another step forward. She was very close now, the tip of the blade almost touching the hollow at the base of Tara's throat.

'Put the knife down. Please.' Tara's vision had narrowed until all she could see was that blade.

The Red Suite was so silent, so well insulated. No one would hear her scream. She might die here, in this hotel room.

Tara took a chance, she moved, backing away from the

knife. The edge of the coffee table pressed against the back of her knees. 'You said that Carl kept looking at the door. Who was he waiting for?'

For a moment, Jade looked confused. Her hand trembled as she clutched the knife.

'Did someone else come into the room?' The half an hour must be up now, surely. Please, let Risha not decide to give them extra time. Tara thought she heard sirens, but maybe she was hallucinating. 'You said you *wanted* to remember. You asked me to help you. That's why we came back here, together.'

'How do you know I didn't bring you here to kill you?' The girl smiled as she took a step closer. It was Ruby's unfeeling eyes Tara was looking into.

Tara braced herself against the edge of the coffee table and reached behind her. Her fingertips brushed the neck of the wine bottle. 'Is that true? Do you want to hurt me?'

The look in those eyes told Tara she was capable of anything. When Jade was in this state, when she was Ruby, she was deadly. Tara gripped the bottle and lifted it a little. It was a good weight. The muscles in her arm were ready to swing. Just like one of those kettlebells. But when she imagined aiming at Jade's head, that felt very, very wrong. She couldn't do it. She set the bottle down.

'You came to me for help. I won't leave you alone here, I promise you.'

Tara could only hope she had not imagined the connection between Jade and herself. There had been a genuine trust. She had to keep talking until someone came looking for them. Someone had to come through that door. The police. Even Ray Jameson would do at this point.

'Jade, can you hear me? There's nothing to be frightened of now, I promise you. Please do something for me. Breathe. Just breathe. In and out. In for three counts, out for five.'

Tara forced herself to keep looking straight into those eyes, hoping they might change and become gentle again. 'Stay with me. Breathe. You'll feel less afraid.'

Jade's eyes flickered. Maybe. The knife dropped an inch. Tara held out her hand, feeling a glimmer of hope, and then there was a rush of air as the door flung open and Risha was screaming and running at her sister, grabbing for the knife, the blade slicing at her hands. And Lucy, behind her. All Tara could see was red. The red of Lucy's waistcoat, the red of Risha's lipstick. Blood.

Jade would not let go of that knife, she kept lashing out. Tara grabbed a cushion from the sofa, trying to get in between Risha and the blade, and then Lucy was pinning Jade's arms from behind.

'Enough now!' Lucy said. 'That's enough. Everyone needs to just settle down.'

At the sound of her friend's voice, Jade's fingers relaxed. The knife dropped to the floor and Tara picked it up.

FIFTY-FOUR

Jade was sitting on the sofa in Risha's office. She looked dazed, as though she had just emerged from a deep sleep. All of the fight and the fear had drained out of her.

Risha was in the chair behind her desk, trying not to show how much pain she was in. Lucy had fetched the first aid kit and was tending to the cuts on her hands and arms. Risha kept saying these were only superficial, but the one on her left palm was bleeding through the bandages far too quickly and she clearly needed stitches. She had called Noor, who was on her way and would take her daughter to see a discreet doctor who was likely to accept the explanation that the cuts were accidental. Risha had no attention of bringing the incident to the attention of the police.

'Was it that medication you gave her that set her off?' she asked Tara.

'It wasn't the meds,' Tara said.

'How can you be so sure?' Risha allowed Lucy to put her arm on top of two cushions stacked on her desk.

'Because I didn't give her anything. Those were just over the counter nose drops. Decongestant. It was too risky to use psychedelics for the first time without a doctor here, but I needed Jade to believe she'd taken the drug. That way, she was more likely to remember.'

'A placebo,' Lucy said, helpfully. 'The power of suggestion.'

'Is she going to be all right?' Risha said.

Tara did not know. She was keeping a close eye on Jade, who had seemed calm, at least on the surface, ever since she'd let go of the knife. But she wasn't making eye contact with anyone and she wasn't speaking. Her father was on his way; Risha had no choice but to call him.

Risha had tried to persuade Tara that it would be best if she wasn't there when Ray arrived, but Tara couldn't leave Jade in this state.

Lucy was applying yet another dressing. 'Risha, please. You need to keep this hand elevated.'

'I'm sorry.' These were the first words Jade had spoken since leaving the Red Suite. She was looking at Risha. 'I didn't mean to hurt you.'

Tara was so relieved to hear her voice.

'I know,' Risha said. 'It's not your fault. It's our fault. All of us. We waited too long to get you proper help. It's going to be different now, I promise. You will get better.'

'Jade, when we were in the Red Suite,' Tara said, 'and you had those memories of being in the room with Carl Ress, you said your name was Ruby.'

Tara watched closely for any reaction, but Jade remained calm. She nodded.

Lucy came across and sat next to her friend on the sofa. She reached for Jade's hand, patting it reassuringly. Lucy had shown no fear, not even when Jade was holding the knife. She seemed to be comfortable around Jade, in all her states.

'Can you tell me about Ruby?' Tara said.

'When I was younger, I thought she was real. Like my big sister. She was with me at Paula's place, and she took care of me. When things got really bad, we'd hide in this cupboard together in the kitchen. Ruby would always take a knife in there, to protect us. After I went to live with Ray and Sandra, she mostly disappeared. Ray once told me we were going to leave her behind, on one of our holidays. He said she would be happier there. She wasn't supposed to come back to London.'

The two girls were huddled up together on the sofa.

Risha stayed very still, her arm extended on the pile of cushions, listening. 'So Dad knew about this Ruby person? And Sandra too?'

Jade nodded. 'After I got Ziggy, I only saw Ruby like once or twice in high school, when I was feeling anxious. By that time, I knew she wasn't real. But she still feels real – it's hard to explain. Then, after I met Carl Ress, I started blanking out again.'

'Blanking out?'

'Sometimes when Ruby is with me, I can see what she's doing and saying. But sometimes she takes over and I don't remember. That night when Carl Ress was killed I wasn't there at all. I swear.'

'Lucy, have you met Ruby?' Tara asked.

Lucy nodded. 'There were always two of them. Ever since we shared a bunk bed at Mrs Martin's.'

'Can you tell when it's Ruby and not Jade?'

'Easy. Ruby's a pain in the butt. She's difficult, she argues all the time and she's always pissed off about something. But mainly, her eyes are different.'

It was fascinating that Lucy saw Ruby as a different and distinct personality.

Although for the most part Jade functioned so well in everyday life, there was significant damage to her personality. When she was very young, she must have experienced terror with no escape. Unable to get away physically, she escaped using her mind, developing a persona that was both protective and unafraid. Jade was the angel and Ruby was a raging spirit.

'When we were inside the Red Suite tonight,' Jade said. 'I saw what Ruby did. Carl had his back to her, he was facing the door, and she stabbed him in the shoulder.'

'Did you see someone else come into the room?'

'Only Risha and Lucy. But that was tonight, right?' Jade looked at Lucy. 'You can tell us if you know anything more. It's all right.'

'When I came into the room and saw Carl Ress's body,' Lucy said, 'I knew it was Ruby standing over him. She had the knife in her hand and she told me to take it and get rid of it. I panicked, I didn't know what to do, so I just did what she told me. I wrapped the knife in a towel and ran up to the roof to throw it over the side.'

'Only she didn't get that far,' Risha said. 'Because I took it from her. My father had called me and told me to sort it out.'

They all knew. The whole family.

'How did your father know what had happened?' Tara said.

'No idea. And I didn't ask. My mum came past the hotel, and I gave her the knife and as far as I know, it went back to Ray and Sandra's place in St John's Wood and through a very intensive dishwasher cycle.'

Tara felt as though someone had poured a trickle of ice water down her back. She knew everything now. Or almost everything. She wondered what Ray Jameson might do about that, and what price there would be to pay.

'I told you,' Risha said, 'loyalty is everything in this family. Loyalty and secrecy. Welcome to our very exclusive club. You're practically one of us now.'

'When I came back into the room after going up onto the roof,' Lucy said, 'Jade was back but she didn't remember anything. She's been telling the truth.'

'I didn't know Ruby would hurt any of you. I swear,' Jade

said. 'If I did, I would have tried to stop her. I tried, I tried to push her arm down when she—'

'I was there,' Tara said. 'I know you tried to come back and take control.'

'Jadey?' Ray Jameson was in the doorway, his bulk filling the frame.

Jade burst into tears; she stood up and went over to hug him. Over her shoulder, Jameson glared at Tara.

Jade had remembered stabbing Carl Ress, but only once. And Ress had been stabbed eleven times in total. It was possible that someone else had come through the door of that hotel room. Someone who had stabbed Carl Ress another ten times, to ensure he didn't survive. A person Jade desperately, even unconsciously, needed to protect. Her beloved father.

Jameson would have to be a true psychopath to let his own daughter believe she'd committed a murder, and possibly even go to jail for it.

Jade was holding both of her father's hands, facing him. 'Dad, you can't be angry, okay?'

Ray nodded through gritted teeth. He was still staring at Tara, his fury contained only because of his daughters in the room. If the two of them had been alone, Tara thought, he might have been inclined to throttle her.

'I asked Doctor Black to help me remember,' Jade was saying. 'I know I stabbed him.'

Ray hugged Jade close into his chest, kissing the top of her head and closing his eyes.

It was possible that Ruby not only protected Jade from danger in the outside world, but also from her own memories, the ones she wasn't yet ready to face. Maybe Jade could not bear to see her father commit a murder and then leave her there to take the blame.

'I want to go home,' Jade said. 'And Risha needs a doctor.'

Ray had not reacted to his older daughter's bloodied hand. All his attention had been focused on Jade.

'Noor's waiting outside for Risha,' Ray said. 'And I'll send a car for Doctor Black.'

'That really won't be necessary.'

'And Lucy's coming for a sleepover,' Jade said, still holding her father's hand.

Lucy broke into a grin.

FIFTY-FIVE

SIX WEEKS LATER

Dr Anthony Edwards was an unassuming man in a white shirt and black suit. He was trim and bald with friendly eyes. Nothing about him stood out and Tara might not have noticed him at all if she hadn't been looking out for him.

He had spotted her too as she walked into the café, and he stood up and waved. 'Doctor Black?'

'Tara, please.'

He held out his hand to shake hers. 'Tony. I'm so glad we could talk.'

Edwards looked quite well, Tara thought. If he had been seriously ill a matter of months ago, he'd certainly made a good recovery.

He had sent her a couple of further emails, after the night of the reconstruction, apologising again for not getting in touch sooner. He had suggested they meet up, as he was attending a conference in London. They had arranged to meet at the National Theatre Café, near Waterloo Station.

'I took a chance and ordered you a coffee,' he said. 'The queue is so long.'

He handed her a takeaway cup. The coffee was strong, just

the way she liked it. The place was crowded though, and it was difficult to talk without shouting.

'Shall we take a walk?' Tara said.

They headed out towards the river. The sun was out on an unusually warm day in late autumn.

'I want to apologise again for not responding to your earlier emails,' Edwards said.

'Did you know I was working on the Jameson case?'

He nodded. A note of caution crept into his voice. 'I understand you stepped back as well? I heard Caroline Collins took over in the end.'

'I was in an accident. A hit-and-run. The man I was with died that night.' Tara felt numb. Partly it was the painkillers she was still taking, partly that was the way she needed it to be.

She often saw Sabine's desperate eyes at her front door. *Don't come to the funeral.*

'Or the police believe it was a hit-and-run,' she said.

'You don't?'

'No.'

Tara had had no further contact with anyone in the Jameson family since the night of the reconstruction. She knew from Lucy that Jade had taken the manslaughter plea, and that somehow the Youth Offending Team had been persuaded that the best place for her to receive treatment was at a secure clinic in Germany. Tara assumed that Ray Jameson was satisfied with this outcome and so had decided not to exact any further revenge on her for defying him.

They walked on, past the market under the bridge, with tables and tables of second-hand books. Tara told Edwards how Daniel had died on the same day Jade's stepsister had told her about a previous knife attack, and on the same day Jade Jameson had asked her parents for permission to go to Tara's office to take a drug that would help her recover her memory. Anthony Edwards was a calm, focused listener. Tara knew of him by reputation, and she thought she'd be intimidated, but she didn't feel that way at all. There was something grounding in unburdening herself to him.

'I think Ray Jameson tried to kill me.' It was the first time Tara had said these words out loud. 'Tell me that's ridiculous. Tell me the concussion and the grief and the painkillers are making me crazy. Tell me you think I'm paranoid.'

'I wish I could.'

Tara was starting to feel the cold, with the wind blowing off the river. She saw her cottage in darkness, her notebook open on the kitchen table, the text from Jade. *I can come to your office tomorrow morning.*

'Why did you not answer my messages while I was still working on the Jameson case?'

Edwards sighed. 'I wasn't planning to share this with anyone. But clearly, I owe you.'

They had been walking side by side along the river as they spoke. Now he broke away and went to sit on a bench. Tara went over to sit next to him, pulling her coat tighter around her.

'A few weeks after I'd become involved in the Jameson case, my son was mugged. He's fourteen. It was around five thirty in the afternoon, and he was walking across the hospital car park after school. On Wednesdays, after football practice, he'd meet me at my car, and I'd drive him home. That was our routine. Every Wednesday.' He looked at the concrete ground as he spoke.

'Is your son all right?'

'Physically, yes.' He turned to face her. 'A man in a balaclava came up behind him and held a knife to his throat. He didn't say a word at first, just held it there, right over his carotid artery, pressing down so the knife drew a little blood. All he had to do was press down a little harder and he would have killed him. He said, "Say hi to your father."'

'And you think Ray Jameson was involved?'

'I thought he was sending me a clear message. The day before my son was attacked, I'd had a long session with Jade. I had managed to convince her to come into my offices in Oxford, I thought the physical distance from her parents would help. I'd managed to make a connection with her, and my impression was that she'd come to a point where she *wanted* to recover the lost memories. She wanted to face what had happened in that hotel room. She confided in me that she'd had other absences in her life, and that those had started happening when she was very young. Like you, I felt I needed something extra, to help Jade's memory. I suggested we ask the hotel for permission to go back there, and Jade was keen. And then my son was attacked.'

Tara was quiet for a few moments, absorbing all of this. Anthony Edwards had got off lucky, with a warning. A knife to his son's throat. He had known when he was beaten. Tara had been arrogant. If she had listened to Daniel, he might still be alive.

The pain of losing him twisted deep inside. Tara bit her lip so as not to scream.

'I've lived and worked in Oxford for over twenty years,' Edwards was saying, 'and I've parked in that car park for most of that time, and nothing remotely like that has ever happened before. And, coincidentally, the CCTV in the hospital car park had been vandalised, so it wasn't working that day.'

Neither of them spoke for a few moments.

Edwards held up his left hand. He was wearing a wedding ring. 'My wife died two years ago, of breast cancer. My son has suffered enough. The day after the mugging, I decided to withdraw from the case. I emailed Valerie with my excuses, I said there were health issues.'

Tara nodded. She stood up. She had to move. They began walking again, continuing on in the direction of the bridge that led to Embankment Station.

'Did you tell Valerie about the mugging?'

'No.'

'By the time I was injured and withdrew,' Tara said, 'she must at very least have suspected something, having lost two expert witnesses in quick succession?'

Worst-case scenario was Valerie Bennett knew everything and was in Ray Jameson's pocket. Best-case scenario, perhaps criminal acts went with the territory, being a criminal defence attorney, and she couldn't get involved.

'Like you, I thought I was paranoid,' Edwards said. 'Or, I hoped I was paranoid. I'm so sorry I didn't answer your messages.'

They had stopped and were leaning against the railings, looking across to the Houses of Parliament and Big Ben. A tourist boat chugged along the river.

'The night Daniel was killed, he tried to convince me to withdraw from the case. He knew what Jameson was capable of and he begged me to walk away. It's my fault he died.'

Edwards reached out and laid a hand on her arm, briefly. Tara welcomed the icy wind on her face, freezing the tears that wanted to come.

'You blame yourself for Daniel's death,' Edwards said, 'and I blame myself for what my son went through, and for not warning you. But I can assure you that Ray Jameson feels no guilt at all.'

The wind was picking up, blowing her hair across her face. 'I think about this case all the time, and what I could have done differently.'

'You need to understand that you are not responsible.'

'What if I can't let it go?'

'I've worked on hundreds of criminal cases,' Edwards said, 'and there is always an element of risk. Clients are angry because you are part of the system, family members are furious because you're helping to put their loved ones in jail. It goes with the territory. I've felt fear before, especially working with people who have committed violent crimes. But I've never had a case where I have felt afraid the way I did working with Jade Jameson. The attack on my son was sophisticated. The work of a professional. So please, tell me you are not considering getting involved again, in any way.'

'I keep thinking about going to the police.'

Edwards turned around, bracing himself against the railings. 'Do you really think you can win in a battle against Ray Jameson?'

'No.'

But Jade Jameson may have confessed to a killing that she wasn't responsible for. And Daniel deserved justice.

FIFTY-SIX

Even if Tara had listened to Anthony Edwards' warning, it seemed the case would not let go of her. A few days after their meeting, she received a phone call from Carl Ress's widow, asking her to come over to the house to talk about a 'sensitive matter.'

When Tara been working on Jade's assessment, she had appreciated Penny's generosity in speaking with her, even though at the time, Tara had been working for the defence team. And Penny had sent her the video clip that ultimately unlocked Jade's memory. It was the right thing to do to return the favour.

In the kitchen of the house in Chiswick, Penny reached up to take two mugs down from a cupboard. Her hands seemed shaky as she set these down on the counter. 'I understand the charges were dropped to manslaughter, for the Jameson girl?'

'That's right, but as I explained on the phone, I'm no longer working with Jade and I wasn't involved in the final report.'

Moving slowly, Penny filled the kettle and set it to boil. She was struggling to broach whatever issue was troubling her.

'The last time I was here,' Tara said, 'I had the sense you

were having a complicated reaction to the loss of your husband. I'm not judging you, but I'm curious. I felt there might be something else you didn't mention to me at the time, that might have helped to understand what went on between your husband and Jade Jameson.'

Penny placed a teabag into each mug. She could barely look at Tara as she spoke. 'When I was married to Carl, I felt like I was losing my mind. I started to have all these thoughts, like: Why would he want to be with an older woman? And why was he so happy to take on the responsibility of my teenage daughter? And then, the thoughts got darker. I started to worry that maybe Carl was with me not despite Freya, but because of Freya. He was far more interested in my daughter than he was in me. They were always playing video games together, he'd offer to give her lifts to meet her friends, or he'd tell me I should take time off, you know, go to the spa, the hairdresser, out with the girls.'

Penny stopped speaking and stared into the middle distance in silence.

Tara waited.

Penny started moving again. With some effort she lifted the kettle and poured boiling water into each mug. 'I started to suspect he was lying to me. But you see, I doubted myself. My first husband always said I was too insecure. Too needy. And Carl would get angry if I asked questions, he'd accuse me of not trusting him.'

Penny picked up the mugs, walked over to the dining table and sat down.

Tara came to sit opposite her. 'Do you think that Carl was abusing your daughter?'

'I never knew for sure. And nothing ever happened to Freya, I swear. Or I don't think. I'm sure she would have told me—'

'What made you call me now? Has Freya said something?'

Penny shook her head. 'Nothing like that. But you see, when I started to have these... concerns, I went to talk to Carl's father, to try to get some information, anything that would help me understand my husband better. Carl was always close to his father, always desperate for his approval. He would go down and visit him often, in Devon. Anyway, his father told me that Carl wasn't discharged from the police because of stress, the truth was, he left under some cloud. Carl's dad wouldn't tell me the details but he kind of implied that I should be careful, and that I needed to look after myself and Freya. He wouldn't be any more specific than that. At the time I had the impression it was more about money.'

Penny was looking behind Tara, at the photographs of her daughter on the wall. 'One Saturday morning, we'd had a couple of drinks the night before and I woke up late, and the house was empty. Carl was gone, with Freya. I panicked; I nearly had a heart attack. In the end it turned out that nothing was wrong, I called Freya on her mobile and Carl had taken her out for breakfast and shopping, to give me a chance to lie in. When he brought her back everything seemed fine, but after that, I knew I had to do something. I couldn't live with a man I didn't trust. That's when I started talking to lawyers. And then, he was stabbed to death in a hotel room with a seventeen-year-old girl. But I didn't have any proof, you see, that's why I didn't say anything.'

Tara understood now why Penny seemed to feel no anger toward Jade for killing her husband. She been carrying a secret fear, a sense she had failed her daughter.

'I need to know if Carl molested Jade Jameson,' Penny said. 'Please.'

'I don't know. So far, there's no evidence that was the case.'

'I need to show you something.' Penny stood up. 'Wait here.'

She disappeared upstairs and Tara could hear her walking around on the floor above. When she returned, she was carrying a camcorder in one hand and a power cable in the other.

'Carl's dad gave this to me after he died.' Penny set the camera down. She opened a flap on the side, revealing a memory card which she removed and placed on the table between them. 'Carl had asked his father to keep this locked in his safe. I got the feeling his dad wasn't entirely comfortable about it. If you ask me, he didn't want it on his property, that's why he passed it over to me about a week ago, when the police were finally finished searching this place.'

'Do you know what's on there?' Tara wondered if this might be the mysterious video that Carl had promised to Jade.

'I've no idea. And I don't want to know. Since you're here, and you're a psychologist... I thought... maybe you could take a look.'

Tara picked up the memory card, reached for the camcorder and put it back in the slot. Penny stopped her, placing a hand over hers. 'Not here. Take it with you. Get it out of here.'

'You're worried there's something on there to do with Freya?'

'You watch it and then you can let me know... if—' She stopped, putting her head in her hands. 'If there's something I need to do.'

'Of course. I will.'

'I'm giving it to you in case my daughter needs some kind of help. And also, in case this could help Jade Jameson. I've always felt sorry for her.'

Tara packed the camcorder and the power cord into her bag. 'I'll call you as soon as I've looked at it.'

Penny walked her to the front door. 'You were right. I wasn't grieving when Carl died. I was relieved. I'll never know if he was using me for my money and my house and my daughter, or if he really loved me, will I?'

'You were right to trust your instincts,' Tara said. 'Don't doubt yourself.'

'Thank you. Not exactly what I wanted to hear, but thank you.' Penny had visibly relaxed now the camcorder was out of her possession.

When Tara got back into her car, she took the memory card out of the camcorder and inserted it into her laptop. It contained a single video file. She dreaded watching it, in case Penny Ress's fears about her daughter were justified.

After a few minutes' hesitation, she opened the file and clicked play.

FIFTY-SEVEN

Paula and Sandra are sitting next to each other on an orange velour sofa. Sandra opens her bag and takes out a small plastic packet secured with a knot. It contains a ball of white powder. She lays this on the coffee table.

'I'm clean,' Paula says. 'I've been clean for months.'

Sandra takes out a syringe and a tourniquet. 'We'll do it together. Like old times.'

Paula backs away from her sister and the syringe, pushing herself into the corner of the sofa.

Sandra opens the plastic bag, heats the white powder up in the teaspoon, and then draws it up into the syringe. 'How could you even think of bringing Jade back here to live with you after what happened before?'

'Please,' Paula says. 'Please don't.'

'I know what the last boyfriend of yours did to your daughter. Jade told me. She told me everything she didn't tell those useless social workers. Ray and I managed to settle her down, but she can't take much more. She's not well.'

Paula closes her eyes. 'It's different now. I'm better, I'm

clean. I have a partner who supports me. Carl's going to get us a decent place to live—'

'Carl? Are you serious?'

'He loves me.'

'You're deluded.'

'I'm sorry Sandy. She's my baby, and I need her back. Carl knows a lawyer, a good one.'

'He's your fucking pimp!' Sandra is shouting now. 'What do you think he wants you for?'

'Please don't be angry. I hate it when you're angry with me.' Paula's eyes are fixed on the needle.

Sandra lifts the syringe upright and pushes the plunger into place. 'How dare you fuck up our lives, again? Jade is in a good school, she has friends. She sleeps without nightmares and she doesn't fucking hide knives and crawl into cupboards at night anymore.'

Paula is barely listening now. Her knees are jiggling up and down as though she can't control them. She pulls up her sleeve.

'You manipulate Ray. You'll never stop. You'll always be there, dragging us down into the sewers with you. You'll destroy your daughter.' Sandra ties the tourniquet tight around her sister's arm.

'I know I'm useless. You've always been much stronger than me. You're better than me.'

'I can't let you hurt her anymore,' Sandra says. 'Jade is safe with us.'

'I love you. And Jade. I love you both so much.'

'You did this to yourself.' Sandra doesn't look at her sister's face as she slides the needle into a bulging vein.

Paula's knees become still. She slumps back against the sofa, before she starts convulsing, foaming at the corners of her mouth.

Sandra doesn't react. She wipes down the syringe.

Paula is no longer moving.

Sandra stands up and puts her bag over her shoulder. Before she leaves, she pauses. She leans down and kisses Paula on her forehead. 'Jade is my baby. Ours. Mine and Ray's.'

FIFTY-EIGHT

Tara opened the window of her car and took a deep breath. She felt a sense of unreality. She had just witnessed a murder. Sandra had killed her own sister.

You do not want to uncover something that you would then have to disclose to the solicitor or worse, the police.

Daniel's prediction had come true.

Carl Ress must have been blackmailing the Jameson family with that video and Tara had no doubt that was what had led to his death, one way or another.

As the shock wore off, the main thing Tara felt was sadness. For Jade, who had lost Paula and been betrayed by Sandra. For Daniel's children. For all of her own losses.

She had to think. She closed her window and considered what to do next.

She could simply destroy the memory card. In terms of self-preservation that would be the safest and most sensible course of action.

She could drive to the nearest police station and hand the memory card over.

If she did give this video over to the authorities, she had no way of knowing the outcome, and Jameson would retaliate. Even if Tara did survive, she had no doubt that Jameson would carry out his threat to expose her past and destroy her reputation.

And then there was a third option. The one that made sense.

Tara had thought she would feel fear. Instead, she felt lighter. She was simply going to do the right thing.

Tara called Penny Ress to reassure her that there was nothing on the video relating to her daughter. She started her engine, checked her mirrors and pulled out.

What happened to her no longer mattered. It was too late, almost everyone she had loved was gone. But there was still time to save Jade Jameson.

FIFTY-NINE

As usual, the London streets were clogged with traffic and it took Tara over an hour to get across to Soho. She barely noticed her surroundings as she drove on autopilot, following the voice of the navigation system. She was rehearsing a conversation in her mind.

It was late afternoon and darkness was falling earlier. Up on the roof terrace of The Onyx, soft lamps lit up the branches of the olive trees in their terracotta pots. The only sound was the distant pulsing of traffic down below.

Sandra and Noor were sitting at one of the tables, waiting for her.

Tara was surprised. She had asked Sandra to come alone. She took a breath as she walked towards them.

'Thank you for coming.' Tara pulled out a chair; metal legs scraped against concrete. 'Sandra, I think it would be better if the two of us talk in private.'

'I want Noor to stay.'

Noor smiled nervously at Tara. Sandra looked anxious too. She had a fleece on over Lycra leggings and trainers, as if she'd dashed out in the middle of a class.

Tara set her briefcase down next to her chair. Noor being present wasn't in the plan and Tara felt uneasy with both women there. She wondered if Sandra had also let her husband know about the meeting. But she had to continue, she would use whatever time she had. She took out her laptop and placed it on the table. 'I have just been to see Carl Ress's widow.'

'Why?' Sandra said.

'I really do think we should discuss this in private.'

Sandra shook her head. 'Noor stays.'

'Fine.' Tara opened her laptop, turning it to face the two women. 'Penny Ress gave me a memory card that had belonged to her husband. She had concerns about what was on there and she didn't want to watch it herself.'

She clicked on the file and the image of Paula and Sandra sitting on the orange sofa appeared. On the screen, Sandra reached into her handbag.

Tara paused the video. 'I think you know what happens next.'

Sandra stood up. She went over to the edge of the roof, standing with her back to Noor and Tara. 'I did what was right for my family,' she said. 'Paula would have destroyed Jade.'

Noor went over to her, putting a comforting arm around her waist. Sandra leaned her head against Noor's shoulder.

Sandra had not been concerned about hiding the video from Noor when it had started to play. So Noor already knew the truth behind Paula's death.

'Carl Ress was using the video to blackmail you?' Tara said.

'Ress was a monster,' Sandra turned around. 'He was my sister's drug dealer. He was her pimp. Later, when he'd been kicked out of the police, and Ray and I were trying to adopt Jade, he saw an opportunity. He moved in with Paula and convinced her to try to get Jade back. He was using my sister and Jade to extort money out of us.'

'Why would he wait until now to use the video?' Tara said.

'Because he knew Ray would kill him.'

Noor stayed close to Sandra, her arm protectively around her friend's waist. 'Something must have happened to make him do something so stupid.'

'Carl was desperate for money,' Tara said. 'His wife was divorcing him.'

She took the memory card out of her laptop and laid it on the cold metal surface of the table. 'That night, when I took Jade back to the hotel, she saw herself stabbing Carl Ress once, in the shoulder. That was all she could remember. But she also said that Carl was expecting someone, she believed he was waiting for someone to walk into the room. Jade has never been able to remember who that was. I believe it was your husband. Ray found out that Ress was blackmailing you, and he killed him, just as you said he would.'

'My husband has nothing to do with this.' Sandra brushed her hair up from her face, putting it up into a ponytail with the scrunchy she wore around her arm. She seemed calmer.

Tara didn't want to feel the fear creeping in around the edges of her thoughts. 'Does Ray know how Paula died?'

Sandra shook her head. 'My husband always had a soft spot for Paula.'

Those were the same words Risha had used. *A suspicious little soft spot.* On some level Sandra must have been jealous of her sister. Maybe she too had suspected Ray was Jade's biological father.

'So I've misunderstood,' Tara said. 'You wouldn't have sent Ray to deal with Carl Ress because you wouldn't take the chance that Carl might show your husband the video.'

Tara had missed something crucial. Ray had been so dominant and so controlling; she had seen what she believed was his coercive control in that family. She had misjudged Sandra, overlooked her.

A weight pressed down on Tara's chest, making it difficult

to breathe. If Sandra was capable of killing her own sister, she was certainly capable of killing Carl Ress. And it was hard to imagine Sandra was going to let Tara walk away now she had seen the video. There was a reason she had wanted Noor to stay.

Tara had to get off that roof. She stood up, heaving her bag over her shoulder, but as she did, she felt an electric surge, a power flowing through her muscles. An outrage.

On the outside, she would stay calm, she was good at that.

She put her bag back down and stood up straight, one hand braced on the ice-cold metal of the chair. 'Jade can't heal until she knows she isn't guilty. She needs to know that she didn't kill Carl Ress.'

'She would have killed him if I hadn't been there.' Sandra had somehow painted herself a picture that would help to bury any guilt she might feel about what she'd done to her daughter.

'But Jade didn't kill him,' Tara said. 'You did.'

'Jade almost killed a man before. With a kitchen knife.'

'That was self-defence.'

Sandra took a few steps forward. 'She was only ten years old, and already she was capable of anything. We let Jade pretend she forgot about that time too, but I knew it was a mistake. I knew we should have taken her to see someone then. But Ray is so stubborn. He likes to pretend as much as she does that everything's forgotten. That everything's all right.'

'Jade is not pretending,' Tara said. 'When the terror gets too much, she lets Ruby take over. She dissociates. It's a self-protective mechanism that extremely traumatised children develop.'

Tara wasn't sure if Sandra was listening any more. She had her hands pushed deep into the pockets of her fleece, and she was walking back and forth across the short space between their table and the edge of the roof.

'We all need to stay calm,' Noor said. 'We need a little time to think, that's all.'

Noor reached into her tote bag and took out a stainless-steel thermos. She unscrewed the lid and filled it with the thick white liquid. She offered it to Tara.

'No thank you.'

'Shardaayi,' Noor said. 'I remember how much you liked it last time.'

'No.'

Tara was thinking about Sandra Jameson's tranquillisers, she had the idea they were crushed up in that drink. She was trying not to think about what Sandra had done to Carl Ress's body with that knife.

'Drink, please,' Noor said. 'Let's all stay calm.'

'All right,' Tara said. 'Noor's right. We need to stay calm. We can find a way out.'

She picked up the cup and took a small sip, buying time. It was much sweeter than she remembered. The last thing she wanted was for Sandra to panic. The edge of that roof seemed suddenly very menacing. Even though Sandra was dangerous, Tara did not want to be responsible for her death.

'Please,' Tara said, 'come and sit down and tell me what really happened that night in the Red Suite.'

SIXTY

FOUR MONTHS BEFORE THE KILLING

Carl Ress turned up in Regent's Park one morning while Sandra was running. It was a chill, foggy day and she couldn't see very far ahead. She became aware that a man had come up beside her and was keeping up with her pace. When Sandra sped up, so did he.

'Your daughter's really attached to that ugly dog of hers,' he said. 'She always did love animals, even as a tiny thing. And congratulations by the way, that house of yours is something.'

Sandra turned her head to get a look at him. He was in joggers and trainers and had a cap pulled down low over his forehead. She hadn't laid eyes on him in years, but she remembered his face well. Sleazy. Corrupt. Vicious.

'If Ray finds out you've been anywhere near his daughter, he'll kill you.'

He laughed. 'I have a video you might want to see, before you get your husband involved.'

Her breath came out in plumes of steam. 'What do you want?'

The answer was obvious. Money. Carl always wanted money. The question was only how much, and what exactly he had to bargain with. Sandra was hoping against hope that he was bluffing, but she had a very bad feeling.

'I don't know. I need to think about that. I mean, this video would traumatise Jade. For sure. I'd hate for a beautiful, innocent young girl to be scarred like that. And I think it might even traumatise your husband. I'm guessing he doesn't know the full story.'

'Get to the point.' Sandra ran faster.

Next to her, Carl's breathing grew heavier as he struggled to keep up.

She had no idea what he might have on video. Herself, she supposed. In a compromising position. Paula, maybe. Something that would hurt Jade and be of interest if it came out now. Lots of things were of interest to lots of people, now they had money. It was a miracle nothing had surfaced on the internet so far. Ray probably had a team of people keeping an eye on that.

'Let me give you a bit of background,' Carl said. 'You remember that night Paula came over to your place, and asked you, no—begged you—not to take her daughter away? You and Ray had the money, the big house, the fancy lawyers. And all poor Paula had was Jade.'

'I remember a lot of nights like that. In between, she'd be off her head on heroin. Probably supplied by you.'

Carl stopped moving. He stood with his hands on his waist, catching his breath. 'Paula was desperate to get her daughter back. She never would have let that adoption go through.'

'Oh fuck off. You're a psychopath. You saw a mark in Ray and Paula was one of his weak spots.' Sandra jogged on the spot to keep warm. 'You put ideas in my sister's head that she wanted Jade back. But Paula never wanted to be anyone's mother. It was never about Jade. You thought you'd get money out of us by using Jade. Ray always told me everything.'

'But did you tell him everything? I've always wondered about that.'

Sandra swung at him, but he caught hold of her wrist. 'And then Paula died. How convenient, for both of you.'

He held on and she couldn't get free of him. The bastard was still strong. But Sandra wasn't afraid. He wasn't going to hurt her, not physically. He needed her alive. He was just going to make her life an ongoing nightmare.

'Let go of me or I'll kill you. I swear.'

'I believe you. You always were the tiger.'

'You're such a fucking coward,' she said. 'Still preying on women and children. You come to Jade and to me, but you're too afraid to talk to Ray.'

'If it was the old Ray,' Carl said, 'I would not walk out of that little talk alive, would I? Now though, he's a family man with a legit business. He has his beautiful wife and daughter to think of. Ray's a big pussy these days, right?'

'Unlike you, macho man. Still preying on women and children after all these years.' Seriously. If she had something to do it with, she would have killed him right then. Right there in the park. And she would have felt no guilt. Nothing.

They were right in the heart of the mist and she couldn't see anything or anyone around them. She might have got away with it, too.

'I lived with Paula those last few months,' he said. 'I was the only one helping her.'

'You were kicked out of the police. You had no income. You were setting yourself up for the big payoff. From Ray.'

'I think a lot about the way she died,' he said. 'I wish I could have done more. I blame myself.'

'Oh you do? And now here you are, making our lives a misery again after all these years.'

Carl squeezed her wrist so tight it hurt. His fingers would leave a bruise. His face was right up close so she could smell the rotten stench of him.

'I don't think you understand me,' he said. 'I was there. I

was in the bedroom when she came home that last night. With a camcorder.'

He let her go. Sandra stopped, the air punched out of her lungs. She leaned forwards, hands on her thighs, catching her breath.

'Does your husband know what you did?'

He was enjoying every moment. He always was a sadist.

Sandra had been warm from running, and from fury, but now she was freezing. She unwound her jumper from around her waist and put it on, trying to stop the shaking. Carl was watching her face. He knew.

'You know how these things can spread if they go viral. I've been really careful though, so don't worry. I kept it on the original memory card from my camcorder, that's the only copy.'

'I'm very reassured.' She had to keep moving. She forced her muscles to take her forwards, one foot in front of the other. They were walking now, two people strolling casually through the park. 'Get to the point. What do you want?'

'Let's not settle on a final amount just yet,' he said. 'We'll nail down a payment plan and a payment method. All in good time.'

He would hold this over her for the rest of her life. Whatever she gave him would never be enough.

'And if I say no?'

'Jade and I have met a few times now. She likes my stories about Paula. I think she might be interested in the one about how her mother died.'

'Go to hell.'

'I beg your pardon?'

'You always were a liar. You have nothing. And if you think you can go up against my husband and win, good luck.'

Sandra turned and began running back towards the entrance to the park. There was no video. She picked up the pace, feeling her heart pumping. She was right at her edge and

Carl was falling behind. He was lying Sandra told herself, he was bluffing.

'Say hi to Noor for me,' he yelled. 'I remember the way Ray used to look at her. It was never quite the same when he looked at you.'

SIXTY-ONE

Most people liked to tell their story. Even killers.

Sandra was back at the table, sitting down, and Noor was beside her. Neither of them had touched the thick white liquid in Noor's thermos.

'Carl had someone phone me that night,' Sandra said, 'to tell me he was going to the hotel to meet Jade. If I didn't get there with the money by a certain time, he threatened to show her that video.'

'Did you plan to kill him?'

'I wanted to kill him, that's for sure. But no, it wasn't planned.'

'Sandra,' Noor said. 'I think you've said enough. We're not here for a therapy session.'

Tara wondered what else these two women might be capable of. The thick white liquid had left an unpleasant aftertaste in her mouth. She was dizzy; she told herself it was anxiety, that was all. She had only taken one sip. All she had to do was breathe. But she couldn't stop thinking that Sandra wasn't going to take any risks now Tara had seen that video.

'I wasn't sure what I was going to do when I got there,'

Sandra was saying, 'but in the end, Jade started the job for me. Carl was in shock from that first stab wound. I took the knife and I finished it.'

Ten stab wounds. Sandra was full of so much rage.

Daniel was dead.

Matthew was gone, he was never coming back.

It still didn't seem real, sometimes. Daniel, her brother, her parents. All gone. Tara had not been able to save a single one of them. Who would miss her, when it was her turn?

'How could you leave Jade alone in that room, to take the blame?' The words slipped out, unguarded. Tara hadn't meant to say them out loud. She wasn't feeling entirely in control of herself.

'I had no choice,' Sandra said. 'When she's in Ruby mode, she won't listen to me and I couldn't get her to leave the room. I had to call Ray to come to the hotel, he's the only one who can handle her when she's like that. I wasn't exactly thinking straight, but I knew better than to use the phone from the room to make the call, and I'd turned my mobile off. So I went down the back stairs, to Risha's office, to use her phone and to clean myself up. And then it all got out of control. Lucy went into the Red Suite, and she called the paramedics. All hell broke loose.'

Noor picked up the memory card. 'Are there any copies of this video?'

Tara shook her head. 'I came straight here from Penny Ress's house. You can check my laptop. I haven't sent it to anyone or copied it. No one else knows.'

'Jade has no idea what I did to Paula,' Sandra said. 'And she can never find out. But I didn't care about Carl. I would have confessed, I wanted to go to the police, I really did. I was going to say I was protecting my daughter, which was true. I begged Ray to let me talk to a lawyer. But he wouldn't let me. He asked me to wait. He said he would keep both me and Jade out of prison. He promised.'

'He was right,' Noor said. 'He kept his promise.'

Noor had her own agenda, Tara thought. She might be as jealous as her daughter that Jade was Ray's favourite. Maybe it suited her to have Jade locked away and to have all this information about Sandra. Whatever the reason, she was unperturbed about what Sandra had done.

'If Jade finds out what I did to Paula,' Sandra said, 'she'll hate me. I'll lose her. And Ray too. I'll lose my family. I'll lose everything.'

Tara sat up straighter. 'I would never tell Jade about her mother's death. That would be cruel, coming from me. Destroy the video if you want to. But if you want a real relationship with your daughter, you have to tell the police what happened to Carl Ress. Your first instinct was right. You need to confess.'

Sandra looked at Noor. Noor shook her head.

'Jade is in the right place,' Sandra said. 'She's getting the treatment she needs.'

'Jade does need to be in a hospital,' Tara said, 'but she cannot get better until she knows the truth.'

'Sandra's right,' Noor said. 'Jade has the best doctors in the world caring for her.'

Tara's anger was rising. 'If someone had called an ambulance after Jade had stabbed Ress once, he would have lived. If you hadn't stabbed him another ten times, he would have lived. But now Jade is living with guilt she doesn't deserve. You let your daughter believe she's a killer. Do you know the damage you've done?'

Sandra was silent. Maybe Tara was getting through to her.

'All I am asking is that you help Jade. Tell her the truth. I can go to the clinic with you.'

Tara had a vision then, of Sandra and Noor dragging her to the side of the roof, pushing her over the edge. That was crazy, she told herself. But then, Sandra had killed twice already. Tara swiped her arm across the table, knocking over the thermos and the lid. Noor dashed forwards to pick it up. Thick white liquid ran all over the ground.

She had to hang in, for Jade. Despite the fear.

Tara heard footsteps. Maybe she was imagining them. But they were so familiar, and her heart swelled up.

'Daniel?'

When she turned around, Ray Jameson was striding towards them in his pinstripe suit.

'What the hell?' he said, when he saw Tara in his hotel, once again.

Tara stood up. 'Do you remember you once told me that Jade was the centre of your world, and that nothing else mattered?'

Confused, Jameson nodded. Sandra and Noor sat in silence.

'Lucy's been in contact with me, she's been updating me about Jade's progress. I know that Jade is not getting better. I know that Ruby is there with her at the clinic, all the time. And you know it's not safe for Jade to come home until Ruby's gone. Jade is only seventeen. She could have a good future ahead of her. I know how to help her.'

'I'm listening,' Jameson said. He was looking behind her, at Sandra and Noor and at the laptop and the memory card on the table.

Tara had to keep talking. Talking was her strong point, only now her tongue felt leaden. She focused every last drop of energy on Ray, speaking only to him. His love for his daughter was Jade's best hope. As long as Ray was listening, Jade might have a chance.

'If Jade doesn't get the right treatment, Ruby will stay. She might even take over. If that happens, Jade will need to be in a hospital forever.' Tara's thinking was clear now. The dizziness was lifting. She had barely drunk from that thermos, it had been fear affecting her mind. 'Jade won't ever be well until she integrates Ruby back into herself and to do that, she has to allow herself to know the whole truth about what happened to Carl Ress. She has to accept her own violent impulses, and Sandra's too. Let me help her do that. You can trust me.'

Ray and Sandra were looking at each other. Slowly, Sandra stood up. She walked over to her husband, put her arms around his neck, and her head on his shoulder. 'Ray, she's right. Let me talk to Valerie. She'll know how to handle it.'

Sandra was holding on tight, her head on his chest, but Ray was looking at Tara.

'You've always been there to rescue Jade,' Tara said. 'Don't abandon her now. I know how much you love her.'

Tara kept her eyes on Ray's face. He was wavering.

'Jade is disappearing. If you don't do something, she may not survive.'

Ray nodded. Tara closed her eyes a moment, flooded with relief.

While Sandra clung on to her husband, Noor packed the thermos as well as Tara's laptop into her tote bag. Then she came over and slipped the memory card into Sandra's palm. Ray did not ask any questions.

'One more thing before I go,' Tara said. 'Whatever you decide to do now, remember that if anything should happen to me, you could lose the only person who might be able to bring your daughter back to you.'

SIXTY-TWO

ONE MONTH LATER

On her way to Heathrow Airport, Tara stopped off at the hospital to see Neil. His door was open and he was sitting at his desk, working at his computer. The collection of abandoned mugs in his office had multiplied. Tara counted five of them, all balanced on different piles of papers and books around the room.

She knocked lightly. Neil stood up and waved her inside and they sat down opposite each other in their usual places in the armchairs.

'How long do you think you'll be away?' Neil said.

'Around three to six months. I'll be in Germany, working, for most of the time, but afterwards I'm hoping to also take some time to travel.'

'Where will you go?'

'I'm not exactly sure yet. There's this yoga retreat I've heard about.'

'My wife keeps telling me I should take up yoga.' Neil crossed and re-crossed his ankles. He clasped his hands on his lap. 'So, this is another goodbye?'

'Only for a while.' This man, this hospital, had been a haven for her. 'I'll miss you.'

But Tara wasn't sorry to be leaving London for a couple of months. Olivia was already on maternity leave and the new office building felt lonely. Ray Jameson was going to cover any shortfall on the mortgage for as long as necessary, and would also pay Oksana to check on the place and clean as usual. Tara and Anthony Edwards had been in contact regularly, and he had been keen to use her Marylebone clinic as a London base from time to time while she was away. Tara hadn't told him that she was once again involved in the Jameson case.

From what Tara understood, Sandra had engaged Valerie Bennett and made her confession about the killing of Carl Ress, claiming she had been desperate to protect her daughter and had panicked. Sandra had also claimed that memories of being abused herself as a teenager had resurfaced in the hotel room.

Jade had been told that she was not ultimately responsible for Carl's death, but she was still being held and treated indefinitely at the secure clinic. Her doctors did not think it was a good idea to break it to her that her mother was the killer. They believed it was better to wait and see if Jade remembered Sandra's role in her own time, when her already fragile psyche could handle it.

'You're going to be working with the patient from the medico-legal case?' Neil said.

Tara nodded. 'I was wondering if you had a view, about the diagnosis of dissociative identity disorder?'

'You mean do I believe in multiple personalities?'

'Yes. I know it can be controversial.'

'I've never personally worked with a case before, and I think most clinicians will probably never come across a case in their entire career. But some of my senior colleagues do find it credible. A response to extreme, early trauma.'

'Either that,' Tara said, 'or my patient is an extremely

talented actor with psychopathic tendencies. But my instinct is that her symptoms are genuine. I'm hoping she'll respond to treatment.'

'You'll write up the case?'

'I'm not sure yet.'

Neil fell silent. He was looking at his hands, clasping his fingers one way, and then the other.

'What are you thinking?' she asked.

'You never came back to see me again, after you began to have those memories about your parents.'

'I know.'

'Did you talk to Olivia, about the psychedelics?'

'I did. She was encouraging.'

'But you're not ready?' he said.

'It isn't that.'

'Go on.'

'It's strange, but I don't feel the need to remember so strongly anymore. My family is gone, whatever happened to them is in the past. It's hard to put into words but right now, all I want is to move forwards.'

Tara stood up, not waiting for Neil to respond. Her mind was made up. She was tired of living that way, of hiding who she was, and at the same time, clinging to her old self on the inside. 'So, are we going to the canteen? I have to leave for the airport in half an hour.'

Neil got up from his chair. He crossed the Persian rug, put his arm around her shoulders and squeezed her in close.

SIXTY-THREE

Tara flew to Berlin on a first-class ticket. A limousine with black-tinted windows picked her up and took her to a five-star hotel in the city centre, where she had a suite booked for as long as she needed it. She could get used to this lifestyle, she thought.

The next morning, the limousine took her out to the clinic where Jade was being treated. The facility was in an isolated location, about an hour outside the city, set behind tall electronic gates and an eight-foot wall. A uniformed guard checked their licence plate and identification documents before letting them through.

Beyond the gates was an unexpectedly lovely, winding drive, with neat lawns and oak trees, eventually opening out onto a gravel forecourt. On the outside at least, the building did not look or feel like a secure psychiatric unit. It was more like a stately home. When she stepped out of the car, Tara took a moment to appreciate the sprawling red brick building, with its windows and doorframes draped with ivy.

Inside though, the clinic had a different feel. It had been gutted and modernised and the level of security was more obvious. The reception desk was set behind thick glass panels. A locked iron gate prevented further access into the building and signs on the walls carried strict reminders, in several different languages, that use of mobile phones was not permitted anywhere in the facility.

Tara spoke into a microphone at the front desk. 'I'm Doctor Tara Black, I'm here to see Jade Jameson.'

A young female nurse arrived to take her through to the visitors' area. She was only in her twenties, not much older than Jade, and her cheerful demeanour and swinging ponytail seemed incongruous with the setting. After being buzzed through the heavy gate, Tara had to go through a metal detector. She surrendered her bag and mobile phone. It was unsettling, being so completely cut off from the outside world.

She was taken into a communal living room with sofas and coffee tables and bars on the windows. There wasn't another soul in there.

'Doctor Black, it's so good to see you!'

Jade was wearing her usual outfit of jeans and white T-shirt. She rushed over and gave Tara a big hug, squeezing tight, almost to the point that Tara could not breathe, before abruptly letting go.

Tara knew immediately that this was not the shy young woman she'd first met in the house in St John's Wood.

'Let's go outside for a walk,' Jade said. 'The fresh air does us patients good, apparently.'

A door led out from the living area into a well-tended, walled garden. They walked side by side along the path that led around the perimeter.

'How are you finding it here?' Tara asked.

'It's not so bad. Everyone is really kind. I miss Ziggy like mad though. My dad's trying to see if he can bring him over for a visit.'

'And what about Jade, how is she feeling?'

Those calculating eyes stared back at her. 'Jade can't handle it in here.'

Even in the secure unit, Tara did not feel entirely at ease being alone with her patient.

Staff reported that Jade had been on her best behaviour since being admitted. She was participating in the required activities and therapy groups and taking her prescribed medication without protest. So far, it would appear that Ruby hadn't caused any problems. She had also stayed out of sight of the team at the clinic; Lucy seemed to be the only person who knew that Ruby was present most of the time.

'Can Jade see us and hear us?' Tara said.

She shook her head. 'Not now.'

'You mean you've taken over?'

'I didn't take over anything. I was here first. Jade only comes when I need to get Ray to do something. Or when we need to talk to teachers or police or psychologists. They all love her.'

'Right. I see.' This was unexpected. Tara had been certain that Jade was the primary personality. 'So, you said that Jade can't see or hear us right now. But what about on the night Carl Ress died?'

'She wanted me with her at the hotel. It was my idea to bring the knife from the kitchen at home. When Sandra came into the room, I gave it to her, to finish the job.'

For a moment, Tara was stunned.

'You know about Sandra?' Tara said, cautiously.

The girl nodded.

'Jade told me she couldn't remember if anyone else was in the room.'

'That's because Jade can't handle real life. If you want the truth, it's me you need to talk to.'

'I'll keep that in mind.'

The two personalities were so distinct that Tara kept having to remind herself that there weren't really two people involved. This was one terribly fragmented mind. Love and hate and pain, all split into separate selves.

'You like Jade, right? You want to help her?'

'I do,' Tara said.

'But how do you feel about me?'

'I think you hold a lot of pain and anger. I think you could be dangerous.'

Ruby laughed. 'But you'll need to convince the staff I'm cured, so my dad can get me out of here.'

'I'd like that to be true.'

Tara had been researching cutting edge treatments for dissociative identity disorder, and she was aware that the process could take years. The main task would be to integrate Ruby's personality and feelings into Jade's own. Once Jade could accept Ruby's aggression, she could work on containing that without acting out dangerously.

Ray Jameson of course wanted fast results. He wanted his daughter home.

They had begun another circuit of the garden. Ruby hooked her arm casually through Tara's as they walked. Tara suppressed the urge to pull away. This was not the patient she had been expecting.

'How do you feel about working with me?' Tara said.

'I'm happy you're here. You remind me of home.' Those gentle, guileless eyes were back then, for a moment or two. 'I want your help to get out of this place, and to go back to my life. To my family. To veterinary college.'

Tara had known that working with Jade would be a challenge, but Ruby's dominance took it to another level. Jade, or Ruby, was communicating, in her own unique way, that she could not be trusted to control her own violent impulses. That made her a dangerous patient. But she was also a young woman in desperate need of help and potentially the most fascinating client Tara would ever get to treat.

'Time to go in for lunch,' the nurse called from the doorway.

Ruby looked towards the clinic building. She waved at the nurse, but didn't move. 'I know all about you. My dad told me what happened to your family.'

Tara did not want to believe that Ray had shared her personal information with his daughter. If he had though, it would not come as a major surprise.

'The police think your brother is like me. They think that maybe you are too. That's how I knew you'd understand.'

The girl was working her way deep under her skin.

Matthew is not a killer.

I am not guilty.

Ruby reached out her hand to Tara. An involuntary reflex made Tara draw back, at first. But Jade's eyes were in there too, desperate. The girl's palm was still outstretched, upturned.

Tara reached out. Jade's hands were always so cold. Maybe hers were too.

'Do I feel like a killer?' she said.

SIXTY-FOUR

Ray Jameson was waiting for Tara in the parking lot of the clinic. He was standing next to her limousine and Ziggy was beside him, sitting obediently on his haunches.

'How is she?' he said.

'She's adjusting well to the clinic. And she's keen for us to start working together. We had an interesting first meeting.'

'That's good news.' Jameson bent down and patted Ziggy's head. 'You know I had to hire a private plane to get this mutt out here. And he needed a passport. The red tape was unbelievable.'

Jameson straightened up and opened the back door of the limousine for her. The driver sat motionless in the front, wearing a cap and staring ahead.

Tara paused. Then she shut the door again. 'You once asked me about my relationship with Daniel Franks.'

'I remember the name.'

She was trying to read his expression, but he was inscrutable.

'Daniel died in the hit-and-run,' Tara said. 'The so-called accident I was involved in.'

Jameson brushed his hair away from his forehead. 'I'm sorry for your loss.'

'You knew that Jade had an appointment with me the morning after that accident. You knew she wanted to take a drug that could have unlocked her memory of the killing of Carl Ress. You wanted to put a stop to that appointment. You succeeded.'

He looked baffled. 'I don't follow.'

'Were you driving the car that killed Daniel?' She was reckless, after so much loss.

'You think I tried to kill you?'

If Tara didn't know him, she might almost believe his surprise was genuine.

'Maybe it was Sandra driving the car?' she said. 'Or Marco?'

Jameson sighed. 'Okay. If it makes you feel better to hear it from me, I can assure you that neither myself, nor my wife, nor any of my employees had anything whatsoever to do with any hit-and-run. We didn't need to take that kind of risk, because Sandra and I never had any intention of sending Jade to that appointment. We only agreed to it so she'd go to bed. Once she was asleep upstairs, I emailed Valerie Bennett, detailing everything about your past and all the inappropriate things you'd done while working with Jade, and informing her we wanted you taken off the case. Which is precisely what I told you I would do. I am an honest man, Doctor Black.'

Tara was mute.

'So maybe you should ask yourself who else might feel – let's say – aggrieved by you and your gentleman friend?'

Tara felt like she had brain freeze, a sudden piercing pain between her eyes.

'I'm afraid that Mr Franks was involved in some dubious business dealings in Switzerland. He was also married. He had a wife and two children. As a teenager, he was interviewed by

the police about your parents' deaths. Not exactly a straightfor-
ward kind of a bloke. But then neither are you.'

An orderly emerged from the clinic and put a bowl of water
down for the dog. Ziggy drank eagerly, slurping loudly. Jameson
seemed quite relaxed. Unperturbed by Tara's accusations.

Tara was still silent, trying to process what Jameson was
saying. Trying to work out if she was being manipulated, or if
there might be an element of truth behind his words.

Once the orderly was gone, Jameson said, 'I have full confidence in you, Doctor Black. Full confidence that you will bring
Jade home. As far as I'm concerned, you are practically a part of
the family.'

Ziggy lay down, panting, looking up at her with what
seemed to be a smile on his brutish face.

'Now,' Jameson said. 'What I suggest is this. Let's meet up
at the bar of your hotel later and drink to my daughter's health.
If you'd like, we can talk about your concerns that someone
killed Daniel Franks. I meant it when I said I could be the best
friend you've ever had.'

Ray's eyes were strangely warm. Tara felt safe for the first
time in a very long time.

A LETTER FROM LUANA

I want to say a huge thank you for choosing to read *The Perfect Patient*. If you would like to keep up to date with my latest releases, please sign up at the following link. Your email address will never be shared, and you can unsubscribe at any time:

www.bookouture.com/luana-lewis

Before becoming a writer, I was a clinical psychologist for 20 years. Like Tara, I took on medico-legal cases and worked with families where children suffered abuse and neglect, and where society failed to protect the most vulnerable. This was where the idea for *The Perfect Patient* began.

While this is a work of fiction, I have done my best to handle these very real issues sensitively.

If you enjoyed *The Perfect Patient*, I would be very grateful if you could write a review. These make such a difference in helping new readers to discover one of my books.

Thanks,

Luana Lewis

ACKNOWLEDGEMENTS

I am deeply grateful to my editor, Helen Jenner, for her sensitive and insightful editing. My thanks go to the entire Bookouture team, whose warm welcome and professionalism have made this writing experience so positive. I could not be more pleased to have entrusted the manuscript to your care.

My friend and fellow writer Emma Smith Barton offered support, a sounding board, and constant encouragement. I am so grateful to know you. Thank you to my long-time colleague and mentor, Dr Rob Neborsky, who talked through the implications of using psychedelics to recover traumatic memories. The author and crime fiction advisor Graham Bartlett guided me through aspects of policing. Any errors in psychiatric or police procedural details are mine alone. I have, at times, prioritised storytelling over absolute accuracy. Genna Lewis helped me think through some of the knotty issues in plot as the book developed. Malcolm Fried and Sarah Fisher were early, encouraging and forgiving readers, and Joseph Fried gave me brilliant input during the writing of later drafts.

I have had the privilege to work with many writing teachers along the way. I am grateful to all of them, in particular: Sophie Hannah, John Truby, Tricia Wastvedt, Sam Simkin and Alexandra Shelley.

Printed in Great Britain
by Amazon